GLOBAL TIME ZONE

A NOVEL

WIDALYS L. DESOTO-BURT

GLOBAL TIME ZONE
A NOVEL

iUniverse books may be ordered through booksellers or by contacting:

iUniverse
1663 Liberty Drive
Bloomington, IN 47403
www.iuniverse.com
1-800-Authors (1-800-288-4677)

ISBN: 978-1-5320-9906-9 (sc)
ISBN: 978-1-5320-9905-2 (e)

Library of Congress Control Number: 2020907070

Print information available on the last page.

iUniverse rev. date: 04/22/2020

To my family and friends,
who always support me,
no matter how wild my dreams may be

CONTENTS

1

There's a new driver behind the wheel of my school bus on the way home. I'm not surprised. People vanish and get replaced by others all the time. The bus pulls up in front of my house ten minutes earlier than usual. I step down and almost don't notice the car a few houses down the street. It's parked under a large maple tree, as far away as possible from the one functioning streetlight, almost as if the driver selected the darkest spot on purpose. But the night is so dark that the faint reflection of the bus's rear taillight bouncing off the car's side mirror draws my attention. *Is it truly the same car?* I wonder. *It has to be.* Around here, we don't see cars often.

That means he must be here. My heart accelerates with excitement. I remove my backpack and hold it tightly against my chest. The bus is now gone, taking with it the dim light that moments earlier lit my path. I quickly scan my surroundings, checking for signs of life.

There's no one around, at least not within sight. I'm used to navigating in the darkness; I've known nothing else. An owl hoots in the distance as I reach my house. If it weren't for the car parked about a hundred feet away, this would seem like any typical school night. Assuming the owner of the car is inside, I grab the handle of my front door and softly but firmly turn it, holding my breath, hoping the door won't make a sound. To my dismay, it lets out a soft creak, and I make a mental note to spray lubricant on it later. *Maybe no one heard it*, I think as I close the door behind me.

A medium-sized black-framed mirror hangs from the wall across from the door. With the foyer light off, the mirror reflects only my silhouette. I can barely see the steps of the L-shaped stairs to my left. I tiptoe across the small foyer and turn the corner into the hall, listening for any signs of activity. At the end of the hall, a faint ray of light coming from the kitchen barely illumines my way.

I stop halfway down the narrow hall and turn to my right as I hear whispers coming from my father's study. I inch forward, careful to avoid stepping on the floorboards that I know are a bit loose and will produce loud creaks. The door to the study is closed. I lean my ear toward it. My heartbeat speeds up. I recognize my father's voice and confirm he isn't alone. There's another man with him, most likely the owner of the car. *But who is he, and what does he want with my father? This is all so confusing.* I wish I could walk in and demand some answers, but of course, that's not an option.

"How long before the plan is executed?" I hear the man whisper.

"Not much longer," my father responds softly, and he sighs.

"I'll see you again next week then," the man says. "Same location as before?"

"Yes. I don't think we should meet here again, in case we run over," my father answers. Soon after, I hear a door open. A few seconds later, I hear the door close.

My eyes widen. *His study has a secret door! Where is it? Where does it lead?*

"Yvanya, come in," my father says loudly.

I jump backward. My heart races. *When did he first notice I was here? Is he upset? Maybe I should pretend I didn't hear anything. Will he believe it?*

"Yes, Father?" I ask, opening the door as I try to compose myself. I feel my face flushing, and I hope he doesn't notice it. I squint for a few seconds as my eyes adjust to the change in lighting. His muscular six-foot figure moves toward me. It's been a few days since his last shave, and his face looks a bit rougher than usual.

"How was your night?" he asks, shifting his voice to a kinder tone, sounding more like the father I know.

"It was fine. Nothing out of the ordinary," I say, swinging my backpack over my shoulder.

"Did you just arrive? You're earlier than usual." His steel-gray eyes study me suspiciously.

"New driver. He seems to have a taste for speed. Anyway, I just came in. Would you like me to start dinner?"

"Sure," he says slowly, raising an eyebrow, probably trying to figure out how much I might have heard. He seems to believe me, and within a second, he relaxes his facial expression. "Go wash up, and get a head start. Your mother and sister should be on their way," he says, and as I turn to leave, he adds before shutting the door behind me, "And turn some lights on. You're going to trip and fall walking in the dark."

That was a close one. Who was that? What plan were they talking about? And the secret door—where is it, and where does it lead to? A train of questions runs through my head as I walk into the small bathroom and turn the lights on. I squirt soap onto my hands and rub them under the cold water, building up a gentle cloud of suds. I stare at my reflection in the mirror: dark hazel eyes, light brown lashes and bushy eyebrows, wavy dark blonde hair, and a pale complexion with no scars or birthmarks. I look more like a young teenager than an eighteen-year-old. As always, the humidity has given my hair a layer of frizz. I dry my hands with a white towel and smooth my hair down. *I wish I had my sister's beautiful straight hair. Instead, I got this thick mane that seems to defy gravity*, I think, biting my thick lower lip.

I enter the kitchen to start preparing dinner. A round black dinette kitchen table with four chairs around it sits in a corner. "Home Sweet Home" reads a simple black-stained wooden sign hung on one of the walls of our medium-sized eat-in kitchen. The remaining walls in the house are beige, unadorned. "Beige is a good neutral color—holds resale value well," my father said when I suggested painting a few walls a different color some years ago. *As if we're ever going to move*, I thought at the time. The top and bottom antique-white cabinets with white metal handle pulls seem to fade into the walls, into a sea of cream. The only contrast comes from the dark hardwood floors and the countertops, which are made of brown-and-black granite—the only features they splurged on when building the house. Everything is sparkling clean. My mother takes pride in that.

I set my backpack by the small kitchen island and open the pantry to evaluate the options. Once again, my mind wanders, wondering about my father, the stranger, and the secret door. *Focus on dinner*, I tell myself. There are five shelves in the pantry, three of which are pretty much empty. A bag of potatoes lies on the bottom shelf. I grab a few of them and set them on the counter. Sprouts have begun to grow, and one of them has a bad bruise—nothing that a knife can't remove. I scan a row of canned vegetables. Each has a simple white label with the words written in thick, bold black letters across it: *Carrots*, *Green Beans*, or *Corn*.

Let's see. Overcooked green beans, carrots, or corn? Which one do we feel like tonight? None? Well, that's not an option; we need some vitamins, if there are any left in here, I think, and I grab the last can of carrots. I look at the best-if-used-by date and notice it's a month expired. *Oh well. It'll still be good enough. How I miss the days when we had fresh produce,* I lament, and then I move on with my cooking chore.

A few minutes later, my mother and my sister, Heidi, walk into the house with a couple of brown bags. "We got some Swiss cheese," Heidi announces.

Ugh. I hate Swiss cheese. "Did they not have cheddar or mozzarella instead?"

"Only Swiss. That's always the only one left," my mother replies.

Yes, that's because no one likes it. Why can't they just use that milk to make more of the cheese that people actually want? And thank you, Price-Setting Board, for setting the prices of the good cheeses so low that the first people in the store buy it all up, leaving nothing for the rest of us, I think, but then I quickly readjust my attitude. *Swiss cheese is better than no cheese. Stop your whining. Plus, it'll go well with the potatoes.*

Heidi sets her bag on top of the counter and leaves to wash her hands.

"They're still out of milk and flour," my mother says as my father joins us in the kitchen. "Every day there's less and less food on the store shelves. We may want to start conserving." She pulls her wavy, shoulder-length light brown hair into a low ponytail. Her blue eyes sparkle as she smiles, seemingly trying to stay positive. Life has been rough in the past few years, and although she's only in her late forties, she looks a few years older in the face. Although she has an athletic build and her muscles seem to be well defined, she is thinner than ideal.

Start conserving, she says? I thought that's what we were doing already. I keep the thought to myself, as I know my parents won't appreciate my sarcasm. Still, I look at the pot in which I'm boiling the potatoes and wonder how much worse things will get before they start to turn around, as everyone keeps promising.

I start unloading one of the brown bags, pulling out a couple of jars of vitamin D, which I line up in single file on one of our pantry's shelves. It's kind of funny that I'm lining them up in single file, when the whole shelf is pretty much empty. I could spread them through the shelf's length, yet I continue to hope that maybe tomorrow we'll be able to purchase more groceries, so I continue to make space for them.

"Those keep getting more expensive too," my mother says as I straighten the jars one more time to make the shelf look neat and tidy.

"It will get better," my father assures her, and he slowly kisses her cheek. She closes her eyes and smiles, obviously enjoying his touch. I smile but look away, feeling as if I'm intruding on their private moment. "The government's working to make things better. They just need more time," he adds as he takes a seat at the dining table.

"Sure they are," I mutter under my breath.

"Yvanya, show more respect," my father says, and I immediately lower my eyes.

"There's barely any water flow in the upstairs bathroom," Heidi announces as she reenters the kitchen. She's pulled her long, straight blonde hair back into a French braid. With her big baby-blue eyes, dark lashes, and fair complexion, she looks more like a porcelain doll than a young teenager.

"I forgot to tell you—they're expanding the rationing to our neighborhood," my mother says. "I heard it yesterday. I filled a couple of buckets a few hours ago, so we should be okay until it's back tomorrow."

We're in the middle of a drought, and the reserves have been low for a while, so the government has been restricting how much water some areas get. Up to now, our neighborhood has been spared, but it seems the levels are getting near critical, so they're expanding the rationing area.

As my mother starts setting the table, the phone rings, and my father rushes to answer it. "Yes, this is James McKenzie," he says, extending the phone's cord so he can take the call outside the kitchen. Roughly a minute goes by as he pays close attention to the caller without saying a word. "Mr. Zhu, can you please repeat that?" he asks, and even from a few feet away, I can hear Mr. Zhu yelling. "Are you talking about Mitchell?" my father asks, covering his other ear with his free hand to focus. "Okay, I think I've got it now. Yes, I understand." After a few seconds, he adds,

"No, sir, it won't happen again." He finally completes the conversation and drops the phone into its cradle forcefully.

"Is everything okay?" my mother asks, setting a stack of plates on the table and turning her complete attention to him.

"Yes, Beatrice, everything is fine," he replies with a deep furrow on his forehead. She accepts his answer and resumes setting the table. We get these calls all the time. It's nothing new; however, this time, I can't help but wonder if the call has anything to do with my father's mystery guest.

Heidi and I finish preparing dinner quietly. When we're done, we bring it to my father, who is now flipping through the newspaper at the table. He closes the paper and drops it onto the floor. As the paper lands, I catch a glimpse of the headline on the front page "Mitchell Arrested and Sent to the Dungeon without Trial."

"The Dungeon" is what people call our maximum-security prison. No one has ever managed to escape from it. Before, only the most vicious criminals were sent there; however, lately, we keep hearing of more common criminals and even civilians being sent there as well. The media and our government call them traitors, terrorists, and anarchy lovers—a danger to our system and our way of life. Basically, anyone who has the guts to speak out against our government or the Empire earns the title.

My father works for one of the government branches, the Empire Bureau of Investigation, also known as the EBI.

I'm not exactly sure what he does. His job requires security clearances, so he's not able to share any details with us. "That's classified," he usually replies when dismissing our questions. We rarely ask any questions anymore. By the way he sometimes talks about the news, I wouldn't be surprised to find out he's behind some of the arrests. He constantly assures us that our local government officials are fighting to protect the citizens' rights and that they're the best chance we have at improving our lives. It's all a bunch of blah-blah-blah if you ask me. As our ancestors would have said, "Show the people some results, and maybe then they'll start drinking the Kool-Aid," whatever that is.

"How was school?" my mother asks, clearly trying to ease some of the tension in the air. She spreads a thin film of butter on her potatoes.

"It was great," Heidi says, grabbing a slice of cheese. She places it on top of her potatoes, and it quickly starts to melt. "I got an A on my literature exam." Her eyes sparkle with delight.

"Great job," my mother replies, and my father nods in approval.

"What about you? Didn't you have an exam last week?" my father asks, pointing his fork at me. A piece of potato, barely stuck on the fork, threatens to drop back onto the plate.

"Yes, a history test. I did okay. I got a C," I say, looking down at my plate. *Here we go. Bring on the lecture.*

"That's not acceptable. If you want to go anywhere, you need to do better than that," he says, and I keep my eyes down as I nod.

"I had a problem with one of the essay questions," I say. "The teacher didn't agree with my answer—said it was controversial and gave me no credit for it."

"Avoid being controversial, Yvanya," my mother replies. "It will lead to nothing good."

"I know. I'm sorry," I say, and I continue chewing my food quietly. I've never been a great student, so I'm not sure why they still act surprised every time I share a less-than-ideal grade. They should be used to it by now.

It's not that I'm not smart or capable of getting good grades. I'm sure I could if I wanted to, but the reality is that the options for what to do after high school are not exactly enticing. The boys with the highest grades are selected by the government to get higher education. They are sent far away from their homes for a few years until they complete their studies, after which they are assigned careers. Their interests are not taken into account. The government's rationale is that at eighteen years old, you're too young to know what's good for you or our society. They also don't want too many people choosing the same career, as that would leave a gap in one area and a surplus in another. Our system claims to be more efficient at matching the right skills to the right jobs. I hope they're better at this than they are at predicting which types of cheese people want to buy.

Unlike boys, girls don't get secondary education, no matter how smart they are or how excellent their grades are. Those who excel in school do so more for bragging rights and personal pride than anything else—or, in Heidi's case, to please our parents.

"Well, I have some great news to share," my father says, changing the topic and immediately drawing our attention. He sets his fork on his plate. His eyes light up, and he sucks his lips inward, waiting for us to react.

"What is it, sweetheart?" my mother asks.

"Remember Paul Anderson, one of my supervisors?" he says.

I don't, but I nod anyway, as it seems irrelevant. My mother and sister nod as well.

"Well," he says, shifting his attention to me, "he has a son who recently graduated from secondary studies and is now back home and looking for a wife. And—" He adds a dramatic break, likely to heighten our intrigue.

I don't like where this is going.

"And?" my mother asks, meeting his excitement.

Please don't say it. Don't say it, I think, preparing myself for what I assume is coming.

"Well, after seeing a few photos of Yvanya, he's very interested in meeting her," he says with pleasure.

My fork slips out of my hand as my fears are confirmed. "What?" I ask, hoping I have misheard him.

"Really?" my mother asks, clasping her hands together with exhilaration.

"Nothing is final, of course, but at least he's interested," he adds, still staring at me, as if hoping for me to smile and jump with joy.

You promised! I want to scream, but I restrain myself. Instead, as politely as I'm able to, considering how angry I am, I reply, "I'm not interested." I push my chair back and run to my room.

2

I lie on my bed in complete darkness. There are no windows in my room, so it's always dark when the lights aren't on. In fact, there are no windows in the entire house, except for a small twelve-by-twelve-inch box with a thick double-glass pane a few feet to the right of the main entrance.

How dare he try to set up an arranged marriage for me, especially after he promised me he would never force me to marry someone I didn't love? Doesn't he know me better than that? What makes him think I'm going to go through with it? I'm not the typical girl; I want to own my own future. It's bad enough that almost every aspect of my life is controlled by the Empire. Now my father also wants to micromanage my personal life and determine what's best for me. What does he know? I cross my arms and stamp one of my feet on the lumpy mattress.

I lie like that for what seems like forever, hearing nothing but the sound of my breathing, which is fast at first before gradually slowing down to a normal pace. *What if the guy is a complete jerk? What if I never learn to love him? What if he never loves me?* My anger changes to anxiety. My eyes get watery, and a few tears roll down the sides of my face. *How could Father betray me like this?*

Suddenly, the light turns on, and I pull my arms over my eyes to block the blinding light. "Turn it off!" I yell, feeling a new burst of anger run through me. I quickly wipe the tears away.

"Sorry," my mother replies, turning off the light and walking to my bed. She sits by my side and, after fumbling for a few seconds, finds the switch for the lamp on the night table between my bed and Heidi's. The softer glow of the smaller lamp is kinder to my eyes. "Yvanya, don't be mad at your father," she says, running her fingers through my hair.

"How can I not be?" I reply. "Mother, he promised he'd never do this to me. How dare he now change his mind and try to decide who I'm supposed to marry?"

"I know he promised, but that was years ago. Things have changed. You know how things are now. It's the only way to move up, to ensure a plate of dinner every night. You know he just wants what's best for you," she says, still playing with my hair.

"Maybe I don't want to move up. Maybe I'm okay with staying where I am." I sit up and look at her. The soft yellow glow from the light shines on her face, making her skin look softer and her cheekbones higher. The crow's-feet at the corners of her eyes seem to disappear, giving her an overall younger appearance. For a second, I get a glimpse of what she must have looked like when she was younger, and I'm amazed at the resemblance between her and my sister.

"Sweetheart, you're smarter than that. You know what we have is not sustainable. Life is getting harder every day here. I'm sure you can tell."

"You guys got to pick each other." I change my argument, as I know the economic one will get me nowhere. "Why can't I pick my own husband? Why should I give up on finding love before I've even tried?" I'm surprised by my question, as I realize it's not just an excuse I'm making up to go against my parents' wishes but something I truly care about. I've had crushes on boys before, but for some reason, I've never thought of myself as the marrying type, likely because I've never had a boyfriend. With my petite figure and flat chest, I've never felt confident around boys. Grasping the possibility of marrying a complete stranger triggers the fear of losing something I didn't know I could have or might want.

My mother sighs as she looks me in the eyes. "Things have changed. Back then, things weren't this bad." She holds my hands between her own. "Just please give this guy a chance. At least meet him, and afterward, if you decide you just can't do it, you can call it off. No one's going to force you. But your father has worked hard to get this man to consider us, so please, at a minimum, out of respect for your father, give the guy a chance."

"Fine," I say as I softly nod once.

"Thank you." She kisses my forehead.

As she walks out of my room, fresh tears roll down my face.

I lie on my bed motionless as my mind runs through endless questions. Eventually, my thoughts wander back to what I witnessed some hours ago. *Paul Anderson—so that's who my father was meeting earlier tonight when I came in. Planning my future without consulting me.* Deep inside, I know my father means well, but I can't help but feel trapped. *Well, mystery solved.* At least that's what part of me wants to believe. Another part of me still wonders, *But why all the secrecy? Nowadays arranged marriages are seen everywhere. Why would mine require secret meetings and secret exits?*

I push the questions aside, close my eyes, and eventually fall asleep.

🕐 🕐 🕐

I wake up as I hear Heidi moving quietly around the room. "What time is it?" I ask.

"Sorry. Didn't mean to wake you," she says.

"That's okay. I feel like I slept for a very long time," I reply, and she turns on the night table lamp. Again, I shield my eyes with my arm.

"It's bedtime. You must have fallen asleep right after dinner. Father was upset that you left the table without being dismissed, but he's okay now." She pulls her sleeping gown out from our dresser. "I'm sorry about them trying to set you up."

"Can we not talk about it?" I say, wanting to forget it.

"The news channel said it's going to be one of the hottest days of the year. I looked out the window right before coming upstairs, and already it looks pretty sunny," she says as she changes into her gown.

"Glad we get to sleep through it then." I roll back onto my other side to avoid the light.

"Yvanya, do you really believe what Father says? That the government is working to make things better?" she asks as she gets into her bed.

"I don't know. Lately I don't believe much of what the government says." I immediately regret saying it, as I don't want to scare her. As a thirteen-year-old, she already has enough things to worry about. The truth is that once upon a time, I used to believe in the government's promises, but those days are long gone. They keep coming up with excuses for why things aren't working and asking for more time and more money to fix the problems, but nothing seems to get better. I used to give them the benefit of the doubt, thinking that maybe the issues were so complex that they truly needed more time, but regardless of what the government or my parents say, it doesn't take a genius to see that the system is broken and corrupt. For the longest time, my family has been somewhat sheltered, but I'm not sure how much longer that will last.

"I overheard kids at school talking about some people planning a revolution against the Empire," she says softly.

This is not news to me. A lot of talk goes on during recess when the teachers aren't around. Many kids repeat what they hear at home or on the streets. You need to be careful, though, as that sort of talk can easily land you in detention. Spreading conspiracy theories is not tolerated. As for the revolution rumors, it seems that every year there are people seeking to overthrow the government to gain independence. It never works out. They always end up arrested, charged with treason, and then sent to the Dungeon. Whatever followers they might have had in the beginning dwindle and disappear as if nothing ever happened. Our society has become complacent, realizing that nothing's going to change. Our future lies with the government and the hope that they'll do the right thing for our country.

Although we still get to vote for our government officials, we don't get to nominate them; the Empire does. No one gets on a ballot without the Empire's approval, and that's where the conflict of interest lies. Our democratic system is nothing more than an illusion to give us a false sense of hope and security. Everyone with half a brain understands this, but of course, most of us are smart enough not to talk about it.

"What do you mean?" I ask as I roll over to face her. I don't want to encourage her, yet I don't want to dismiss her either. I hate it when people talk down to me as if I'm a kid. I don't ever want to make her feel that way. I like that she trusts me and tells me what she's thinking.

"The kids were saying that this global time zone thing was designed by the New Orientals to get revenge on us for treating them unfairly for so long. They said our government is trying to get us to believe we got a good deal when they switched our work hours to nighttime, while the New Orientals get to enjoy the daytime."

"I'm not sure, Heidi. I hope that's not the case. Father says the government's working to protect us. After all, if it weren't for the New Orientals, we would be in a much worse place. Things will get better. They're doing everything they can. If they were lying, Father would know about it, so I wouldn't worry too much," I tell her, feeling nauseated at repeating the same propaganda I don't even believe myself.

"I'm not a kid, you know," she says softly. "You can tell me the truth."

"I know. I am." I try to sound convincing, but Heidi knows me better than anyone. I can't fool her. However, it's late, and looking tired, she lets it go.

"Okay." She turns the light off.

A few minutes later, I hear her start to breathe in a rhythmic pattern, indicating she's fallen asleep.

So Heidi has lost her innocence, I realize with sadness. I was a bit younger than she is when I started questioning the world around me. *I hope she's better than I am at hiding it.*

According to our history books, about forty-three years ago, our nation, which used to be called the United States of America, as well as the countries in what used to be called the European Union, found themselves in a deep financial crisis after decades of incurring unsustainable levels of debt at artificially low interest rates. Life started becoming difficult for people around that time as inflation skyrocketed and erased most people's life savings overnight. Crime became rampant, and conflicts erupted as those who were now poor started fighting the few who were still rich, whom people referred to as the One Percent. To make things better for everyone, many countries united under what used to be called the United Nations, while New Orient, a newly formed country in Asia, became the new world leader. As it was one of the few stable countries at the time, it became our savior, helping to stabilize us by tying its currency to ours. This kept the dollar from plummeting further. Eventually, they suggested we take their currency to enable more effective business transactions. Everyone knew it wasn't much of a choice.

Prior to that, the world had been divided into different time zones, with each having a different clock time at any one particular moment. I guess they thought that was helpful because it allowed everyone to work while the sun was out and sleep at night. Because the world's economy was in such bad shape and given the need for easier and faster connections, New Orient mandated that a single time zone be imposed worldwide, based on the time in its capital city. Not having to deal with time differences of up to twelve hours made everything much more efficient.

Our world leaders agreed that moving to a single time zone and aligning our work schedules were good ideas, so the global time zone, or GTZ, was established. By that point, they had agreed only to move to the same working hours and not what those working hours would be. Fights soon erupted over which countries would get to work during daylight hours.

At the same time, scientists from our government conveniently discovered a series of holes in the ozone layer over our country's sky. They claimed the holes were leading to an alarming rate of skin cancer, so to protect our people, we were given the night shift. Thanks to our government and our top-notch scientists, we came out with the safer schedule, or at least that's what our books will say. I've heard conspiracy theories that the ozone holes and the cancer stories were lies fabricated to manipulate us, but most of the population opted to go with the better-safe-than-sorry mentality, especially since the government produced a lot of data supporting the claims.

Not long after we adopted the global time zone, New Orient merged with a few neighboring countries, establishing what we now call the New Orient Empire. They've since grown across the world, taking their culture and financial help to other nations who would otherwise be poor and under severe social distress. To make the world more inclusive for everyone, we dropped all the old country names and instead go by region numbers. My region is

Region 12 because we shifted our clocks by twelve hours to match the global time zone.

"Working together for a better tomorrow" became the Empire's slogan, and by "working together," they mean working together at the same time—no exceptions.

For the first few months, there were many upheavals. They started as peaceful manifestations, with people marching in front of government buildings while carrying placards and chanting for a repeal of the global time zone agreement and the new working-hours schedule. As they noticed the protests were going nowhere, they turned more violent, which led to bloodshed and incarcerations. Little by little, the revolts dwindled, until all finally seemed to have accepted their new reality—all except those who are part of the Daylight Militia. The government doesn't acknowledge their existence, but we hear about them here and there through informal means. Nobody knows who they are, but we believe they're a small pocket of people who have gone dormant but are waiting, looking for an opportunity to overthrow the government so we can go back to the independent country we used to be. Some argue they're just a bunch of fools, because we gave democracy a try, and clearly, the experiment didn't work.

Nonetheless, whether we like it or not, the New Orient Empire has saved us and the rest of the world, so we owe them our loyalty for everything we have. At least that's the message we've grown up hearing every day of our lives.

I open my eyes and am greeted by the darkness of my room. I have no idea if it's time to wake or not, but feeling as if I can no longer sleep, I get up and sneak out of my bedroom. With bare feet, I walk down the stairs and into the kitchen, where the oven's clock indicates it's just a little past 4:00 a.m. GTZ. Our clocks always reflect the time in the Empire's capital city. Since it's early morning for them, the sun will still be out here.

Decades ago, before we became part of the Empire, when the people in our country lived in a diurnal society, the clocks for those who lived in this area and within its original time zone were twelve hours behind those of the New Orient capital city. Once the country became part of the Empire and they established the global time zone, they not only moved our country to the nocturnal schedule but also moved the clocks up by twelve hours; thus, what used to be 4:00 p.m. before is now 4:00 a.m. and vice versa. Every time zone was adjusted so that now it is exactly the same time everywhere within the Empire. I bet it must have been a significant adjustment for those around at the time, but for those like me who weren't around yet, it's normal.

I walk to our house's only window, which we keep covered with a thick, heavy curtain. Removing windows from houses was another idea the Empire suggested. After all, who needs windows when it's so dark while you're awake that you can't see anything outside? And when it's daytime, we're trying to sleep, so windows are nothing more than a nuisance. Windows are also inefficient for temperature control. With the high cost of electricity, few people objected to their removal. Scientists also discovered that the radiation coming through windows was enough to cause skin cancer, which was yet another reason to get rid of them altogether. Most houses don't have any windows at all, but our mother insisted we add this one by the door so we could see who's outside before opening it. I guess with the crime and all, she became a little paranoid. My father finally agreed to it, although he insisted we add the curtain covering to block the sun's radiation. We were all okay with that compromise.

I pull back the curtain enough to get a glimpse of what the outside world looks like during the day. I'm always intrigued when I see how many shades of green there are. As we avoid the outdoors during daytime, I rarely get to enjoy the beautiful colors and scenery.

Wanting to see more than what the small window allows me to, I look up the stairs to make sure no one is coming and then unlock the door. *I shouldn't be doing this. I might get caught and get in trouble. Plus, what if it's true? What if even a few minutes of sun exposure gets me sick?* Worried, I start to lock the door again, but my curiosity is stronger than my fear, so I change my mind once more. *I'll be quick, just to remember what it feels like.*

It has been months since the last time I was outside during the peak of the day. On that occasion, my sister cut her finger while dicing an apple with a dull knife, and no matter how much pressure we put on it, her finger wouldn't stop bleeding. My father rushed her to the hospital to get stitches, and I insisted on going with them. Prior to our leaving, my mother covered us with sunscreen lotion, even while we applied pressure to Heidi's wound—apparently, the sunscreen was as critical as the wound itself. Heidi was fine afterward, although she still has a scar. She's been shy around knives ever since.

I shake the memory away and open the door slightly. Its creaking sound reminds me of the need to spray lubricant on the hinges. A blast of warm air meets my face, and I smile. I walk outside and quietly close the door behind me. I walk a few steps away from our house and stop to enjoy the sidewalk's heat against my bare feet. I curl and uncurl my toes as the heat transfers to my body, relaxing my muscles.

I glance at the cream-colored cookie-cutter houses of our neighborhood. Most have stains and areas where the paint has chipped away. The once cheerful-looking community is now showing how hard these past years have been. Our houses are separated by less than twenty feet, yet despite the proximity, we rarely see our neighbors. Socializing is not common in our society, particularly because people never really know whom they can trust. It probably doesn't help that my father works for the government, which makes those around us even more cautious.

Unkept trees line the streets; overgrown grass and weeds cover every yard. Not much maintenance goes on. What would be the point? With the little lighting we have at night, no one notices it anyway.

I roll up my gown sleeves and savor the feeling of the sun's rays kissing my skin. My arms are so pale. I lift my face and close my eyes as all thoughts escape from my head, leaving nothing but the warm, comforting feel on my cold ghost-white skin.

"What are you doing out here?" My sister's angry whisper brings me back from my reverie, and I reopen my eyes to see her standing by the door. "Get back inside," she says as she looks over her shoulder.

With disappointment, I follow her inside and gently shut the door.

"Why were you outside?" she asks as we move into the kitchen.

"Don't you wonder what it's like to be out there during the daytime?" I ask, pulling a cup from one of the cabinets and pouring myself some water from the sink. The flow of water is slower now, and it takes forever to fill the cup.

I look around the kitchen and notice a piece of paper held by a magnet against the refrigerator's door. "Phototherapy Tuesday at 1:00 p.m. GTZ" is written in black cursive letters. My mother has suffered from depression for years. A combination of vitamins and phototherapy are among the most prescribed treatments. She's not the only one to suffer from depression; many in our society are afflicted by it. Wealthy people often purchase special lights to get the therapy at home. The lights are not expensive, but they consume a lot of energy, which is expensive. It's a lot cheaper just to go to one of the phototherapy clinics. They're all over the city, and it's easy to get an appointment.

"The sun—it's not safe," Heidi says, but I can tell she also questions this well-known so-called fact. I can also see she's curious and wants to be outside as much as I do. "Father will be mad if he finds out you were sneaking out."

"Then don't tell him, and he won't know," I reply, and she smiles, assuring me with a nod that my secret is safe with her.

"But what if the police saw you? You know we're not allowed outside during daytime," she says, referring to the new daytime curfew the Empire has enacted. Unless you have a rightful reason to be outside during those hours, you will be fined or detained if caught.

"They don't frequent our neighborhood," I say.

"You don't know that for sure."

"All right. I'll just stick around the house. That way, if

I see anyone coming around, I'll be able to dash back in on time. I'll be fine. Don't worry."

"Just don't do it. Period," she insists.

"Oh, Heidi, it feels so much better without sunblock on," I tell her as I run my hands over my arms, which have retained some of the heat.

"That's even more dangerous. Even a few minutes of exposure without protection can lead to cell mutations," she says, reciting the propaganda we've been fed over and over again.

"I thought you weren't a believer," I say with a mocking smile.

"Better safe than sorry. Let's go back to bed. Mother will be waking us in less than an hour," she replies, and we both tiptoe up the stairs to our bedroom.

As I walk down the hall to the stairs, my eyes focus on the door to my father's study. I need to find a good time when he's gone to sneak in there and look for the secret entrance. *What could he possibly be hiding from us?* I wonder as I climb the stairs.

4

As I ride the bus to school, I stare out the window into the darkness. Once again, the sun has set, so there's not much to see, only field after field of corn hidden by the black veil of night. Visibility is poor out here due to the lack of functioning streetlights. With electricity being so expensive, few areas have the luxury of spending tax dollars on such things, especially when there are food shortages and hungry people in plain sight. Not surprisingly, the crime rate started to increase when the cuts to street lighting were enacted, since criminals benefit from the added anonymity.

A couple of weeks ago, I heard in the news that a young mother was mugged for a loaf of bread right outside the supermarket in a nearby town where lower-income people live. It turned out she had bought the last loaf of bread. As expected, the assailant—a woman in her sixties—was never found. This is not surprising, as the police have more important things to worry about, such as the growing list of home invasions, murders, and kidnappings.

My family and I live in what is considered a middle-class

neighborhood. Things haven't gotten that bad in our area yet. Since a few government officials live in our neighborhood, we were able to keep one streetlight per block, which might be contributing to our security—that or the thieves haven't fully exhausted all the resources in the areas they've been targeting. It's probably just a matter of time before they migrate to our area.

We go to school all year long. Before the Empire existed, most countries used to give kids a break during the summer. The Empire saw that as a waste and an opportunity to accelerate our learning. Back when they suggested the change, not many people complained about it. In a way, most parents were somewhat relieved, as they no longer had to find alternate arrangements to keep their kids busy during the summer months. I'm surprised they haven't decided to get rid of weekends. It seems like the most logical next step. Until then, like most teenagers, I plan on sleeping late to catch up on my sleep during those nights.

From what I've heard, schools have changed quite a bit in the last half century. Instead of principals, we have school headmasters who are appointed by the Empire. They come straight from New Orient and are firm in their discipline philosophy: "Shaping the young while it's early will save them from a lifetime of pain." Teachers need to complete four years of strict training at the New Orient Empire Academy before they're allowed to teach. The Empire wouldn't want them to teach the wrong things, of course.

Our history books are only a few decades old. The former ones were destroyed and rewritten to ensure their accuracy. All publishing presses need to be registered with the Empire and are subject to on-the-spot audits. A few of the older history books still exist but can only be found circulating in the black market. Possession of one of those could cost you a few years in jail, if you're lucky.

The bus hits a large bump in the road, and I'm thrown off my seat. Road maintenance is not a government priority either. I regain my balance and turn my attention back to the cornfields. The workers are gone. We rarely see them, as they work during the day, when we're sleeping.

"Poor bastards," my father sometimes says, referring to them. "They have no choice but to work the fields, with no hope for a future."

These workers make up our society's lowest class. Most are uneducated and illiterate, and most of the land they farm belongs not to them but to the government, who provides them with what are referred to as "modest living arrangements." We can sometimes see their houses from the road. Most look dilapidated, which makes me wonder how anyone can live under such inhumane conditions. In exchange for their work, they are also able to keep a small portion of the crops, enough to keep themselves and their families alive. Some people refer to them in a derogatory way as the burned ones because they have darker skin, burned by their daily exposure to the sun. I hate that term. I can't understand how someone could call another human being such an awful name.

Attractive women from the middle class have a chance of rising to the higher class, but it requires marrying a wealthy man. Burned women have virtually no chance, as no respectable man from the higher class would look at a woman with substantial skin damage. Who knows what other mutations might have taken place inside her body and whether her children will be affected? It's not a risk many affluent men want to take.

Other than through marriage, there are few opportunities for women to rise on their own. I've read that once upon a time, women used to hold high-paying jobs similar to men. When I was growing up, I secretly liked to think about what job I would have if I had a choice. Sometimes I would imagine myself as a doctor helping to cure the sick or as a scientist in a lab, coming up with new inventions to help improve people's lives. When I was ten, I dreamed of flying high above our planet on a spacecraft, looking out through a small window at Earth. It looked majestic, just like in a schoolbook picture I had seen the night before. I woke up crying, as even at that young age, I realized I would never see anything as beautiful in real life. Those thoughts and dreams became fewer and fewer as I realized they were nothing but futile fantasies.

Most women in our country stay at home, fully relying on their husbands to carry the financial load. The ones who are unmarried or still have to work to make ends meet do so by working as clerks in stores, waiting tables, or doing other low-paying jobs. Our options are not exactly empowering. It wasn't always like that. During the pre-Empire days, women were regarded as equals to men. Some extremists even claimed superiority over them. They tended to be more vocal and demanding, which the Empire saw as a threat. Fearing the rest of the women would follow, the Empire leveraged the financial aid that our country needed so badly as a tool to put them back in their place. They redefined the role of women in our society, restricted the jobs we can hold, and in some areas even limited the number of children we can have. When having to choose between food for their families or civil rights, most women had little choice but to give up their rights. Interestingly, one right that did not get revoked was the right to vote, which the Empire claimed proved their willingness to let us choose our own leaders. Of course, given that they select the candidates, it is clear that neither women nor men truly kept that right.

As we drive through the center of town, we pass a military tank. We've always had soldiers patrolling our streets, but it seems the numbers have increased recently. Even in the dark, I notice the Empire's flag painted on the side of the tank: a red rectangle with a large blue stripe in the center, surrounded by a thinner white stripe above and below. A large yellow star sits in the center of the blue stripe. Speakers around the main plaza are playing the New Orient

Empire's national anthem. We all know it by heart. You can't graduate the first grade without reciting it from beginning to end. Every night at school, we start by reciting the pledge of allegiance to the New Orient Empire, followed by singing the national anthem. They play it as background music pretty much everywhere: elevators, stores, government offices—you name it. It's as if they're afraid of silence, as if silence might allow for unpatriotic thoughts to creep into our heads and corrupt our beliefs. I hear it so often I've become desensitized to it, but tonight the speakers seem to be playing it louder.

"Hey, Anya," Daphne says as she sits down by me, pulling me from my state of nightdreaming. Only Daphne calls me Anya. As a toddler, she couldn't say my entire name. It eventually became her nickname for me.

"Hey," I say.

"Want to sleep over at my house today?" she asks, winking at me.

"What's the wink for?" I ask, never knowing what my unpredictable friend is planning.

"Just sleeping and doing our nails, of course," she replies with a daring smile. Daphne is not the type who cares about manicures or pedicures. Neither am I.

Knowing she's not going to tell me, I decide to drop it. "Fine. Count me in." I hope my parents won't object. It's Friday, after all, and a great way to start the weekend.

"Okay, it's been an hour since they went to bed," Daphne says. "They should be fast asleep by now. Let's go." She gets up from the floor, where we were watching her old black-and-white TV set. The big, bulky box, which probably weighs more than fifty pounds, sits on her distressed white dresser. Decades ago, there used to be fancier, more modern TVs, but they came with integrated cameras and microphones, which the Empire demanded be left on at all times so they could monitor the population. I guess citizens judged that a higher-resolution picture was not worth the loss of privacy and reverted to the older technology.

A twin-sized bed with a white metal frame in the corner and a small table with a lamp next to the bed sum up the furniture in the room. A Hello Kitty poster hangs on one wall. Her father got it for her years ago on a business trip to Asia, back when we were kids and it was on trend. She's no longer a fan but hasn't found a better poster to replace it. The process to make paper is expensive because it requires specialized equipment, plus a lot of water and energy, so making new posters is not a priority. I once asked her why she didn't take it down, and she just shrugged and said she didn't like the look of the bare wall. Other than her childish poster and my bedroom's two beds, our bedrooms look pretty much the same. Our society is minimalistic. There are not many things to buy, nor is there money to buy them.

At five feet eight, Daphne is half a foot taller than I. She has shoulder-length dark brown hair and brown eyes. Her skin is several shades darker than mine. Her exotic looks are courtesy of her multiracial ethnicity. Her mother is of Hispanic descent, and her father is Asian. She often gets second and third looks from the boys. Although I'm often called cute or pretty and have gotten compliments on my hazel eyes, I've never been called hot, as most guys would call Daphne. It doesn't bother me, as I don't like to call attention to myself anyway. She's not into calling attention to herself either; it's just something that seems to happen when you look like that.

She opens a drawer from her dresser and pulls out a bottle. "Catch," she says as she throws it at me.

Automatically, my reflexes kick in, and I'm able to catch it before it hits the floor. I look at my hand to find out it's a half-empty bottle of sunblock.

"Where are we going?" I ask, finally confirming my suspicion that she is up to something.

"Out," she says with a smile as she pulls another bottle from her dresser and starts to apply sunblock to her face.

"What about the curfew? What if we get caught?"

"There are never guards around this part of town. We'll be fine," she says. "Here. Wear this shirt instead." She pulls a couple of long-sleeved gray shirts from her dresser and hands me one. She pulls her hair into a low ponytail and gets close to her dresser's mirror as she applies lip gloss to her lips.

As I change my shirt, I catch a glimpse of my reflection in her dresser mirror. My ribs are more prominent than they were a few weeks ago. I quickly pull down the shirt over my chest and brush the image aside. The words "Keep Calm and Carry On" are printed in white on my shirt. A picture of a crown is centered on top. I have no idea what this means, but I don't bother to ask. Daphne probably won't know either. The selection at the stores is limited, so as long as clothing fits, graphics and their meanings are secondary.

After we change our shirts and apply the lotion, she packs a few items into a black backpack. She then pulls an olive-green bucket hat from a drawer and offers it to me. "You can have this one."

I put it on and examine myself in the mirror. It has hooks and other small items hanging from it. "I look like a fisherman," I reply, and I hand it back to her.

"Just in case," she says, and she stuffs it into the backpack.

We carefully open the door to her bedroom and sneak through the house in complete darkness.

It's 11:15 p.m. GTZ, and the sun is close to its highest point. I squirm the moment we step outside as my eyes work to adjust to the bright light. Within thirty seconds or so, I'm able to see again. I smile as I feel the day's heat against my face.

"Let's go," she says as she starts to jog down her driveway, which is full of cracks with weeds and other small plants growing out of them. Suddenly, it occurs to me that I don't know why our houses have driveways and garages, as almost no one owns a car. Maybe back when the houses were built, people had them, but nowadays a vehicle is a luxury few can afford. Some people used to use their garages for additional storage, but given how the economy keeps declining, rarely does a house have enough things to need the space anymore.

Looking at the deteriorating neighborhood houses, I remember a time when my mother, Heidi, and I planted some flowers in an attempt to brighten our house's exterior. Back then, almost all the streetlights on our street were on at night, so you could see clearly what the houses looked like. We went out at dusk, when the sun was low enough not to be a hazard yet provided enough light that we could see fairly easily. Heidi and I had grown the flowers from seeds in small pots. It had taken us about a month to get them strong enough to transplant to the front yard. The following day, a government notice was taped to our door, stating that if we were caught wasting water on the plants, we would be fined. The flowers were dead within a week.

Not wanting to call attention to ourselves, we jog quietly for about a mile, staying close to trees and bushes along the road that offer some cover, until we exit our neighborhood. Although the roads seem deserted, I keep glancing back over my shoulder, watching for soldiers or anyone who might be a curfew enforcer. So far, the coast seems clear, but it's not enough to ease my concerns. *We shouldn't be doing this. We're gonna get caught. Why did I go along with this? It's one thing to go out for some sun right outside my house, but venturing this far is completely different.* As we leave the safety of our neighborhood, I consider turning back, but my curiosity is piqued, and part of me wants to see what she's up to, so I continue to follow her.

We slow down our pace as we reach a narrow gravel road. We take shade by some bushes on the side of the road, and Daphne pulls out a couple of water bottles from her backpack. She hands me one, and I take a couple of sips, realizing how thirsty the jog has made me. It's probably another record-breaking day for temperature. So far, we have not seen one human being along the way.

"Where are we going?" I ask Daphne, who seems ready to go again.

"You'll see. We're not far," she says, shoving the bottles back into her backpack and swinging it over her shoulder.

I walk behind her as she speeds up, and I notice the rips on the back of her jeans: right under her knees, extending a few inches into her calves. *Her family must be doing worse than mine*, I think for a second before catching up with her. Like my father, her father is a government official, only he works in a different division: the armament department, which secures weapons for the police and the Empire military. Only they are legally allowed to possess guns. If anyone else gets caught with a gun, he or she will win a one-way ticket to the Dungeon. It's safer that way—who knows what desperate people might do if they had access to guns?

We continue down the gravel road for another mile or so until we reach the edge of a cornfield. *Where the heck are we going? There's nothing here. Where is she taking me?* I keep wondering if I should just turn around and go back, but then the change in scenery intrigues me. I've never been in a cornfield. The stalks are as tall as we are.

Daphne finds a wide-enough opening and cuts through it. I continue behind her, wondering where she is leading us. I look back and realize I can't see the road anymore. I worry we might get lost. I'm not typically claustrophobic, but being surrounded by tall cornstalks is not necessarily relaxing.

"Okay, where are we going?" I yell, losing my patience, as I pull her by the backpack. She comes to a stop and turns around to face me. "And don't tell me it's a secret!" I snap.

Right as she's about to open her mouth, I hear voices approaching, and I tense up.

"There she is," a guy's voice says, and an arm wraps around my friend's waist. His grinning tanned face appears over her left shoulder, and I stare at him, confused and scared.

"Matt, this is Yvanya. Yvanya, meet Matt." She grins at me.

I'm still a bit shocked, so I just stare at the stranger, not knowing how to react.

"Come on," she replies as the two of them start walking hand in hand down the cornfield aisle.

I follow closely behind, shielding my face from the leaves and twigs that snap back as Daphne and Matt push them in their walk. *What's going on? Who's this guy? What's she doing with him?*

After about five or six minutes of nonstop walking, we reach a clearing, and the corn plants stop. I'm relieved by the change of scenery.

"Over there are our houses," Matt says, pointing to what look like old shacks. Boards are missing from some of the structures, making me wonder how these people stay warm during the winter. Now that we're out of the cornfield, I'm able to see him better. He's about half a foot taller than Daphne, with olive skin, wavy dark brown hair, and light brown eyes. I notice Daphne staring at him as if she's hypnotized, and I feel annoyed. *Seriously?*

As Matt moves on, pointing to some farm equipment, I notice another guy approaching us.

"This is my cousin Clayton," Matt tells me, and Clayton raises his hand to wave at us.

"Clay, this is Yvanya, the friend I was telling you about." Daphne grins at him as she points to me, still holding Matt's hand.

I give him a small smile, pretending to be interested. I study his face. His skin is as dark as his cousin's, but his hair is a much lighter color. Light locks of blond hair highlight his otherwise light brown hair. He's slightly shorter than his cousin and has hazel-green eyes the same shade as mine.

With a good scrub, this guy could be considered good looking, I think as I try to imagine him without all the dirt and grime on his face.

"It's great to finally put a face to your name," he says. "I

43

would shake your hand, but I'm covered in grease and oil." He wipes his hand on a dirty rag. "Welcome to the farm world," he jokes, raising his arms to the sky.

Daphne hands me her backpack, and then she and Matt walk away hand in hand toward some trees, leaving Clayton and me alone in the open field. *Great, Daphne. Thanks for abandoning me here.*

"How long have those two been seeing each other?" I ask him, pointing to Daphne and Matt, who continue moving away from us.

"Matt brought her over about a month ago," he says, wiping the sweat off his forehead with his forearm. "I think they had just started seeing each other."

She kept this secret from me for over a month? I can't help but feel a bit hurt.

"You know each other pretty well?" he asks, studying my face.

"Best friends since babies," I reply.

"By the way you look, I'm guessing you just found out about him," he says, probably noticing my disappointment.

"I'm sure she had a good reason."

"What's it like?" Clayton asks.

"What's what like?"

"Living in the shadows of the night, never seeing the sun," he replies, staring at the horizon.

"Well, you know, as they say, 'It's all in the name of progress, the sacrifice we must make to drive our economy

and dig ourselves out of the hole our ancestors put us in,'"
I say, reciting the same lame excuse we hear everywhere.

"Does it really make any difference?"

"I dunno, but we don't really have a choice. Do we? My
father is constantly getting calls from New Orient. We get a
lot of interruptions during dinnertime, but he says it's better
than being asleep and getting woken up, which would be the
case if we weren't on the same time schedule."

"I just can't imagine not being able to enjoy the day."

"Well, it's the only thing I've ever known." I shrug. I
don't want him to feel pity for me, so I look for a way to
change the subject. "How old is he?" I ask, having noticed
that Matt seems older than us yet also secretly wondering
how old Clayton is.

"If by 'How old is he?' you mean to ask how old he and
I are, he's twenty-one, and I'm nineteen," he says with a
wink and a smile.

"No, I meant just him," I reply.

"Daphne was right. I like you already—so charming,"
he says, and I shake my head.

Now in the open, I feel the sun beating against my head,
and I reach into Daphne's backpack, pull out the bucket hat,
and put it on.

"Nice hat. The pond's over there," he says, pointing to
his right.

"Thanks for the sarcasm." I pull the bottle of sunblock
from Daphne's backpack.

"You should avoid that. It's been tampered with. You know that, right?" Clayton says.

"What do you mean?" I ask. The bottle has the G&NOEA stamp of approval, meaning it's government and New Orient Empire approved. It's the certification added to all consumer products, medicines, and supplements as a guarantee of their efficacy and safety.

"The government adds chemicals to sunblock to change its composition. Plus, contrary to what you've probably been told your whole life, in moderation, sunlight is actually good for you. It helps your body release endorphins, which can help improve your mood and make you feel happy. It's also a key player in mineral and vitamin production and absorption, especially vitamin D, which is critical for bone and immune system health," he says, as if reciting from a medical journal.

"Thanks, Doctor," I say. *How does he know all this?*

"I know it sounds insane, but the government's manipulating the sunblock's chemistry to block the positive effects of the sun's rays," he says.

"And why would they do that?" I am in no way a government defendant, but something about this guy and his arrogance stir in me a desire to contradict him.

"One of the main reasons is that in moderation, sun exposure can help you feel better and more energized, but also because for some people, sunlight can become addictive. By changing the chemistry, they make sure you don't get addicted, and they eliminate any desire to be outdoors during daytime. It also makes you more dependent on supplements and other chemicals they're likely tampering with as well. It's all about controlling the population."

"I've never heard of sun addiction."

"That doesn't negate its existence," he replies. "I wouldn't be surprised if they were behind the recent higher incidence of skin cancer either."

"So how deep does this conspiracy theory of yours go?"

"Well, think about it. You apply your sunblock before going out in the sun but later find out you're now sick. You'll never blame the one thing that's supposed to protect you, right? You'll blame the sun because it's what they've taught you to think," he says, crossing his arms.

"No offense, but your theory sounds a bit far-fetched."

He looks at me with a smile and shrugs. "The facts are out there, baby; you just need to look at them with an open mind."

"So if you're concerned with them altering your supplements, what do you take for vitamin D? You just agreed that it's critical for our health," I say.

"I don't need to take any of that garbage. I get it from the sun," he replies, stretching his arms up to the sky.

His know-it-all attitude gets on my nerves, and I say the one thing I never thought I would repeat. "Have you not heard that sun exposure causes cancer?" As the words escape my mouth, I feel cheap and brainless, as if I'm nothing more than a puppet. This is exactly the type of propaganda the government wants us to believe. I've always had my doubts about the government's true intentions, and sharing them with the wrong people has led to nothing but trouble. Now in front of me stands a person who is saying just what I have been suspecting for years, yet rather than agreeing with him, I find myself challenging him and getting irritated.

"Maybe that crap in your bottle is what's causing cancer. Just consider it," he says with a smirk. Maybe my words don't bother him, or maybe he can see right through me. I can't seem to figure him out, which upsets me even more. Still, I refuse to let him have the last word.

"I'll take my chances," I say, and with a swift motion of my finger, I open the cap, squirt some lotion onto my palm, and rub it on my cheeks.

"Your choice," he says with a laugh. "You know, you should get some sun. Some real sun without that garbage lotion on. It'll make you feel happier." He turns away from me and starts walking toward Matt and Daphne, who have finally reappeared.

"You shutting up will make me feel happier," I whisper under my breath. I take a look at my friend, and seeing her radiant smile helps me regain control of my emotions. I don't think I've seen her this happy in a long time. *Be civilized. For Daphne*, I think.

"We're having dinner soon. Would you girls like to join us?" Matt asks as he and Daphne reach us.

48

Dinner at this hour? We should be sleeping. As if on cue, my stomach grumbles, reminding me I haven't had enough to eat in a while.

"We wouldn't want to take your food from you," I say, assuming these poor people probably have little for themselves and even less to share.

"We have plenty," Clayton says.

"We'd love to," Daphne says, and she and Matt start walking toward one of the shacks.

With the damaged wood and chipping cream-colored paint, the structure looks at least a hundred years old. A brown door is centered on the front, and there's a pair of windows to each side. One of the windows has been boarded. *I hope this place is structurally sound and doesn't collapse while we're inside.*

"After you," Clayton says with a ridiculous, grand gesture as he and I follow behind the lovebirds. In the distance, we can see small children running and playing. A chicken crosses our path, followed by a row of chicks, all moving in single file. This is all foreign to me. I don't remember the last time I saw a farm animal outside of a book.

I enter the house and am immediately surprised by how normal it looks. I'm not sure what I was expecting, but this is definitely not it. Although the house appears to be dilapidated from the outside, it's not much different from mine inside. Actually, it's a bit better, as it has windows throughout most of the living space and vases with flowers adorning the tables. I can't remember the last time we had real flowers inside our house. The natural light and soft breeze from the open windows give the place a bright and welcoming feel, making my house feel dark and gloomy in comparison. The sound of birds chirping throws me off, as I've never heard them while inside a house.

"Not what you were expecting, huh?" Clayton asks me, likely noticing my surprised look.

"No," I admit with a bit of embarrassment. "It's very nice inside."

"We make the outside look bad on purpose," he says with a smile.

Why would anyone do that? I think, and just as I'm about to ask, a woman in her late forties walks in, so I hold my question. She has curly, shoulder-length dark brown hair and big brown eyes. Freckles are sprinkled across her cheeks and nose.

"Daphne and Yvanya, meet my mother, Rebecca," says Matt.

"Finally, I get to meet you," Rebecca says, smiling at us. "Matt talks about Daphne all the time."

"Okay, enough embarrassing me," Matt jokes. "Hope you don't mind I invited them for dinner," he says to his mother, and again, I worry they might not have enough food for us, regardless of Clayton's assurance.

"That would be lovely," she replies, smiling at us. She then turns her attention to Clayton. "Is your father joining?"

"No, he's busy working on one of the tractors and said he'll eat some of the soup you made for him yesterday."

"Okay then," Rebecca says with a nod. "Maybe you can take him some lemonade afterward. Boys, go clean up." She walks into the kitchen. "Girls, go ahead and sit at the table," she says from the kitchen to Daphne and me.

A few minutes later, a cleaner version of Matt walks in.

"So who lives in these houses?" I ask him as I look out a window at the closest house, which is probably fifty yards away.

"My mother and I live in this one, and my uncle and Clay live in the one next door. A few other friends and relatives are in the other ones around ours," he replies as Clayton walks in and joins us.

Not bad, I think as he takes the seat in front of mine. With the dirt and grime gone, I can now appreciate his attractive face. I feel my face getting hot, so I turn it away so he can't see me blush.

A few minutes later, Matt's mother brings out the food. Once again, I'm expecting minimalistic options, and the lavish offerings surprise me.

"Chicken? You have chicken?" Daphne exclaims, examining the contents of a bowl.

"Yeah, who doesn't?" Clayton asks.

"We don't," Daphne replies.

"Sorry. I thought it was a standard," he says, blushing, seemingly embarrassed.

"It's okay," I say as I put a spoonful of carrots on my plate. "The shelves of most grocery stores are missing a lot of things. Meat is scarce, as is fresh produce."

"Well, we have plenty, so please eat what you want," Matt's mother says, bringing out a plate with ears of corn on the cob and butter. Daphne and I smile at each other, and we go for a second spoonful of everything.

Twenty minutes later, I'm fuller than I've been in a long time.

"Do you want to take some food home?" Rebecca asks, pointing at the leftovers.

"We'd love to, but we'd have a lot of explaining to do," Daphne says.

"Our parents don't exactly know we're here," I admit.

"Of course. Then you'd better head home soon, as the sun sets in less than an hour," she says while I stare out the window. The sun is starting to go down. The sky's colors are changing, and the horizon has taken on a beautiful light pink color. I haven't seen a sunset in a long time.

We finish our food and prepare to head home after thanking Matt's mother for the wonderful meal.

"Here. From now on, use this one instead," Clayton says as he hands me an unlabeled white plastic bottle.

"What's in it?" I ask.

"Sunblock. Just the much healthier type. Non-government approved," he replies with a wink.

"Fine," I say, and I sigh before stuffing the bottle into Daphne's bag.

As Daphne and I walk back to her house, I can't help but wonder who the low-class citizens in our society really are.

5

The events from the previous day run through my mind as I work on my homework. I can't shake away the fact that Daphne kept her new boyfriend secret from me for so long. Was she afraid I would lecture her on dating a farmer? She should know me well enough to know I wouldn't judge her.

Or would I? How would I have reacted if she had told me?

And all that food! How is it possible that those who are supposed to be at the bottom of our society have more food than the middle class? It makes no sense. *And their houses.* Clayton said they intentionally make their houses look unappealing from the outside. But if they have decent places to live, why do they make them look that way? What's the point, and whose idea was it?

I also can't shake Clayton from my mind. Something about him intrigues me. *Too bad he's so arrogant and a know-it-all.* I don't know what to think. My head spins as I try to process it all. To add to it, the lack of sleep is not helping me concentrate on my work either. I've read the same passage in my chemistry book three times already and can't remember what it was about.

"Yvanya, your father called. He's arranged for us to have dinner at Paul's house tonight." My mother's enthusiasm is evident as she enters my room. Heidi walks in right behind her.

"Paul?" I ask.

"Paul Anderson. Father's boss and your potential fiancé's father," Heidi responds with a sympathetic smile as she pats my shoulder.

"Oh, right. That Paul," I say, not making any effort to hide my disappointment.

"Please show some enthusiasm." My mother gives me a pleading smile.

"I know. I'll do my best to impress," I reply, lowering my face and closing my book. *I'm definitely not getting any homework done now.*

"Let's get you ready. Dinner's at five," she says.

"What am I going to wear? I don't have anything that's appropriate," I say, wondering which of my two sundresses I should wear. Both are old, faded, and a bit too small for me, as I have been wearing them since my early teenage years.

"I have just the right dress," my mother replies, and she disappears from our room.

About an hour later, I'm in my bedroom with my sister, who is curling my hair, when my mother comes in with a hanger and a black bag around it.

"Here," she says as she removes the bag to unveil what's underneath.

"Wow, it's beautiful!" Heidi and I both exclaim as she shows us the dress. It's a baby-blue sundress with crystal beads stitched along the bustier. It's a sweetheart cut, with thick shoulder straps, and should hit right above the knees. It's perfect.

"You can wear it with these," she says, giving me a pair of barely worn heeled strappy nude sandals.

"Where did you get these?" I ask, as I have never seen her wear them.

"It's a long story for another day. They're a family heirloom, so please be careful with them," she replies.

"Okay," I say, and I give her a quick hug.

When I'm fully dressed up, I stand in front of the swiveling mirror in my room and am pleasantly surprised by its reflection. I don't look cute or pretty, like I usually do. This time, I actually look beautiful.

I'm so thrilled to be showing off these gorgeous clothes that I almost forget the real reason for the occasion: meeting a man I have zero interest in so he can decide if I'm worthy of marriage, in exchange for reassurance of food and a roof. Hopefully the roof is large enough to take care of my entire family in the future. By the way things are going, we're going to need it. Only then will it have been a choice worth the sacrifice.

The only issue with the outfit comes when I try to

walk in the shoes. I've never worn heels, so my ankles keep twisting. *I hope I don't fall flat on my face*, I think as I carefully make my way down the stairs.

After the oohs and aahs from my parents and my sister, we're finally ready to leave. As the Andersons live in the rich part of town, we would have a long way to walk, but thankfully, my father has arranged for their driver to pick us up in their car.

The moment I get in the car, I'm once again filled with excitement since I can count with one hand the number of times I've been in a car. A strange yet pleasant smell adds to the surreal experience.

"Leather," my father tells me as he notices me trying to identify the smell.

"Expensive leather," Heidi says. My mother hushes her, and Heidi and I chuckle.

We sit back and enjoy the ride. The night is cloudless, so the full moon helps illuminate the streets as we drive through them. As we leave our neighborhood and enter a rougher part of town, I can hear in the background faint remnants of someone yelling through a megaphone. Five minutes into our drive, a military vehicle rushes past us, heading in the opposite direction. Within fifteen seconds, gunshots break the silence. My sister and I exchange worried looks, but our father assures us that all is fine. We've felt this type of tension in the air before, but now it's starting to feel more common.

I sense a weird feeling in my stomach but can't pinpoint the origin. So many things are happening at once. I try to distract myself by focusing on the scenery around us. Overgrown trees obscure many of the worn-down buildings and houses. Most of them have at least a window or a door boarded up and have graffiti sprayed on them. I see people walking on the sidewalks; some of them move slowly, as if they're in no rush or have nowhere to go. We slow down at an intersection, and I notice a woman wearing an oversized dress and pushing a grocery cart. Inside it seem to be a blanket and some bags. The homelessness problem has reached the highest level our society has seen in decades.

As we turn a corner, the environment changes abruptly from houses that are falling apart from years of neglect to houses whose owners likely have never uttered the words *not enough money.* Thoughts of hungry, desperate people flash through my mind. *How can life be so unfair? Why do some need to have so much, when so many others have nothing?* I don't have a problem with people having money if they've truly earned it. Most of them, however, have it just because of their good connections with the Empire. Word among my school classmates and others in the street is that these people set barriers for the ones on the bottom to keep them there, dependent, slaves to the system. All people, regardless of where they come from, should have the freedom to choose how far they want to go in life.

About ten minutes later, we're driving through big iron

gates and down a long driveway lined by old hundred-foot-tall trees. I look out the car's window to see a huge white brick mansion. Black shutters adorn the many windows lined across the front of the house. Spotlights on the ground direct beams of light onto the house, highlighting different architectural details. Although it's dark, I can still see the huge gardens surrounding the house. Apparently, when you're rich, no one is concerned with how many gallons of water you use on your plants.

After the car stops, a man opens my door and gives me his hand, helping me out of the car. The night is clear, and a cool breeze of air blows through my hair as I take a few steps toward the house.

These people are not just rich; they're filthy rich, I think in disgust as my parents and sister join me on the front steps.

We enter the house and are greeted by Paul Anderson and his wife, Elizabeth. He's wearing khaki pants and a navy-blue polo shirt. He's medium built, looks to be in his fifties, and has blue eyes and receding brown hair.

"She's more beautiful in person," he says with a kind smile as my father introduces me.

His wife looks like she belongs in this house. She's extremely thin, probably by choice and not from lack of food, and has pale skin and shoulder-length, straight dark hair. She's wearing a tight red dress that hits her right above the knees and some seriously tall high heels. For some reason, her red lipstick makes me think of vampires. *Wow,*

I thought we were coming to dinner, not to a runway fashion show. I wonder if she always dresses like this.

"Hello there," she says, eyeing me and the rest of my family up and down, and despite wearing my mother's beautiful dress, I feel as if I'm wearing rags.

What am I doing here? I wanna go home. "Hi. Nice to meet you," I say cordially, forcing a smile.

The foyer is spectacular. The floors are made of shiny white stone, probably marble. A glass chandelier seems to hover over us as it lights the room. The walls are perfectly white, except for a couple of large paintings that adorn them. A double round staircase connects the first level with the second one.

"Yvanya," my sister calls.

I turn my head to see them walking toward another room. I follow them as I continue to take in my surroundings. Before I enter the new room, a furry white ball approaches me and starts rubbing against my legs.

"You'd better not venture outside," I tell the cat as I bend down to rub its back. "There are a lot of people who'd be happy to eat you." Although I've personally never seen anyone eat a cat or a dog, word in the street is that some are so desperate for meat they've succumbed to this disturbing practice. It's probably the reason we no longer see strays in the streets. As if thanking me for the advice, the cat lets out a soft meow and continues on its way.

I proceed after my family and enter a formal-looking

living room. A ridiculously large white sofa anchors the furniture in the room. Across from it is a smaller white sofa. Multiple silver, gray, and black cushions are perfectly lined on the back of the sofas. A zebra-patterned rug lies between the two sofas, and a few glass tables complete the furniture. A crystal vase with white orchids lies on top of one of the tables.

Is everything in this house white or made of glass? I so do not belong here, I think, impatient for the hour when we get to leave.

"Preston, darling, say hello to our guests," I hear Elizabeth say, and I turn around to see one of the most attractive men I've ever seen in my life. He has jet-black hair and his father's bright blue eyes. His skin, like that of most of us who live at night, is ghost white. Although nice looking, it doesn't have the nice glow that Clayton's has.

Wait—why am I all of a sudden thinking of Clayton? Focus on this guy instead. Preston's wearing a blue shirt the same shade as his eyes and has his sleeves rolled up to his elbows. Khaki pants complete his magazine-perfect look. As he looks at his mother, he smiles, showing off his perfectly white teeth. *Ugh. Mama's boy.*

"Hello," he says with a serious face to my father as he shakes his hand. He gives a polite nod with a small smile to the rest of us.

Inside my head, my snob-detection alarm goes off, and

I feel anger rising. *How can my father think this family would be interested in me?* I feel a desperate urge to run away.

Preston joins us at the sofas, and he and our parents talk about the weather, the economy, and the Andersons' recent trip to Europe. Elizabeth goes on and on about all the museums they visited, while my parents ask questions, appearing to be interested and engaged. They talk for what seems like half an hour while my sister and I do our best not to pass out from boredom. Suddenly, the lack of sleep from the previous day catches up with me, and I find myself fighting the urge to close my eyes. I feel a yawn coming, and as I fight it, my eyes start to water. *Will this ever end?* I think, when out of nowhere, I hear my name.

"Yvanya? What do you think?" Elizabeth asks, and everyone seems to be staring at me, waiting for an answer.

"About what?" I ask, my face turning bright red with embarrassment.

"The literary classics you study in school," she replies with a bit of impatience as once again her eyes scan me up and down. Clearly, she's not impressed by what she sees, as her mouth contorts with distaste.

Stop trying to measure me! I want to yell, but I hold my tongue. Instead, I blurt out the first thing that comes to my mind. "I wouldn't know; I just read the CliffsNotes to pass the tests."

Why did I have to say that? I immediately regret being so blunt, knowing it'll only embarrass my parents.

Elizabeth rolls her eyes, and my parents sigh.

Instead of staying quiet, as I should, I try to show off how proper and insightful I can be. "Given the financial state of most of the people in this country, I believe students should focus their time on more practical ways to lift themselves out of poverty, instead of wasting it on superfluous and pretentious things, like art and literature. Besides, *classics* is another word for obsolete, in my humble opinion. They are no longer relevant and don't represent our society or our people, so I don't see any value in spending time on them." *There. I know some big words too.*

I might as well have just cursed like a pirate. The world seems to stop, and the silence in the room would allow us to hear a pin drop. My parents are likely asking for the earth to open up and swallow them right this moment.

"Yvanya, you have quite a sense of humor!" Preston exclaims, laughing, apparently trying to restore the blood to people's faces. "Well, my mother happens to own first editions of some of the most important literary works from the last century," he says proudly, turning his attention to my parents.

Seriously? I feel like asking.

"Yes, Preston darling here just gave me a first edition of *The Great Gatsby* for my last birthday," she says, and I feel like laughing.

This woman is absurd. What planet does she come from?

"Would you care for some caviar?"

I look up to see a blonde girl with tanned skin and freckles. She looks about my age and holds a small tray of what look like crackers with little beads of blackberry jelly on top.

All of a sudden, I become aware of how hungry I am. "Sure," I say as I grab a couple along with a napkin. "Thank you," I tell her, but instead of nodding or saying, "You're welcome," she just gives me a snarl.

What did I do to you? I study her carefully as she moves on to Preston. As she serves him, I see her face transform into a sweet smile and fluttering eyelashes. *Oh, I get it*, I think as I laugh on the inside. *Don't worry, honey. He's not going to choose me. I've pretty much guaranteed that already.*

I take a bite of my appetizer, but instead of tasting the sweet jelly I'm expecting, I'm hit with a salty, fishy flavor. I force myself to swallow it and accidentally spill a bit of it on the sofa.

Argh. I rush to clean it up with my napkin. Unfortunately, instead of cleaning it off, I end up rubbing it deeper into the fabric. I lift my head to look around and see that no one has noticed, so I grab one of the cushions beside me and use it to cover the stain. *This is not going well.*

A few minutes later, we're called to move to the dining room. I feel relief until I see the dining chairs are also white. *What is wrong with these people? Don't they know there are other colors besides white?* I wonder, worrying about not spilling anything else.

We take our seats, and Paul opens a bottle of red wine, which I can only assume cost him more than what we spend on groceries for a whole month. He serves everyone except for Heidi, who looks at the wine with sad puppy eyes.

My mother shakes her head at her, and Heidi pouts. I seem to be the only one to notice. I take a sip of my wine and am surprised by the taste. I've tried wine before but have never been a fan, as it is always a bit too acidic for my taste. This one is smoother and fruitier. I take a larger sip.

"Slow down," my mother mouths as a warning from across the table, so I set my glass down.

In the center of the table lies a basket of steaming bread. We haven't had bread in a few weeks due to the shortage of flour, so it's one of the first things I go for.

"Preston, darling, can you please get the olive oil we bought in Tuscany, so our guests can try it with the bread?" Elizabeth asks.

Her well-trained son immediately pops up from his seat and goes to fetch it. *Good boy! What a good boy you are*, I imagine her telling him as if speaking to a dog. The mental image cracks me up, and I accidentally let out a laugh.

"What's so funny?" Elizabeth looks at me.

"Nothing," I reply nonchalantly, and I look down, trying to wipe the smile from my face. Right away, everyone's attention turns back to Preston, who rejoins us holding a thick dark green glass bottle. We pass it around and experience the smooth, velvety oil.

"Isn't it the best you've ever had?" Elizabeth asks, staring at us in expectation.

We all nod as we taste it. Indeed, it is delicious, although I have nothing to compare it to since I've never had real olive oil before.

Remember your manners, my mother warns me with her eyes as the first plates of food come in.

Keeping that in mind, I make an effort not to dig into my food as soon as the plate is placed in front of me, as I'd like to. I'm starving, and everything looks and smells delicious. We're served a boneless piece of steak, mashed potatoes, and fresh vegetables. This is the second day in a row that I'm eating well. *I could get used to this.* I look around and notice others are now eating, so I feel it's safe for me to begin.

Everything tastes as great as it looks. After the meal is over, my favorite waitress comes in with dessert. It's been many years since I've had something other than fruit for dessert.

"Cheesecake," Paul tells me as I lift my fork. "From my point of view, one of the seven man-made wonders of the world."

"What are the other six?" I ask. I like the lighter mood we're finally enjoying courtesy of the wine.

"Fine wine," Elizabeth says, joining in.

Paul lifts his glass and says, "Cheers to that!" Both my

parents nod, although I wonder if prior to tonight they've ever had fine wine.

"Ice cream!" Heidi says with a giggle, and everyone smiles. We've only had ice cream a few times in our life, but the fond memory of its taste and feel seems to have stuck with Heidi.

"Electricity and plumbing," my mother says.

"Cars and airplanes," Preston says, and once again, I'm reminded of the class difference. They own a car, and we don't; they've flown in airplanes, while I've never even seen one in person.

Even if for some strange reason he still wanted to be with me, I'd never fit in his world, I remind myself as I find myself drawn to his handsome face. *Stop looking at him, Yvanya; he's not for you.*

I cut a piece of the cake with my fork, and the moment it touches my tongue, my mouth turns into water, and the cake seems to melt. The decadent, sweet, buttery flavor sends signals of pleasure through my brain. The texture is perfect. I feel sad when it's all gone, as I know I might never taste anything this good again.

When dinner is done, our fathers excuse themselves and move to Paul's home office. I wonder what they need to talk about that can't wait until Monday. I take advantage of the break and visit the bathroom. My head feels a bit light, probably from the wine, as I'm not used to alcohol. "No more wine for you, girl," I tell the girl with the rosy cheeks in the mirror, knowing the last thing my parents need is for me to make a spectacle of myself, if I haven't already with my lack of cultural appreciation. On my way back, I stop by the paintings in the foyer.

"So what do you really think about my mother's paintings?" Preston's voice startles me.

"Oh, Preston darling, I didn't see you there," I say with a smirk. I normally would have never dared to say something like that, but the wine seems to have taken control, removing my inhibitions.

"Yeah, she calls me that a lot, doesn't she?" he asks, and I shrug.

"They seem nice, although a bit blurry," I say, turning my attention back to the paintings. I move closer to examine one of them.

"Nice, but superfluous and pretentious. Weren't those the words?" he asks with a grin.

"Exactly," I say, returning his grin.

His face softens, and he turns his attention to the painting in front of us. "The style is called impressionist. It's supposed to look blurry up close, but if you step back, it starts to look a bit more coherent," he says, grabbing me gently by the arms and pulling me a few feet back. His touch causes an eruption of goose bumps all over my arms.

Yvanya, compose yourself. It is a beautiful painting. I would love to someday have something just as beautiful in my house. I surprise myself as these thoughts suddenly cross my mind. Reminding myself that this lifestyle is not for me, I push the thoughts aside. Instead, I look at him with a smile and say, "Still blurry." Out of the corner of my eye, I notice the waitress standing by the bathroom door and watching us while pretending to shine the door handle. I ignore her and turn my attention back to him.

"You guys seem to spend a lot of money on things that aren't essential. Out there in the real world, there are lots of people in need of food and clothes, so forgive me for not caring too much about culture or art," I say, pretending to look unimpressed.

I expect him to get offended or say something defensive, but instead, while looking me straight in the eyes, he takes a couple of steps closer to me and lowers his head so his mouth is inches from my ear. I freeze and hold my breath as his breath teases my skin. The hairs on my arms stick up as I feel butterflies fluttering in my belly. For a second, I wonder if it's a side effect of the wine, and I make a mental note never again to drink alcohol in the presence of attractive men. I pretend he has no effect on me and force myself to breathe again.

"I know what you did to the sofa," he whispers in my ear, and then he slowly pulls backward, seeming to wait for my reaction.

"That was an accident," I whisper back, trying to hide a smile.

"Was it?" he asks, raising an eyebrow, which makes him look even more handsome, if that's possible.

"Yes, it was. And who ever thought white was a good color for furniture? It's begging to get dirty."

"It's my mother's favorite color. As a kid, I wasn't allowed near pretty much anything in this house," he jokes. "By the way, what did you think of the caviar? I'm guessing it's the first time you've tried it."

"Yeah, that was some funny-tasting jelly," I say, and he bursts into laughter. "What's so amusing?"

"Caviar's not a type of jelly. It's fish eggs," he says, and my face turns in disgust. After pushing aside the thoughts of eating such a repulsive thing, I join him in laughter.

I turn my attention toward one of the windows in the living room. It's open, and a light breeze is gently blowing the curtains. I stand in front of it and let the air blow through my hair.

"You're not like the other girls," he says, staring at me.

"What do you mean?" I don't dare to meet his gaze, as I know it'll make me blush.

"You have spunk. You don't try to impress."

Is that supposed to be an insult or a compliment? As I don't know for sure, I pretend I didn't hear it and continue to stare out the window.

"You have beautiful hair," he says as he gently twists one of my long blonde locks around his index finger. Once again, his touch induces a foreign yet wonderful sensation.

71

"How come you guys have windows? I thought all health-conscious people had gotten rid of them." I change the topic, trying to distract myself from his proximity.

"Our windows have shields that we lower during the day. There's no risk during nighttime, so we can open them safely then," he says as he points upward to rolls that hang over each window.

"What was college like?" I ask.

"Don't tell my mother, but between you and me, I'll admit it was boring. Nothing but a lot of studying and hanging out with a bunch of males."

His answer makes me smile. I want to ask him more about school, what he studied, and what his plans for a job are, but before I have the chance, we are interrupted.

"Yvanya, we're leaving," Heidi says.

We both turn toward her as my parents enter the living room. After exchanging hugs and handshakes and thanking the Andersons for their hospitality, we walk toward the door.

Preston pulls me aside as my family continues moving toward the car. "I enjoyed our conversation. It was great meeting you," he says, touching my arm with his index finger, which makes me stiffen.

"Yes, it was nice meeting you too," I reply with a sad smile, wondering if I'll ever see him again. As I walk toward the door, one of my heels turns under my weight, and I fall to the floor. *Way to make an exit, Yvanya!*

Preston rushes to help me up, and I hear his mother

sigh loudly. Feeling everyone's eyes on me, I feel myself turn the brightest shade of red possible. Out of the corner of my eye, I see the green-eyed-monster waitress smiling. *I bet she's enjoying this*, I think with bitterness.

Preston lets go of my arm, and I continue walking to the car, where my parents and sister are waiting for me, likely sinking their heads into the floor with embarrassment over my big mouth and lack of grace. Far away on the horizon, the sun is rising. I avoid looking at the spectacle of colors and focus on walking, as my pride can't afford another misstep.

I climb inside the car and keep my eyes on the house as we drive away in silence. Slowly, they close the windows one by one. Next, I assume they will lower the sun-radiation shields. I see Preston standing by the door. As we drive away, I can't tell for sure, but it appears to me he's smiling.

6

A bit more than two weeks go by without any news from Preston. I wasn't expecting him to call our house, but I haven't heard any updates from my father either. I'm not entirely surprised, but I'm still unsure how to take it. Part of me feels relieved and happy he's not interested in me, while another part feels rejected. *Am I not good enough for him? I'm from a completely different social class. I have no money and nothing to offer to him, other than entertainment if he happens to enjoy sarcasm and clumsiness.* Even Daphne has stopped asking me about him.

I think of our conversation right after I met Preston and his family. She was thrilled for me, as she recognized what the possibility of my marrying him represented in terms of stability for me and my family. She confided that part of her was a bit jealous it wasn't her, but at the same time, she was relieved she didn't have to choose between having her basic needs satisfied for the rest of her life and finding real love.

"What's he like?" she asked, intrigued, as we folded her laundered clothes in her bedroom. Her mother had hung them out to dry in the early-morning hours while it was still dark and then brought them in soon after sunset. They felt a bit stiff.

"He's a very attractive snob," I replied, folding one of her old pairs of jeans. "His parents' house is preposterous to the point that it's embarrassing. These people have spent so much money. I don't even know how they can afford it."

"They may have a lot of debt," Daphne said, and she pointed to one of the drawers in her dresser. I opened it and placed the jeans in it. There were just a couple of items inside.

"Maybe, although I doubt it," I replied.

Decades ago, people used credit from banks to buy things they otherwise couldn't afford. They teach us in school that many people got into so much debt they were unable to repay it. That debt is part of the reason we ended up where we are today. Few people have access to bank loans nowadays. The practice still exists informally as part of the underground world, but you need to know whom to deal with. If you get a loan from the wrong guys and can't repay it, you or a member of your family might end up as their slave, badly beaten up, or, in the worst case, even dead. Few people take this type of risk, and it's usually for emergencies or life-or-death situations, not for frugalities or luxury items.

"What does his father do for a living?" Daphne continued her interrogation as she folded a long-sleeved gray T-shirt. I recognized it immediately. It was the one I'd worn to the farm the day I met Clayton and Matt, the shirt with the white crown.

"He works with my father. He's one of his managers. I don't know what he does, but there's no way he makes enough money to afford what they have. He seemed pretty nice, though."

"And his mother? What's she like?"

"She's probably the one who's loaded. You should have seen her. She hated my guts the moment I walked through the door. She'd probably have a stroke if I ended up marrying her bratty son." I let out a snicker. "I should marry him just to spite her. Oh, and the servant girl!"

"They have a servant?" she asked with interest. Prior to the Andersons, neither of us had ever met somebody with one.

"Yeah. She's probably about our age. The little witch was drooling over him the entire time, though he probably doesn't even know she exists. I'd feel bad for her if it weren't for the nasty looks she kept giving me the whole night."

We were down to the last pieces of clothing: two nonmatching socks, one gray and one white. I lifted them to her and asked, "Where are their partners?"

"Broken beyond mending, so I finally had to trash them. Those now go together," she said, and I tied them together. She opened a drawer, and I threw them inside. "Well, you just wait. I'm sure he's going to call you in the next couple of days and surprise you with a huge diamond ring," she said, clearly trying to encourage me. "Imagine that. Then you can move into their extravagant mansion and become just like your mother-in-law," she joked, poking my side.

"Ha, that's not going to happen. If I were to end up living there —"

"And you managed not to end up in jail from trying to kill each other," Daphne said, interrupting.

"Exactly! Challenge number one." I laughed. "I would probably first kick the servant out of the house, and then I would sell all their *amazing* first-edition books," I said in a highly nasal tone, imitating Mrs. Anderson's voice, "and give the money to charity. I would feel too guilty otherwise. No one should have that much, especially if they haven't done anything to deserve it."

"Aren't you being too fast to judge? Maybe they've worked hard to get what they have. Isn't that a possibility?" Daphne said.

"Trust me. That woman has not worked one day of her life. I can tell," I said. "I'm a pretty good judge of character. And again, government people don't make that much."

"Well, if Preston makes the worst mistake of his life and passes on you, maybe you can marry Clayton. We could even have a double wedding!"

"You and I marrying farmers? Yeah, I bet our parents would be thrilled."

"I know. I'm not sure how I'll ever be able to bring the news up to them if it ever gets to that," Daphne said.

"You really like him?"

"I think so. He's different from the other guys I've dated. He's much more mature. He's responsible and knows what he wants. He's very hardworking too. But I don't wanna get too carried away yet. You know how men are—nice one day and then total jerks the next."

"True. Can you do me a favor? Don't talk about Preston or the whole possible engagement thing to anyone. I doubt anything will come of it, so it's better to just not say anything. That way, I won't have to deal later with awkward questions and conversations," I said.

"No worries. I won't," she said.

After our initial conversation, she asked almost every day for an update. As the days went by, my responses became more tainted with disappointment and resentment, and she stopped asking altogether.

I shouldn't care. No, actually, I don't care. I'm glad he's not interested in me. Looks and money aside, he's a nobody, a mama's boy. I could never respect a man like that. He's inherited what he has. He hasn't done anything to earn it. I need a husband who's self-made—a hard worker who's not afraid to get his hands dirty. And most importantly, a husband who loves and appreciates me.

That's right. Preston, you can take your sorry ass away from here because I'm not interested. You're not rejecting me. I'm rejecting you!

79

Hanging out with Daphne and the guys at the farm during the day has messed up my biological clock. I'm starting to turn diurnal. Daphne and I have started taking power naps during our lunch break at school. We skip lunch altogether and go to the library, where we hide among the never-ending aisles of books.

Decades ago, the Empire conducted an evaluation process on our books, and those that didn't find favor in their eyes were removed from circulation and destroyed. Although history books dating prior to the Empire were destroyed and rewritten, most fictional ones were spared. Volumes and volumes of thick old books crowd the library shelves, some of them squeezed in so tightly they look as if they're about to burst to the ground. It's almost as if they're begging desperately to be pulled from their shelves. I bet most of them have been closed for decades. I know they're inanimate objects and don't have feelings, but in a way, I still feel bad for them. Maybe in another life, if things were different and I didn't have so much homework, I could have enjoyed sitting down and losing myself in their stories.

I push a book back onto its shelf, worried it might fall out and hit Daphne or me on the head as we rest.

The library's usually pretty empty, so no one interrupts us. The librarian's a sweet old lady with her hair up in a white bun and small spectacle glasses. She walks around with a wooden cane, dusting the books to keep herself busy. She seems lonely, so she probably likes seeing Daphne and me come in on a regular basis, even if only to sleep. She doesn't speak much, but a few weeks ago, she left a couple of beanbags, one bright blue and one red, by the area where we've been hanging out. I had never seen them before, which tells me she might have brought them over from the nearby elementary school's library. I remember the library having beanbags when I was in grade school. I feel kind of bad when imagining how much work it might have been for her to drag them all the way here. I hope someone helped her.

I set my backpack on the carpeted floor and lie down on the blue beanbag. As my body pushes down on it, a bit of stuffing comes out from a tear. I push the stuffing back inside, rearranging it so it doesn't pop out again. The beanbags have some small tears here and there, but otherwise, they're perfect. Beggars can't be choosers, and it certainly beats sleeping on the old, dusty carpet.

I set my wristwatch's alarm to wake me in forty minutes. A minute later, Daphne joins me on the red beanbag. With no time to waste, we close our eyes and doze off right away.

🕐 🕑 🕒

It's late in the morning, and everyone in my house has finally fallen asleep. I creep down the stairs and stand in front of my father's study. I've been meaning to get into his study to look for the secret door, but amid all the excitement with the potential engagement and my father working late from his study, I haven't had a chance. I try the door handle gently but firmly. It's locked.

What were you expecting? If Father's got something to hide, he's certainly not going to leave it right there in the open for you to find. Think, Yvanya. Where could he be keeping the key? If it were me, I would keep it either well hidden in my bedroom, away from peeping eyes, or on myself—maybe around my neck on a chain. I don't recall ever seeing my father wear something around his neck, and I definitely can't go up to their bedroom to check for it right now. I could ask my mother tomorrow if she knows where the key is, but it would only lead to questions.

As I'm about to crawl back to bed full of discouragement, another idea comes to mind. *Where would be the most obvious place Father would keep a key? With the rest of his house keys. But if Father is keeping secrets from us, he's not just going to park them right under our noses. What would be the point of having a lock then?* Still, I decide to give it a try.

I find his key chain in the kitchen cabinet drawer where we keep all our keys. It was my mother's idea for us to drop them off there the moment we come into the house. She got tired of us losing them all the time.

I close the drawer slowly so it doesn't make a sound and walk to our home's only window. I pull up the curtain just enough to allow some light in and then bring the key chain to the light. It contains five keys. I recognize the one for the front door, which is an exact replica of the key on my own key chain. I have no idea what the others are for. They all look different. Some are long and skinny; others are short and wide. I replace the curtain and make my way back to the study's door.

I run my free hand over the door, seeking the keyhole. My index finger moves from smooth hardwood to cold metal, and I know I'm close. An inch lower, I feel the dip and the grooves in the metal plate. I select one of the unrecognizable keys and push it toward the keyhole. It does not go in. I try two more keys with the same result. The keys won't even go into the hole.

Disappointment starts to set in. I pick the last unknown key and push it against the keyhole. To my surprise, it goes in smoothly. I hold my breath in excitement as I try to twist it. But it won't twist. It's not the right key.

I walk back to the window and lift the curtain again. I study the keys one more time, still holding the last key I tried. Upon more detailed inspection, I notice the shape of it closely matches the one for the front door.

Could the key to the front door open more than one lock? I wonder.

I go back to the study's door and insert the house key into the keyhole. Just like the one before, it enters smoothly. With a shaky hand, I slowly twist the key—and it works. My heart accelerates, and I feel a bit of disbelief at how easy it was to get in—too easy, really. I twist the handle, quickly let myself into the room, and then close the door quietly behind me. I run my hands over the wall by the door, looking for the light switch. I find it and shield my eyes from the blinding light. As my pupils adjust, the room comes into focus.

I haven't been in here in a while. Dark tan-colored walls with built-in mahogany bookshelves line the entire perimeter of the small room. An old mahogany desk sits in the center. It's a bit too big for the size of the room. A brown leather chair that has seen better times faces away from the desk. I pull the chair back and scan the desk. Years of scratches and dings have damaged the otherwise attractive piece of furniture. I run my fingertips over the desk's aging surface.

I set the keys down and switch my focus to inspect the items on the desk. My father's work cap; a folded newspaper; a small bronze desk lamp with a green glass cover; a coffee mug featuring a picture of the Empire's flag, holding a couple of pencils and a few pens; and a pad to protect the desk from writing scars are a few of the things that catch my eye. *Should have thought of getting the protective pad before the desk was all scratched up.*

I pick up my father's cap. It's navy blue, with the letters *EBI* embroidered in bright yellow thread. He wears it often to work. Sweet memories come to my mind of him putting it on me as a child. My parents thought it looked cute because it was too big for my small head. I play with it for a few seconds and then set it back on the desk right where

I found it. I pick up the newspaper; the thin pages feel cold against my fingers. I scan the headline and learn there's a sizeable reward for anyone who helps in the identification and capture of Mitchell's followers. If I recall correctly, Mitchell is the traitor who was apprehended and sent to the Dungeon a few weeks ago. I set the newspaper down. To the right sits a globe of the world.

"You girls are the center of my world," Father always told us as he tucked Heidi and me into bed. "Never forget that," he insisted, kissing our foreheads. Mother often stood by the door with a smile on her face. She seemed to love watching him interact with us, especially when he didn't know she was watching. He also read a book or two to us on most nights. We savored every second of it and often complained when he got up to leave, but the moment we heard him say his center-of-the-world phrase, we knew it was time for bed.

I lower my face to the globe and turn it slowly. The areas that long ago used to be called North America, Europe, and Asia are now shown in red, with the words *New Orient Empire* written in bold black letters over them. Vertical lines divide the regions based on their original time zones. The number twelve is written over our region. I slowly turn the globe 180 degrees and see the star over the Empire's capital. I let out a sigh.

I continue looking around the room, but nothing seems unusual. *Where can that secret door be?* I run my hands over the bookshelves. They're mostly empty, but nothing looks out of the ordinary. I decide to pull on some of the books, as I've seen shows in which that sometimes triggers a lever, which then opens a hidden door. I pull at least fifteen or twenty of them, but nothing happens. I look for any buttons or marks by the bookshelves that, if pressed, might lead to something, but again, I find nothing. I also push and pull on the edges of the bookshelves, hoping maybe it's as easy as that, but that doesn't work either.

I make a horrible sleuth.

I turn the chair around and take a seat. The cold leather feels nice against my legs.

Think, Yvanya. Think. I lean forward and rest my elbows on my thighs. I lower my head and stare at the rug underneath the chair. An idea comes to mind, and I push the chair away from the rug. I fold the rug halfway, hoping maybe the door is right underneath me. The floorboards look just like the rest in the study. I gently tap them, wondering if they'll make a different sound from the rest of the floor, but they don't. I feel around for any loose boards, but again, I get nothing but the same disheartening result.

Could it be that I misheard? Could it be there's really nothing here? I start to doubt myself. *No! I heard a man talking to my father and then a door open. It has to be here. I didn't imagine it.*

I stare back at one of the walls. Other than the few books I pulled, there are a few family pictures hung on the back wall of one of the bookshelves. They're a combination of five-by-seven and eight-by-ten black frames spread a few inches from one another. An eight-year-old version of me smiles from one of the pictures, while another frame holds a picture of Heidi. Looking at Heidi's, I can't help but smile. One of her front teeth is missing, and she's sticking the tip of her tongue through the hole. I lift the frame holding my picture, and it comes off its hook. I stare at the wall, but there's nothing behind the picture other than the nail from which it was hanging. I pull Heidi's picture, and again, I see nothing new. I try a few more frames with pictures of the two of us together, but to no avail. I replace the frames where I found them. The last one is an eight-by-ten picture of Heidi and me with our mother.

I still remember the day. We went to a professional photographer and wore our nicest dresses. Heidi had a big pink bow that matched her sundress, while I was wearing a lavender dress with a smocked collar. I was about six years old, and Heidi was a toddler. The camera's flash kept upsetting my eyes, and every time the photographer took our picture, I would close one of them.

"I'm sorry; she keeps blinking," the man kept saying to my father, who wouldn't give up on the hope of getting a nice picture of us.

Eventually, my mother and baby sister started laughing out loud, and the cameraman gave up.

"Forget it. We'll take that one," my father said, pointing

at one of the pictures. "It kind of looks like she's winking, like keeping a secret," he joked.

The picture became one of our favorites, with Heidi and my mother grinning from ear to ear while I wink at the camera. *Back then, life was so much easier*, I think with nostalgia.

I grab the picture frame, but it won't come off. I can't pull it from the wall. I gently push on its bottom left edge, and it rotates about the center of its top edge. I continue pushing until a small keyhole is revealed behind it.

Oh my goodness! I found it! I found the keyhole! And now where's the key?

I look down at the key chain I set on my father's desk and pick it up. My hands shake as I go through the keys. I decide to try them all, certain that one of them must be it. One by one, I try each key, and one by one, each fails to enter the keyhole. *But I'm so close!* I want to cry. I let go of the frame, and it swings back into place. My winking smile now mocks me.

"You know where it is. Tell me your secret, little girl," I whisper. "Tell me where it is."

I search the room for the missing key for another hour or so. *What a terrible way to end this*, I think, giving the room one last scan. I've run out of ideas, and it's late. I should probably get back to sleep. I place the chair back as it was before I moved it and switch off the light. After locking the door, I tiptoe back to the kitchen and return the keys to their drawer. I give the study's door one last glance as I walk upstairs.

So close! I think with disappointment, and I sneak back into my room.

As I lie in bed, too wired to fall asleep, I think back to the night when I followed my father to his secret rendezvous. It was lighter than usual, a full-moon night. School had let out early because we were expecting bad weather, and the school headmaster thought it was safer to get us all home before it turned severe.

"I don't have time to drop you all off in front of your houses, so I'm just gonna stop at the beginning of each block. Please hurry home so you're not caught in the rain," the fifty-something-year-old driver told us as the bus pulled over. I waved goodbye to Daphne and, strapping my backpack on, stepped off the bus. The driver closed the door the moment my feet touched the ground. He was clearly in a hurry. I watched him speed away for a few seconds and then walked quickly toward my house. Although it wasn't raining yet, the wind had picked up. The branches of the trees that lined our street twisted and bent at angles I hadn't known were possible without breaking. Leaves and twigs fell all around me.

As I drew closer to my house, I noticed a figure exiting. It was my father, wearing a gray trench coat and a matching brimmed hat. Even from far, I knew it was him because of his walk. He told us that as a young boy, he was being chased by his older brothers and didn't see a crack in the sidewalk. He tripped and broke a leg when he fell. Although the doctors did what they could to repair it, it never healed quite right, so he's always had a bit of a limp. I found it strange that he would be home so early and, even more, that he was leaving the house in such haste.

For a second, I thought of yelling out to him, making myself known, and asking if I could go with him, but something about the way he looked over his shoulders told me he wasn't looking for company at that time.

Where's he going in this weather? I wondered. There was only one way to find out, so I decided to follow him. I left about six or seven houses between us, allowing enough space to ensure there was always a tree nearby to hide behind if he were to abruptly turn around. A couple of times, he did stop and look back, but quick reflexes allowed me to duck in time to avoid being seen. He picked up his pace once he left our neighborhood. My walk turned to a jog as I struggled to keep up with his long legs. My backpack was bouncing too much, so I pulled it to my front and cradled it with my arms.

In a couple more blocks, he turned into a less desirable part of town full of buildings with boarded doors, graffiti scribbled over the walls, and trash cans overturned with garbage. A raccoon rummaging through one of the garbage cans lifted its head and hissed at me. *Okay, this is not the place where I want to be, especially at night*, I thought, and for an instant, I considered turning around. *No, not going back now. I need to know what he's up to.*

I walked between a pair of five-story buildings. I would have thought they were abandoned had it not been for people hanging out on the balconies. I heard a man on one of the balconies yell some obscenities at another a few floors away. *Wow, I'm definitely out of my element*, I thought with angst.

Past those buildings was another building, possibly an abandoned factory. It was two stories high and covered the length of the entire block. A long sign about six feet by three hung by one of its sides over a boarded door. The words *Employee Entrance Only* were barely noticeable, as the paint had chipped away through the years. The strong breeze threatened to snap at any moment the single cable that supported it. I made a mental note not to walk anywhere near it upon my return. Empire propaganda posters covered most of the first floor's outside wall. Some of the posters were torn, with the back layer of the paper still stuck on the wall, as if someone had tried to strip them off with little success.

In a corner stood a group of scruffy-looking middle-aged men. There were five in all, and one held a bottle of liquor. They ignored my father as he walked by them, but the moment I got closer, they turned their attention to me. I crossed the street to put distance between us.

"Ah, mama, where do you think you're going?" one yelled.

"Are you lost, sweetheart?" another asked.

"Come over here. We just wanna talk to you!" a third guy yelled, and he started crossing the street, walking in my direction. His steps were clumsy, revealing his level of intoxication.

Please stay away from me, I thought, starting to panic and scanning my surroundings to see if there was anything I could use as a weapon if the men got any closer. I looked for a metal trash can lid, a broken board, or glass bottles, but none of those seemed to be around. I saw nothing nearby other than piles of newspapers and some empty boxes. I stuck my hand inside my jeans pocket and wrapped my fingers around my house key. *In the worst case, I can always scratch someone's face with it*, I thought. *As long as I'm not blocked, I'll try first to make a run for it, but if that's not a choice, I can always scream for my father. He'll surely hear me, recognize my voice, and come to my rescue.* I considered my options.

Just then, the man who was walking in my direction tripped and fell to the ground. *Nasty drunk*, I thought with relief. The others started laughing and hooting, and I immediately increased my speed to a jog. Soon their voices faded away, and my nerves calmed down a bit.

Once I had some space between myself and the creepy men, I refocused my attention on my father. He turned a corner, and for a few seconds, I feared I might have lost him. Thunder echoed in the distance, and a few small drops of rain hit the top of my head. I turned the corner and caught a glimpse of him as he slowed down and turned into an alley. I slowed down my pace and stopped altogether when I got to the corner. The last thing I wanted was to have come all this way only to walk straight into him.

An old brick building stood on the corner. The phrases "Death to the New Orientals" and "America Free" were spray-painted on the board that covered what once had been the entrance. Whoever had written those words would face up to life in prison if caught by the police. The Empire takes that type of aggression as a serious offense, and they show no mercy. They take every opportunity to set an example to dissuade others from joining any dissident movement.

I leaned against the edge of the building and peeked around the wall. Chunks of some of the bricks were missing, and the exposed material felt rough against my fingers. My father wasn't alone. In the middle of the narrow alley stood another man dressed in a similar khaki raincoat and hat. Behind him was a dark-colored car. That was the first time I saw it, before it was parked by my house in the dark. On the front of the hood was a figure of a leaping animal, maybe a large cat. It was hard to be certain, as I was at least thirty feet from it.

I felt something move over my feet. Startled, I jumped and looked down to find a rat with its thick pink tail twirling. I held my breath so I wouldn't scream and shooed it away with a kick. It squealed as it ran away. A strong gust of wind blew straight onto my face, and the stench of something rotten hit me. I almost lost what little was left of my lunch. I tried to ignore the distractions and peeked again around the corner, watching as my father opened his raincoat and pulled out a large manila envelope, which he handed to the stranger. The man opened the car's passenger door and tossed the envelope inside. He shook hands with my father and then walked around the front of the car to the driver's door. As he shut his door, a lightning bolt hit nearby, and the sky cracked open, pouring all its contents over us. As the man turned on the car's headlights, I pulled myself back behind the wall to avoid being seen.

What was in the envelope? I wondered, but I immediately realized my questions would have to wait because I needed to hide before my father ran straight into me.

I spotted another alley nearby and made a run for it. I leaned against a boarded door, making myself disappear into the shadows. I watched out of the corner of my eye as my father walked past me. He didn't seem to see me. I waited almost a minute and then resumed my pursuit, staying far enough behind not to be seen but close enough not to lose sight of him. After all, the last thing I wanted was to get lost in that dreadful place.

He took the same route we'd followed in coming there. The drunken men were gone by then, and the balconies were empty. The street was now a ghost town. The road had turned into a shallow river, with the water up to my ankles in some parts.

Once back in our neighborhood, I took a parallel street and raced home as fast as I could. My shoes had soaked up so much water it was hard to get any significant speed. Thick clouds covered the sky, obscuring the moonlight. I was afraid of tripping on something and falling, but I was more afraid of getting caught by my father. I needed to get home before him, so I crossed through a couple of neighbors' yards.

A few feet from my own backyard, I stepped on uneven ground and twisted my ankle. I felt pain shoot through my entire leg but was able to recover my balance. I ignored the discomfort and continued moving as I stuck my hand into my pocket to retrieve the front door key. Without a second to spare, I inserted it into the keyhole and let myself inside the house. I ran up the stairs to the bathroom, leaving a trail of water behind me. *I'll clean it up as soon as I can. Do my parents know we were let out of school early? If so, how am I going to explain my tardiness? I'll think about it in the shower. One thing at a time.*

I could say I was at Daphne's and lost track of time, I thought. *But what if Mother was worried and called her house and knows I wasn't there? Where else could I have gone that would make sense to them—that they wouldn't question? I could say I missed the bus at school and had to walk all the way back, but they might know it's not true. If Mother did call Daphne's mother, she probably already knows I was on the bus.*

This is not going to end well, I thought, preparing myself for the worst. Not having a convincing story, I decided to press my luck and claim I had been at Daphne's.

Ten minutes later, I walked downstairs. My mother, Heidi, and my father were all in the kitchen, sipping hot tea. They were all soaking wet.

"We just got back. It was crazy out there!" Heidi said.

"Yeah, where were you?" I asked, pretending to have been waiting around for them for a while. "I was getting worried," I lied as I pulled a mug from a cupboard.

"Sorry, honey. I heard the market had received a new shipment of meat, and I know it probably wasn't the smartest choice, but I really wanted to get some before it was all gone," my mother responded. "Heidi should have stayed here. I shouldn't have brought her along in this weather."

"No, it was fun. Lightning was hitting all around us!" Heidi said. "For a minute, the store lost power, and some people started screaming. But it was worth it—we got a whole chicken!"

"That's awesome, my love, but please don't do that again," my father said, setting his mug down and caressing my mother's arm. "What about you, Yvanya? I saw a trail of water when I came in," he added, looking straight at me.

"The bus dropped me off at the corner of the street, and by the time I made it to the house, it was raining already," I lied, turning around to pour water from the kettle into my mug. *I can't believe it's going to be this easy to get away with this*, I thought as relief sank in.

"Really? I'm glad you weren't out there putting yourself in danger," he said in an emotionless tone, and I could feel his stare burning a hole into my back. No one else seemed to pick it up.

He knows, I thought. *Did he see me? He must have. But why didn't he say something? Why didn't he call me out? Why would he have kept going if he knew I was following him? Or maybe he saw me as we were returning? Still, why play along if he knows I'm lying straight to his face? Because he doesn't want me to ask questions. He doesn't want me to confront him and ask him what he was doing, of course. Whatever he was doing, he wants to keep it a secret from my mother as well.*

"What about you, Father?" I asked, turning around to face him, trying to look and sound innocent. "Where were you?" *Two can play this game*, I thought.

"At work, of course," he replied casually, locking his eyes on mine. "They didn't let us out early like they did you kids."

"Oh, that's a shame, honey," my mother said, still not seeming to notice the staring contest or the tension between my father and me. "They should have let you all go early as well. Okay, everyone needs to dry up before we all get sick. I'm going to take a quick shower, and then I'll start preparing that amazing chicken. Yvanya, please dry the floor while we go change. I don't want anyone slipping and falling." She took our mugs away and directed my father and sister upstairs.

Father, what are you hiding? And who was that man? I thought as I watched him exit the kitchen.

"Do you guys plant anything other than corn?" I ask Matt as he pours a cup of lemonade for me. A bowl with chunks of warm, buttered ears of corn sits on the middle of the picnic table. It is a bright and sunny day with puffy white clouds scattered across the sky. A hawk flies in circles across the open sky, probably having spotted prey somewhere on the ground. After a minute or two, it dives and disappears between the trees. Although the novelty of seeing birds and farm animals all around has started to wear off, I still enjoy seeing them and am impressed by the variety of colors and shapes they come in. The wind carries the sounds of the neighboring children playing.

A few puddles remain from the early morning rain showers, but most have evaporated by now. The humid air feels a bit stuffy, so we've sought shelter under a canopy of trees by a corner of the yard. Hanging between two large maple trees is a brown hammock, which Daphne has made her bed. "This is the life," she says, kicking her shoes off and letting them drop to the ground.

"Corn, wheat, soy, kale, carrots, beans, broccoli, squash—you name it," Matt replies, smiling at Daphne. "Our neighbors plant a few other things, and we trade."

"How do you plant all these fields? It must take you months," I say, remembering how long it took my sister and me the time we grew our flowers, and we planted no more than a few dozen.

"Not really. We have some pretty handy equipment to help," Clayton says. "If we all work together, we can be done in a couple of days."

"Give her the tour you gave me when I first came here," Daphne says. Sitting up on the hammock, she turns to me and adds, "It's impressive how they run the whole operation."

"Come on. I'll show you our toys," Clayton says, popping up from the bench. He leads me to what was once a red barn about a hundred feet away, and Matt and Daphne follow.

"Is this place safe to enter?" I ask, studying the structure and noticing missing pieces of wood and jagged or rotten edges everywhere. A beam leaning against the ground seems to hold a wall, stopping it from collapsing.

"Yes. It's a sound building. Remember, it's all decoration," Matt jokes.

What do you mean by that? What kind of decoration? I've been wondering for a while why they make their buildings look dilapidated, but for some reason, I haven't asked the question.

Clayton walks to a set of double doors made from wood that is likely more than a hundred years old. Chunks of the wood are missing from the bottom, probably from water damage, termites, or both. He lifts the lever that keeps the doors shut, and they slowly open with a loud creaking sound.

I should expect it, but I don't: as with the house, the barn's exterior is a false front meant to conceal something of greater value inside. Although nowhere near fancy or new, the inside looks just as I would have expected a normal barn to look. It's obvious the inside has been recently painted, since the walls are in much better condition than the exterior. A pile of pitchforks, rakes, shovels, and other tools whose names I don't know stand in a corner, leaning against a wall.

"Trying to fool outsiders?" I ask Matt.

"You catch on quickly," he says with a smile.

"Unwanted visitors are less attracted this way. They're not gonna try to break in if they think there's nothing of value inside," Clayton says. He walks to what I guess is a tractor and, as if introducing an old friend, says, "Meet Anabelle. This beauty has seventy horsepower. She was top of the line back in 2004, when she was made, and can still lift a bale of hay without any hesitation." I'm surprised the paint looks so shiny for being more than seventy years old. They must have repainted it recently.

"How much does a bale weigh?" Daphne asks.

"About fifteen hundred pounds, give or take a few hundred," Clayton responds, pointing at some giant cylindrical marshmallow-looking things neatly stacked a few feet from the barn.

"What are those for?" I ask.

"Food for the animals during winter," says Clayton. "It's usually too cold for them to graze. We break the bales up, and that's what they eat. We sometimes supplement with grain feed too."

"You named your tractor?" I ask, turning my attention back to the piece of equipment. It's bright green, and its rear wheels are as tall as my shoulders.

"Who doesn't? All our machines have names," Matt says, as if it's common knowledge.

"Because that makes a lot of sense!" I laugh.

We then turn to Daphne, who is pointing at another piece of equipment. "What about this one? What was her name again?"

"That's Daisy Mae," Matt responds. "She's a one-hundred-and-ten-horsepower tractor and is now connected to a hay mower, although sometimes we use it with the baler, the cultivator, or the corn chopper." He climbs onto the tractor and turns it on for a few seconds. "Hear her purr like a kitten!" he yells over the loud noise. The engine's sound is much louder than a kitten's purr, so I'm not sure why he would say that. I figure it's probably a farmer figure of speech, so I ignore it.

"So you don't drop the seeds one at a time?" I say, inspecting the machine.

"That would be insane," Matt says.

"Then what do you use to plant corn?" Daphne asks.

"We use a vacuum planter for that. Corn needs better singulation," Clayton replies. He might as well be speaking a foreign language. I just nod, pretending to understand what he and Matt are saying. "Would you like a ride?" he asks Daphne and me.

"Sure!" Daphne jumps at the offer. "Come on. It'll be fun," she tells me, pulling on one of my arms. She moves toward Anabelle and climbs behind Matt.

"Come on, Cricket; you can have fun for once," Clayton says as he detaches the hay mower from the tractor named Daisy Mae. He climbs up and extends a hand out to me.

"Cricket?" I ask, confused.

"Because you're one of those who comes alive at night," he explains, and I shake my head in amusement.

"Is that what you call nocturnal people?" I ask.

"Nah. Just you because you're small like a cricket," he responds playfully, and I can't help but smile.

I let him pull me up onto the tractor. The engine's vibration makes my nose itch. We pull outside the barn and ride through the open field for a few minutes. The tractor approaches a pair of hares, which freeze for a second and then run away into the safety of nearby trees. Young kids run in the distance, enjoying a chasing game. The smallest one runs after one who's twice his size and then stumbles and falls down, only to rebound immediately and continue the chase.

We bounce around as we go over bumps and holes, and I hold on tightly to Clayton's waist, afraid of falling. For the first time, I become fully aware of his proximity, and I feel fluttering butterflies inside my stomach. I wonder if he feels anything. Dried-up stalks, branches, and leaves get flattened under the tractor's weight. We're riding at probably no more than five or ten miles per hour, yet the height and the light breeze blowing on our faces make it feel as if we're moving much faster. Eventually, I get used to the movement and start enjoying the exhilarating experience. We return to the barn and climb down.

"Is that a little smile I'm seeing?" Clayton asks me.

"No," I say as I try to erase the smile, but instead, it turns into a grin.

"You can admit that you liked it, you know."

"It was fine." I let out a laugh.

The tour moves on to another barn, where the animals are kept: cows, pigs, chickens, sheep, and almost every other type of imaginable farm animal. The offensive smell makes me gag, and I try holding my breath. Daphne pinches her nose with her thumb and index finger.

"That's the smell of fresh country air!" Matt says, and he and Clayton take in deep breaths and then exhale loudly.

Are they nuts? I would vomit!

"Meet Lady Abigail." Clayton points to a cow. "We've raised her since the day she was born because she was a twin, and her mother chose her sister over her."

"Why did she not take care of both? That's horrible," Daphne says, getting closer to the cow and stroking her brown fur. The cow turns her head toward Daphne, seeming to agree with her.

"That's the way it is. They can only take care of one calf. This one would have died had we not taken her in," Matt says.

"Is she a dairy cow?" Daphne asks.

"No, we only raise animals for meat," Matt says, stroking the cow's head. Lady Abigail turns her head toward him, unaware of what he's just said.

"Why not keep her for milk instead of killing her?" I ask.

"This breed is best for meat. It won't produce much milk," Matt says.

"Won't you find it harder later to kill the animals if you've named them?" I ask.

"Clayton does! He cried when his father sold his first cow. He's a softy," Matt jokes.

"Hey, I raised that one from the day she was born. I bottle-fed her. No one warned me of what would happen to her," Clayton says. "She used to follow me around. She was like my pet by then."

How cute. I smile, imagining the calf following him around like a puppy or a kitten.

They talk a bit more about the cows, including how they rent bulls to keep the purity of the breed and how they sell them to be butchered somewhere else—which is a good thing because I really don't want a tour of the slaughterhouse. We tour the silo where they keep the grain and learn about the selling process. I'm amazed by the complexity of the entire operation. Who would have thought farming could be so complicated? It's a completely different world to me.

"Has the production been very low this year?" I ask Clayton.

"No, similar to previous years. Why?"

"There's a shortage of produce and meat in the stores. It's hard to find anything other than processed food," I say.

"Not sure why, because at least from what I've heard from my dad, from our side, output has been consistent. The same is true for the rest of the farmers in the area. I haven't heard anyone complain. And trust me, when the yield is low, they complain," Clayton says.

"Interesting. Actually, now that you mention your father, I realize I haven't met him yet," I say. By now, Daphne and Matt have gone to Matt's house to get something to eat.

"Come on. He should be in our house. I'm sure he'd like to meet you," he responds as we head over that way.

I wonder if he's told his father about me.

Similar to Matt and Rebecca's house, Clayton's looks at

least seventy years older on the outside than on the inside. There's no luxury, but it has inviting features, including yellow walls, a brown leather couch and chair, a couple of red cushions on the couch, and a turquoise vase filled with daisies. The windows are wide open, and the sheer white curtains dance gently as the light breeze plays with them.

"My aunt helps with the decoration," he says, and I smile. "She makes sure we have live flowers every week. If it weren't for her, we would have an empty vase or likely no vase at all."

Maybe we should hire your aunt to help decorate my house. She could start by making some holes in our walls and installing some windows, I think with a bit of jealousy.

As he goes off to look for his father, a lone medium-sized frame on a table catches my eye. It has a stainless-steel border and straight lines—it's simple yet elegant at the same time. "Leah and Ashton Jones, June 26, 2052" is inscribed in the metal—it was a wedding present, most likely. I pick it up and study it. It's a close-up picture of a brown-eyed brunette with a nice smile. She's probably no older than twenty-five.

"That was my mother," Clayton says, turning my attention away from the picture. "Died giving birth to me. Complications from the C-section."

"I'm sorry," I say, carefully setting the frame down.

"That's okay," he says with a bit of sadness. A second later, his sad face turns to an angry frown. "When a farmer gets sick or hurt, we don't always get priority treatment at hospitals. She bled too much, and someone decided she wasn't worthy of the blood they had in storage."

"That's horrible! They told your family that?"

"Not directly, but my father overheard the nurses fighting over it. Apparently, there had been a stabbing at a military base, and they were saving the blood reserves for that. They couldn't afford to waste an ounce on a farmer." His frown deepens.

"I'm sorry to hear that. I can't believe anyone would treat another human being in such a way," I say.

"Well, to some people, we're not quite human beings. Second-class citizens for sure," he says.

I don't like the look on his face or the way this conversation is going, so I decide to change the topic. "Is your father around?" I ask, looking around and hoping to distract him.

It works, and immediately, his frown softens. "No, seems he's not here. He's probably at the garage, working on equipment, or at my aunt's place."

"Can I see your room?" I ask, not thinking of how inappropriate the question might come across.

His eyes widen, and he grins. "Why?"

Oh, don't go getting ideas. "I'm just curious. I've never been—"

I want to say I've never been inside a farmer's room, but knowing that might reopen his old wounds, I go with "I've never been inside a boy's room." This is not quite a lie, as I haven't been inside a boy's room either.

"Well, today you won't be inside a boy's room. I'm a *man*," he says with emphasis.

"What? Afraid I'll laugh at your collection of toy cars or action figures?" I say, laughing.

"I don't have many cars or action figures, but I do have some cool toys," he replies, and he leads the way to his room, which is located down a narrow hall, past the small kitchen.

Going into a guy's room? Do you think that's what a lady would do? My father's voice comes to my mind. I shove the thought away and follow Clayton into the room.

Light gray walls with colorful movie posters greet me: *Star Wars, Indiana Jones, ET,* and *Close Encounters of the Third Kind.* Some of these I've watched at Daphne's house. They're classic movies from the last century. I wonder if he's even seen the movies or if, like Daphne, he found the posters interesting and stuck them to the walls without understanding the references.

Many years before the Empire was formed, some people used to idolize movie actors. They held them to high standards, scrutinizing everything they said and did. Actors and other celebrities defined what people thought beauty and health should look like. Getting paid more in a year than a typical person earned over a lifetime, those people put up with the loss of privacy and the constant criticism. But that way of life didn't last long. The Empire closed the movie studios, and soon actors were without jobs. Those who hadn't saved a dime found themselves working tables or cleaning floors like the rest of the country. They were no longer special and soon were forgotten.

The only movies produced now come from the Empire, and they're not very interesting to watch. They're in foreign languages, with subtitles in English. The actors speak quite fast, so it's hard to read along, and the plots are repetitive, as they follow the same old theme: people are hungry and in trouble, and out of nowhere comes the Empire to save the day. If I wanted Empire propaganda, I would just open any history book or magazine or turn on the TV.

I continue scanning the room. Against one of the walls are a full-sized dark brown headboard and a chest with five drawers. Both look old but still functional. A rectangular navy-blue rug lies in front of the bed. I see nothing too out of the ordinary, except for a tall brown bookcase standing against the wall opposite the bed. For some reason, it seems out of place.

"You know how to read?" The words escape my mouth before I realize I've said them.

"Of course I can read. Can't you?" he asks me sarcastically.

"Sorry. I didn't mean for it to sound like that. The stereotype out there is—"

"Yeah, I know. To set the record straight, yes, some farmers are illiterate, but many are not," he says without a hint of offense or discomfort in his voice. "Our community homeschools. My aunt and the other mothers in the area use a cooperative system to distribute the work. Aunt Rebecca has taught math and science for years. They're her true passion. If this had been a different time, she could have been a great engineer or scientist."

His words remind me of my own impossible dreams and aspirations. I don't feel like moping about things I'll never be able to control, so I move closer to the bookcase to study some of the titles. There must be more than two hundred books in total, including *The Scarlet Letter, The Grapes of Wrath, Brave New World, Black Boy,* and *Atlas Shrugged.* Some of them I have studied in school, although most of them I started to read and never finished. I pull another one from the bookcase and feel a bit of nausea after reading the title: *The Great Gatsby.* I can almost hear the voice of Preston's fastidious mother explaining how her darling son spent an insane amount of money on the stupid book. "I know of someone who blew a fortune on a first edition of this book," I tell Clayton, waving the book for him to see.

To my surprise, he replies, "Really? That's so cool. I would love to see it."

"What? How is that cool?" I ask. Clayton is the last person I would have ever expected to think it's okay to spend money on fancy books.

"Yvanya, books tell our history. Whether fiction or not, they define our past, who we were, and who we are as people. If we don't learn about our history, how can we expect to improve our future? We'll just keep making the same mistakes over and over," he says.

"These are fiction. How is that helpful?" I ask, shaking the *Gatsby* book in my hand.

"Fiction is inspired by truth. Whether it's the characters, the setting, or the plot, what happens in a fictional piece of art is inspired by something that actually happened in history. There's no such thing as a book that has zero inspiration from real life. Authors write about the things they know or have experienced in one way or another. They may twist the plots and change the outcomes, but even fiction can teach us about what we know, what we fear, and what we dream of."

The passion in Clayton's voice is evident. I wonder what he would have done with his life if he had been born in a different time. Although I don't quite agree with his view on works of fiction, I understand his point, and it makes me feel ashamed of my attitude and a bit exposed. Maybe I've just been using my arguments as an excuse to be lazy. Maybe I should be more open-minded and less judgmental. Maybe, but I'm too proud to admit it.

"Maybe," I reply, returning the book to the bookshelf. I continue looking around the room and notice a shelf with multiple objects on it. Random items have been carefully arranged, as if on display: car models, a hat, a red can with white letters I don't understand, and a weird-looking rectangular item with a black glass on top. "What are these things?"

"Those are my antique collectibles," he replies proudly. "These are antique car models from the early two thousands."

I interrupt. "Ah, so you do have toy cars. You promised me a man's room," I joke, grabbing one of the cars and waving it in his face.

"It's different. I don't play with them. I just look at them," he says with a grin, taking the car from me and replacing it on its shelf.

"I see. So you just sit around and stare at it. That sounds like fun," I joke, and he shakes his head as he turns his attention toward a hat.

"This is a Cincinnati Reds baseball cap. They were a pretty good ball team back in their time." He points at the hat. It's all red, except for an odd-looking white letter *C*.

Unlike in the past, we no longer have organized sports. The only sports we play are among ourselves and rarely include sophisticated equipment. Playing in the dark is hard to do and often leads to injuries, so we don't engage in those activities much.

Before the fires from the civil revolts, Cincinnati was a medium-sized city near where we live now. Books describe it as a great place to raise a family—not too big and not too small. Not much remains from it, just a few abandoned buildings from its downtown and a yellow bridge that extends over what used to be called the Ohio River. The bridge is so old by now that no one in his or her right mind would dare to cross it. I've never personally seen it, but I have seen pictures. For some reason, I've always imagined myself standing on it and walking across it, when out of nowhere, it collapses, plunging me a few hundred feet down into the murky waters. I shake the thought away and point at the red can. "What's that?"

"A can of Coke," he replies.

"Coke?"

"Coca-Cola. It was a soda drink. People loved it, but it had too much sugar and was blamed for obesity. The country outlawed it years ago. This is one of the last cans," he says, handing me the can.

"Let's drink it!" I joke, pretending to open it.

"Don't you dare!" he yells, pulling the can away from me. "It's worth a lot of money."

"Then why not sell it? Why hold on to all these things?" I ask, pointing at his collectibles.

"They're important to me. Like I said, they're part of our history. I don't want to forget who we were as a nation." He sets the can back on the shelf. "And this last item," he says, picking up the boxy rectangular item, "is a phone."

"A phone?" I ask, examining the object. How can this thing be a phone?

"It's a gadget from the early two thousands. I guess back then, everyone carried one around. They could make calls from virtually everywhere as well as check the internet," he says, handing it to me. "Be careful with it. It's very fragile."

"I've heard about them, but I'd never seen one," I say, turning it around. Its sleek design looks attractive, and it feels heavier than I expected. "Can you turn it on?" I ask, returning it to him.

"No, I don't have a way to charge the battery, if it even works," he says, setting it carefully on the shelf.

I've heard people were obsessed with these things and carried them everywhere as if they were extensions of their own bodies. Special towers, not many of which are left anymore, were required to send the signals. The Empire removed most of them, as they didn't like the idea of people having easy access to one another or to information on the internet. The few that remain are used exclusively for government purposes. I've never been on the internet but have heard about it. Word in the street is that the government thought that easy access to information among the people would be dangerous, as it could lead to disorder and rebellions. That was never said explicitly, but it was what everyone inferred. The official reason for removing most of the towers and the phones was, of course, health-related: they were linked to cancer. Like everything that seems to threaten the Empire's existence, they were demonized and removed. The weird-looking phones went away and were replaced by the old-fashioned corded ones we use now.

"Where did you get all this stuff?" I ask Clayton.

"They belonged to my mother. She inherited some from her father, who lived most of his life before the Empire was formed, but others she added to her collection as she found them. When she died, my father saved them for me," he says, his eyes smiling at the fond view of the items. He looks as if he's lost in his own thoughts and has forgotten I'm standing right by him. I take the opportunity to look at him up close. The apples of his cheeks are a bit reddish from the recent kiss of the sun. His olive-green eyes sparkle; his long dark lashes are completely fanned out. His arm nears mine, and as the hairs come in contact with mine, an electric current seems to flow through my body. I freeze in place; he seems completely unaware.

"What are you guys up to?" Daphne's voice startles me as she enters the room.

"Nothing," I immediately reply, feeling my face flush. I hope Clayton doesn't notice my blushing.

Daphne picks up on it and, with a big smile and a raised eyebrow, seems to ask me, *What's going on in here?*

"Hey, Daphne," Clayton says as he straightens his collectibles one more time.

"Let's go back outside," I say, and they agree.

"Sorry to interrupt," she whispers as we turn around to exit the room.

"You didn't interrupt anything," I whisper back, trying to sound cool.

Once outside, we find out Matt's mother has prepared

a small raised-bed area for Daphne and me to plant a vegetable garden. We say our goodbyes to the guys, who need to return to their chores, and stay with her. Rebecca teaches us the basics of how to space out the seeds and how deep to plant them. We plant kale, parsley, green beans, basil, carrots, and potatoes. A rainwater collection system by the bed makes the watering an easy task. She promises the plants will start sprouting in a few weeks. Soon after, we express our thanks and head back to our homes.

8

For the next few weeks, Daphne and I continue to sneak out almost every other day to hang out with our friends at the farm. Every once in a while, I sneak back some food for Heidi, who has become my accomplice.

I think back to the night when she caught me sneaking back into our room. As always, the room was pitch black. I was quietly closing the door behind me, when her soft voice startled me.

"Where were you?"

I could hear the concern in her voice. "Sorry. I went downstairs for a cup of water," I lied, talking as quietly as I could to avoid waking up our parents.

She turned on the night table lamp and sat upright on her bed with her legs crossed. "Really? For five hours? That must have been one large glass of water."

"You're right. Sorry. I was outside," I replied.

"Yvanya, where have you been going all these nights? You can't possibly believe I haven't been noticing."

"Okay, fine. I've been hanging out with Daphne. We met some guys at a farm, and we sometimes go visit them."

As expected, Heidi's initial reaction was one of disapproval. "Are you guys crazy? What if our parents find out? Father's gonna go ballistic. What if the police catch you? We're under curfew! And not to forget about your skin. Have you been wearing enough sunblock? What if you get sick? I don't want you to die!"

"Heidi, it's fine. I'm not sick. And yes, I'm wearing enough sunblock." I sat on her bed and placed my hands on her shoulders, trying to reassure her. "Calm down, and please lower your voice."

She looked me straight in the eyes and pouted, likely recognizing that she wasn't going to be able to influence my behavior. "So what's it like?" she whispered, seeming to regain control of her emotions.

"It's amazing, really. I love being outside during the day. I've seen things and animals that I didn't even know existed. Everything is just so beautiful. And, Heidi, they have so much food. Good food, not the canned stuff we have to endure. I don't understand how it's even possible. Here. Let me show you." I stuck my hand inside my pocket and pulled out a dinner roll I had taken from Matt's house earlier that day. It was cold and a bit squished, but Heidi didn't care. She peeled off the napkin in which I had wrapped it and immediately took a bite. She moaned as she devoured the whole thing.

Once she was done, she asked, "And what are these people like—the farmers?"

"Honestly, it seems like everything we've ever heard about them is completely made up. To be fair, I haven't met a lot of them, but at least the ones I've met are completely normal, no different from you and me."

"Can you please promise me you won't keep going out?" she asked, making a sad face and batting her eyelashes, likely hoping her cute little face would be enough to convince me.

"You look adorable, but no. I can't promise you that. Sorry."

"Can you at least promise me you'll be careful?"

"That I can promise you," I replied, and she gave me a sad smile. I kissed the top of her head and tucked her in, and we both went to bed.

From then on, I've kept sneaking food in for her, which she seems to appreciate. I would love to bring her to the farm sometime, but I don't think it would be the responsible thing to do. I'm risking myself already; there's no need to get her in trouble as well.

Clayton has toned down his know-it-all attitude and is slowly growing on me, or maybe I'm lowering my guard and giving him a break. I'm not sure which one it is, but I no longer feel as defensive around him as I did that first day. Daphne's feelings for Matt seem to be the real deal. She seems to care about him much more than she ever did for any of her previous boyfriends. I have no reason to doubt

Matt's intentions but hope he feels the same way about her and is not just leading her on.

Up in my room, I remove my watch and earrings and place them in my small jewelry box, the only thing that sits on our plain distressed white dresser. The two small gold hoops my mother gave me a few years ago are my only valuables. They belonged to her mother, so I guess that makes them a family heirloom. I got the stainless-steel watch as a birthday gift last year. The band is somewhat beat up already, and the face has some scratches, but it works beautifully to help me keep track of time, which is essential when Daphne and I sneak out.

I examine my face in the mirror and notice it's looking a bit fuller than a month ago. I've probably gained a few pounds, which explains why my ribs are not as prominent anymore. I turn my attention to the black backpack on my bed and pull out a small loaf of bread wrapped in a white paper napkin. I snuck it in from yesterday's visit to the farm. Rebecca baked more than what we were able to consume, and rather than letting it spoil, she insisted we take it and find a way to share it with our families. I spent some time debating with myself whether or not to bring it down to the table, but eating it by myself just makes me feel guilty. Even sharing food with Heidi is not enough, as I know my parents are just as hungry.

As I help my mother set the table, I unwrap the bread and place it on a plate.

"Where did that come from?" she asks, and her eyes widen with anticipation. It has been a long time since we've had bread at the house, and I can tell she can't wait to take a bite.

"Daphne's mother sent it," I lie.

"Where did she get the flour from?" she asks, possibly hoping there's finally been a new shipment to the store.

"Not sure, but she said it was the last pack," I reply, trying to keep the topic short. The more I talk, the guiltier I feel about lying to her. I need to make sure she doesn't go asking Daphne's mom about it later, though.

"Remind me later to call her and thank her," she says, and I bite my lip.

"Don't worry. I already thanked her and will thank her again when I see her tomorrow," I say. I start to fear that bringing the bread was a terrible idea.

A few minutes later, my father and Heidi join us at the table. Just like my mother, he's inquisitive about the bread's origin, but a bite of it makes him stop caring about where it came from, and he turns his attention toward enjoying it instead.

"Have you heard anything from Paul?" my mother asks, as she knows my father was supposed to meet with him tonight at work.

"Yes, I almost forgot to tell you. Surprisingly, Preston is still interested in Yvanya," he says, raising his eyebrows with delight. "He seemed to like how passionate she is about life."

123

What? Is that what he said?

"Or maybe he's into grand exits," Heidi jokes, and my mother shakes her head with a smile.

The three of them look at me with high expectations, so I give them a small smile. The truth is, I'm not sure how to take the news. In my head, I already decided it was over, admitted he wasn't interested in me, and moved on. Now hearing that he's actually interested in me brings a mixed set of emotions. Secretly, I feel a bit excited about being wanted and maybe even desired. I'm also relieved I didn't entirely blow it for my family, especially given how much it seems to mean to them, but at the same time, I'm still uncomfortable with the idea of marrying someone I don't love or even really know. Yes, the guy is handsome, and I'm sure any other girl would give anything to be in my position, but it's just not how I saw my future turning. I don't even think I have what it takes to be a good wife, let alone a mother, and I'm sure he will want kids. It seems all rich men want lots of kids.

This thought makes me wonder why Preston is an only child. *Maybe his mother decided she didn't want to ruin her figure with another pregnancy*, I think, and my stomach turns as I imagine what it would be like to have her around all the time. I hate the way she makes me feel inadequate and inferior. After my disgraceful performance and not hearing from Preston for almost a month, I really thought it was all off. I thought I was in the clear. Now I'm even more confused than before.

"Yvanya, could you please pass the salt?" Heidi asks, pulling me back to reality.

I stretch my arm across the table and grab the salt shaker, when all of a sudden, my father grabs my wrist. "What is this?" he asks, raising his voice.

"Father, you're hurting me," I say, and I drop the shaker, not knowing what's gotten into him.

He lets go of my wrist. "Please explain yourself," he says, pointing to my wrist, and he takes a few deep breaths, likely to calm himself down.

I examine my arm and notice the suntanned skin, which is highlighted by my missing watch. I pull my sleeve down to cover it up and look down at my plate.

"Do you want to be known as a woman of the day?" he asks, now breathing more normally, regaining his control.

"No," I respond softly, shaking my head while still looking down.

"Do you know what this could mean for your prospects? For the agreement with Paul?"

"I'm sorry," I say, still afraid to look up. "I'm not trying to ruin anything for anyone."

"This is not about us; it's for you," my mother says gently.

I'm surprised and relieved they don't ask how I got the suntan in the first place.

"Eat your food," my father says, and we all resume eating. For the rest of the dinner, no one utters a word.

Under the table, Heidi's hand finds mine, and I squeeze it tightly.

🕐 🕐 🕐

About a week goes by before I risk sneaking out again. By then, the suntan mark on my wrist is almost gone. Soon after the dinner altercation, my mother spoke with Daphne's mother, who also suspected her daughter was up to something. We both got lectured on the dangers of sun exposure and the risks of getting caught breaking the curfew, so we promised not to do it again. We never mentioned the boys, the farm, or the mysterious food. Our parents did not seem to make the connection, or maybe they pretended not to. Either way, they didn't mention it again.

"Don't go," Heidi pleads. "If Father finds out, you're gonna be in a lot of trouble."

"I'll be more careful," I say, and her stomach grumbles loudly enough for me to hear it. I tilt my head and point to her belly.

"It's not that bad, really," she says, but immediately, her stomach lets out another grumble as if yelling, *Yes, it is!*

I grab my bag, toss in the almost empty bottle of sunblock Clayton gave me, and turn the lights out, whispering to my sister, "See you in a few hours."

I walk down the stairs, skipping over the steps I know will creak. As I turn the door handle to go outside, adrenaline kicks in, and I feel a rush of excitement. It's 12:00 a.m.

GTZ, and the sun is at its apex. A block from my house, I meet up with Daphne, who is wearing her same old torn jeans and a navy-blue long-sleeved shirt. I point at the blue baseball cap on her head.

"It's Matt's. He said it was for some old famous team—the Cubs or something like that, I think he called them," she says, handing it to me.

I study it closely. It's bright blue and has a blue bear stitched on top of a red letter *C*, both outlined in white. "Looks cute on you," I say as I return it to her.

We exit our neighborhood and walk quietly down a street just outside town. As we near the end of the block, we hear men approaching. Daphne and I stop abruptly, and as quietly as we can, we rush back toward an alley we just passed. We look for a way out, but there's no outlet. Scanning our surroundings, we quickly find a recessed door about ten feet from the main street. We lean against it, hoping to be out of sight. The one thing I don't like about being out during the day is how much more vulnerable it makes me feel. At night, the darkness protects your anonymity, which gives you a sense of freedom, but during the day, anyone can see you from a mile away.

My heart pounds like a galloping horse inside my chest as the men walk by. While our government's military personnel wear slightly loose bright cobalt-blue uniforms with *Region 12* stitched in white letters over the left side of their chest, the Empire soldiers wear tight-fitted black shirts and slightly loose black pants with red belts. The Empire's flag is stitched on the left side of their chest. They all seem to wear the same black combat boots. Just by looking at these guys' uniforms, it is clear they are Empire soldiers.

For a second, they stand in front of the alley. *They saw us.* The worst thought comes to my mind, but it quickly dissolves as we notice they don't seem to be looking for anyone. They just stand in the same spot, speaking among themselves. Although they're being pretty loud, I don't recognize their language.

We've been part of the New Orient Empire for decades now, but I don't recall ever seeing so many of their soldiers around. The Empire typically delegates military street patrolling to our own people. The few times I've seen them around have usually been at night, and I've never seen them close up. It's always been on the way to school or home. Walking around in broad daylight makes them feel more intimidating for some reason.

A few minutes later, they resume their walk. As they pass, I notice the large rifles hanging across their backs. We stay hidden for a few more minutes until we're certain they're out of sight. We hurry the rest of the way to our friends' farm in silence and much more vigilant than ever before.

"Seeing them during the daytime creeps me out," Daphne says as we disappear into the first row of cornstalks. "Did you notice the size of their rifles?" she asks, and I nod quietly. "Speaking of which, yesterday I overheard my father tell my mother that there's a shipment of weapons unaccounted for. My father's division is under a lot of stress in trying to locate them."

"Are you serious?" I ask. "How can they just lose them? Don't they have good controls on that kind of thing?"

"You would think, right? I just hope the weapons haven't fallen into the wrong hands," she replies, and I shake my head in disbelief.

🕐 🕑 🕒

"You're gonna love this," Clayton says, carefully swinging a dark olive-green camouflage backpack over his shoulder. It has lots of pockets and zippered compartments. Although it's not necessarily full, it seems heavy and makes a loud thud when it hits his back.

"Where are we going?" I ask, grabbing my black backpack, which contains nothing but a bottle of sunblock and my dorky bucket hat.

"A place I bet you've never been to before," he responds without offering any further explanation.

Leave it to Clayton to tell me something I don't know already. I hate how he avoids my questions.

"And what's in the bag?" I ask, knowing there's no point to my question because he's not going to tell me.

"Something I bet you've never used before," he says, winking at me.

I stop in my tracks. "Maybe you haven't noticed, but I don't enjoy suspense."

"Just trust me," he says, tugging on my hand. I become aware of his touch and feel a current of electricity flow through my arm. He lets go of my hand as I follow him, and the current subsides.

As usual, Daphne and Matt have disappeared to do their own thing, leaving me alone with Clayton. I don't mind it anymore. Over the past months, we've become good friends. When he's not being annoying, he can be quite charming. He probably would say the same about me, as I can be quite fun myself when I'm not being stubborn or moody.

We leave the quiet of the farm and enter a wooded area I have never seen before. The terrain turns steep, and I struggle to keep up with him. The heat of the day does not help either. The temperature must be in the nineties. Beads of sweat drip down my back.

"I need a break," I say as I set my backpack on the ground and lean back against a thick, tall tree. I bend over, resting my head between my legs, as I take a deep breath. My white long-sleeved T-shirt is soaked with sweat and sticking to my skin. I pull it away from my stomach and fan it to let some air in, feeling an instant cool.

Clayton sets his backpack near my feet, pulls out a couple of water bottles from the front pocket, and gives me one. As he drinks, I grab the bag by the handle to lift it. Just as I thought, it's quite heavy.

"What are you carrying? Bricks? Lead?" I joke, wondering how he can carry this load while making it look effortless.

"Something like that." He laughs and takes the bag from me. "Unless you want to switch bags and carry mine," he says, extending his bag back to me.

"Only if you want to get there next week," I joke.

"Come on. We're not far from where we're going."

"Easier for you. You have longer legs, and you're used to moving around in this hot weather."

"Come on, Cricket," he says as I take a couple of long gulps from my water bottle.

"Chirp," I reply, shoving the bottle against his chest playfully. I dry the sweat off my face with my shirt sleeve and pick up my backpack, and after adjusting it, I'm ready to continue the hike.

After five minutes or so, the grade changes, and we're going downhill. The ground is wetter, and patches of moss make the gravel and dirt disappear. The air smells different, and the temperature seems to have dropped by at least ten degrees.

"Watch your step, or you'll end up on your butt," he says, and as if he's predicted the future, my right foot loses its grip, and I plummet to the ground. Thankfully, I land on a flat surface, so it's not too painful.

"Anything hurt?" he asks, smiling and offering me his hand.

"My ego," I say as I pull hard on his hand to lift myself up. I shake the dirt off my pants and look at the landscape. "This place is beautiful!" I exclaim, feasting my eyes on the view. A small waterfall probably thirty or forty feet high forms a pool of sparkling turquoise water. As the water hits some of the rocks in the pool, it produces a smooth mist. The rays of the sun interact with the mist, creating a rainbow effect.

"Can we go in?" I ask with exhilaration, having never seen anything quite like this in my life.

"Later. I have something I want to show you first. Come on. Let's go," he says, and he resumes our hike. I follow after him, paying more attention to the ground.

After another five minutes of walking, we stop as we reach an open clearing. By now, I'm completely drenched in sweat and wish we could go straight into the water. While daydreaming about what the cool water will feel like against the top of my head, I watch him open his bag and pull out a water bottle and some empty vegetable cans.

"What are those for?" I ask, and as expected, he ignores my question and walks away from me, leaving me with nothing but the water bottle. I notice a tree stump nearby. I sweep a few leaves from its top and take a seat. I fan my face with my hands and take a few sips from the bottle. The water is warm, but considering how hot I am, it feels refreshing.

He walks for about thirty feet and eventually stops in front of a dead tree. The top of it is missing, and it looks as if its trunk has been split in half by a lightning bolt. A thick branch maybe about four feet from the ground extends horizontally from the trunk. He sets the five cans on the branch, spacing them out with about half a foot separating each from the next. With a mischievous smile, he walks toward me. As he gets close to me, he sticks his arm into his bag and pulls out a gun.

"What are you doing with that? Where did you get that?" I ask, jumping up from the stump.

"Relax," he says with a calm voice. "I'm going to teach you the basics of shooting."

"I'm not interested," I reply, taking a step back. "I don't want anything to do with this."

"Yvanya, calm down. It's not a big deal."

"Are you kidding? Not a big deal? These things are illegal! Besides, why would I need to know how to use it?"

"It's a basic skill that every person should know in times like these. You never know when it'll come in handy." He moves closer to me, holding the gun down.

I'm not necessarily against guns, but the thought of holding one makes me nervous since I've never seen one in person. "These are so dangerous," I say, still unsure whether I want to be part of this. "You'll be arrested if anyone finds out you have it."

"Then I'm going to ask you to please not tell anyone about it," he says, now standing by my side.

"Please don't," I say, moving a few feet away from him.

"Yvanya, it's okay. I need you to trust me. This is important." He looks me in the eyes, pleading with me to agree.

"Fine," I say finally, and he softly approaches me, as if afraid I might run away if he moves too quickly.

"First, let's start with safety." He presses a button on the grip. Something in the handle pops out, and he catches it with one hand. "This is the clip, and as you can see, it's unloaded." He gives it to me to examine. He then puts his hand over the top of the gun and slides something back a few times before locking it back into place. "No round. See?" He shows me, and I nod in agreement. He threads a seven- to eight-inch-long cord through the barrel and releases the sliding part back to its forward position. "Now it's roped, so for sure it can't shoot." He extends the gun to me.

While still afraid, I extend my arm and grab it. It feels much heavier and colder against my skin than I anticipated.

"Two very important rules to stay safe," he says, looking me seriously in the eyes. "Always keep your finger off the trigger, and always keep the gun pointed down."

For the next twenty minutes or so, he shows me the different parts of the gun, teaching me how to stand, how to load and unload it, and how to aim. By now, my fear is turning to excitement as I anticipate the thrill of using it. Adrenaline rushes through my body, and I'm surprised by my desire to practice actual shooting and engage in something that is completely forbidden.

"Continuing with the safety training, you need to wear these," he says, pulling two pairs of earmuffs and safety glasses from his bag. We put them on, and finally, the time has come to shoot the first round. "Remember the safety rules," he says, taking the gun from me and loading it with three rounds.

My heart races. Following Clayton's detailed instructions, I hold on tightly to the gun's handle and lift my arms to eye level. I look through the sight with my dominant eye and slightly adjust my body until I see one of the vegetable cans through the sight.

"Now slowly move your finger to the trigger, and very gently squeeze it," he says as he stands next to me. He places a hand on my lower back, and I stiffen. "Relax," he says, and I take a deep breath.

I follow his instructions to the point, and as the gun shoots, the loud noise startles me—it's much louder than I was expecting. The recoil pushes me back, lifting my arms and causing me to miss the target and hit the tree behind it. A chunk of bark flies off into the air.

"That's a lot of force," I tell him, recovering my stance. Surprisingly, I find the smell of gunpowder pleasant. I still feel nervous, though a bit giddy.

"That's why you need to stand firmly," he says, squaring my shoulders and reminding me to lean forward slightly to keep my shoulders in front of my waist for a forward aggressive position, as he calls it. "If you don't control the recoil, not only are you gonna miss, but it can also cause a jam in the barrel, which in a life-or-death situation can be a fatal mistake."

"Aren't you being a little dramatic?" I say.

"Joke all you want, but this is not just a fun exercise. I want you to learn this skill. So let's try it again," he says, and I become more serious, trying to focus better this time.

The second bullet comes out, and although it also misses the can, at least I'm able to control the recoil better and only miss my target by less than a foot.

"Your aim is a bit off," he says, getting closer to me. "Let me help you with that." He stands behind me and puts his arms over mine, readjusting my aim. His breath tickles the side of my neck, and I laugh involuntarily. "Stay still, and focus on the front sight," he says.

Maybe if you weren't standing so close to me, I could.

The third bullet scrapes the top of the can, knocking it off the tree branch.

"I did it!" I yell with amazement, and I jump in place a couple of times. "By the way, you need a bath; you don't smell too good," I joke, giving him a small nudge on his side.

"News flash: you don't smell like roses right now either," he says, and he winks at me as he takes the gun from my hands. "Great job! Let's try that again."

He reloads the clip, and we practice shooting for the next half hour. He teaches me a few more basics, including what to do in case of a jam and how to draw from a holster without accidentally shooting myself.

As he practices shooting, I study his face. Except for the few freckles on his cheeks and over his nose, his skin is flawless. He has full lips, and as they part into a small smile, I can see his perfectly straight white teeth underneath. His hazel eyes look a lighter green under this light. His brow furrows, and he looks a bit older as he frowns, concentrating on his target. Making it seem effortless, he gently pulls the trigger and hits a can right in the middle.

"Did you see that?" he asks, momentarily looking like a proud ten-year-old who wants to see if his mother noticed him doing something great. I nod with a smile, and he resumes his practice.

We continue taking turns for about a half hour. By the time we're done, I've forgotten how hot and sweaty I am.

"Wanna stop by the waterfall still?" he asks as he walks to the dead tree to pick up the cans, which are now scattered all over the ground.

"Oh yeah!" I exclaim, having entirely forgotten about it.

We collect our things and start the hike back.

"When did you learn to shoot? And where did you get that gun from?" I ask as we walk side by side. I slow my pace to better take in the landscape. He slows down, matching my stride.

"It's my dad's. It's been in the family since before the Empire days. The government confiscated most weapons years ago, but they know that many were hidden and are still out there, although they won't admit it. My dad taught Matt and me when we were in our early teens. We sometimes get coyotes on the farm, so we need to know how to defend ourselves. Plus, farmers are not exactly the most appreciated people in the world, so it's not just coyotes we worry about."

"Has anyone ever attacked you guys?" I ask, coming to a halt.

"Most times we get people sneaking into the crops and taking food. Usually, we don't do much about that because we know they're desperate, and they just grab and go. Sometimes when we have a large harvest and there's plenty left over, we purposefully leave food by the road to keep them from venturing onto our property. But occasionally, we get a soldier or government official who thinks we owe them something, and things can escalate a bit," he replies, standing by me.

"Have you ever shot anyone?" I ask, my eyes widening with fear.

"Oh no, it's never gotten to that point, thankfully," he says. "We usually just let them know we're not easy prey, and they carefully rethink it and leave us alone. One time, though, one of those jerks tried to make a move on my aunt, and she ended up pulling a knife on him. You should have seen the look in his eyes. She's one tough girl. My father was very proud of her. He's the one who taught her how to work the knife.

"There was one other incident when we thought a situation would escalate. Soldiers came over and handed us a notice that we had six months to vacate our premises and move to one of those old ghost cities in the Midwest. We told them we would stand our ground. They didn't like it, of course. One of the soldiers threatened to shoot us all if we refused, but his commander calmed him down. They never came back, and we never got another word on it, so we just ignored it."

His comment brings back distant memories. Years ago, the Empire decided that to accelerate prosperity, they needed to move people from the rural farmlands to the urban developments. They invested ludicrous amounts of money in creating technologically advanced cities, only to find out that forcing people to move there was harder than they had anticipated. Eventually, they gave up on the ordeal and left the cities abandoned. They are now referred to as ghost cities. It's believed there are five to seven ghost cities spread across the country, although no one is exactly sure, as some are said to have been built in isolated places. I've heard from some kids at school that the same experiment was tried about a hundred years ago in a different part of the world with the same result. It didn't work back then, and it didn't work now. *Funny how some people don't learn from history.*

We resume our walk as I try to imagine how tough it must be for the farmers, especially for Rebecca. "Must be tough living on edge all the time," I say.

"We have a tight community, so we take care of one another. That makes it a lot easier," he replies.

I nod and pay closer attention to where I step, as I notice tree branches all over the ground. "By the way, on the way here, Daphne and I saw a couple of Empire soldiers. And I don't mean our soldiers but actual Empire ones. They were speaking a foreign language and wearing the black uniforms."

He comes to a stop and seems to contemplate this for a few seconds before responding. "How close were you to them, if you were able to hear them?"

"Too close for comfort," I reply. "We've seen them before, around the town center, but it's always been at nighttime. This is the first time we've seen them during the day. Oh, and they were carrying rifles, which we've not seen before."

"Maybe you guys shouldn't be coming to see us anymore, especially with the curfew. Maybe it's time we take a break until things calm down a bit," he says with worry showing on his face.

"You mean Daphne and Matt not see each other? They'll die!" I joke.

"Maybe we should come to you guys instead. We could come over at nighttime so you don't have to sneak out. That may make it easier for you guys anyway."

"Maybe," I say, and I silently contemplate the options in my head. No longer visiting the farm would suck. By now, I've grown to enjoy my time at the farm, including the delicious, satisfying dinners and, just as important, the feel of the sun against my skin. I also don't think our parents will be thrilled to see their daughters hanging out with farmers.

Now that I know where I'm going, I no longer feel on edge, and I allow myself to enjoy the view. Mature trees line the pebbled path. The canopy of leaves provides some shelter from the torturous sunrays. As we walk under the trees, the temperature feels at least fifteen or twenty degrees cooler and much more enjoyable than in the open field we just left behind. I look around, and the forest seems to come alive. I see two squirrels jumping from one branch to another, chasing each other playfully. Like skillful acrobats who know no fear, they leap into the air, trusting that the thin branches of the trees will be able to support them. I watch as one misses, and although it falls probably seven or eight feet, it lands perfectly on its feet. Its friend jumps from the safety of the tree to join it on the ground, and as if nothing has happened, they resume their chase.

"Those guys are insane." I laugh as the squirrels run up another tree.

"They have a lot of energy—that's for sure," he says.

Birds chirp happily above in the trees. A monarch butterfly flies in front of me, and I slowly raise my hand near it. It stops to rest on one of my fingers, and I slow my pace to make sure I don't scare it away. I gently lower my arm as I study it. Its bright yellow, black, and white wings are breathtaking. I don't recall ever feasting my eyes on colors so bright.

"You're really not used to this," he says, affirming what we both know.

I turn to him as the butterfly spreads its wings and leaves my hand. "It's not fair. There's so much to life that we're missing. All because of a stupid agreement that might be nothing but a fabrication."

We live our lives in fear, hiding in the shadows of the night, oblivious to everything around us. We're wasting our lives away, missing out on the beauty of the world. But nature doesn't care whether or not we enjoy and appreciate it. Life doesn't care whether or not we live it. Everything keeps moving while we stay behind.

With kind eyes that seem to look into my soul and read my thoughts, he gently nods and places an arm around my back. I lean my head against his shoulder, and we resume our walk.

A bit later, we arrive at the waterfall.

"I'm going to guess you didn't bring a bathing suit," he says with a mischievous smile.

"Yes, because I own so many of those," I joke. "And I'm going to guess you planned that all along so you could check me out in my underwear. But don't worry; that's not going to stop me. Turn around." I grab the bottom of my T-shirt, and as soon as he turns, I pull my shirt off and peel off my jeans. I neatly stretch my clothes over a boulder and move closer to the water.

"Wow, you're pale!" he exclaims.

"I told you to turn around!" I yell. Standing in my beige underwear, I feel completely exposed, so I hurry into the water. I try to pay close attention to the ground, as there are small pebbles all around the pool, and some of them look sharp. The last thing I want is to injure a foot and need Clayton to rescue me while I'm dressed—or, more accurately, undressed—like this.

I reach the water and, without giving it much thought, keep moving until it's shoulder deep. "It's cold!" I yell.

"You'll get used to it." He laughs, still facing away from me.

I watch as he takes off his shirt, revealing strong, muscular arms and a toned back. This is the first time I have seen him without his shirt on. I never realized how well defined his body is. His tanned skin reveals the outline of his shirt. He continues to undress until he remains in his navy-blue boxers.

As he turns around, he catches me watching him. "I see the privacy rule is only one way."

"I didn't get much privacy, so not sure why you should get any," I reply, blushing.

He walks toward the water, dips his feet in, and gradually moves into the pool. He kicks some water in my direction, and I turn my face to avoid getting my eyes wet.

"Really? Take this." I cup my hands and throw water at his chest.

He laughs and disappears under the water. For a few seconds, I don't know where he is. Then he reappears behind me, grabbing me by the waist. He lifts me up and launches me a few feet away. I squeal, startled, and he laughs, pleased.

Wow, Yvanya, you're really turning into a woman of the day. I hear in my head my father's reproachful voice.

I push the thought aside. A year from now, I might be trapped in an arranged marriage in which the most excitement I get is listening to my judgmental mother-in-law talk about all the expensive stuff her darling son has bought her, so I choose to focus on the present and enjoy the moment.

"Is it safe to go under the waterfall?" I ask. The mist gives it a mystical, ethereal appearance, and I'm drawn to it like a moth to light. The sound is loud, but it's more inviting than scary, and I realize it won't matter whether or not he says it's safe; I'll still get as close to it as I can.

"Yeah, the turbulence is not too bad, and it's not very deep," he replies to my relief. "Do you know how to swim?"

"I learned when I was young, but it's been years since I've been in deep water."

"I'll help you. Hold on to me," he says, taking one of my hands, and we move toward the waterfall.

We paddle slowly until we reach it. Moving my arms and legs in circles to stay afloat, I close my eyes and lean my head back until the water hits the crown of my head. The stream feels stronger than expected, and the laminar flow provides the sensation of being massaged. I smile, savoring the moment. I've never felt so much water hitting my head at once. To conserve water, the showers in our homes have low-flow nozzles. Sometimes the pressure is so low you have to collect the water in a bucket and use a cup to wash and fully rinse out your hair.

A minute later, I start to feel tired, but I don't want to move away from here. Clayton seems to notice and moves closer to me. "Hold on to my shoulders," he says, and he places my right hand on his left shoulder. With his other hand, he holds on to a nearby rock. I smile, continuing to enjoy the water.

Being so close to his face, I find myself studying his eyes. Under the bright sun, they look a light shade of green with light brown borders. His lips look soft, and I find myself wondering what it would feel like to have them pressed against mine.

We stare at each other for what feels like a minute, and before we realize it, his mouth moves toward mine. *It's going to happen. He's going to kiss me!* Butterflies move inside my stomach, and I take a deep breath, anticipating the inevitable.

Out of nowhere, a name pops into my mind: *Preston.*

What about that thing with Preston? Clayton's going to find out sooner or later. But what if nothing comes of it? Why push Clayton away when there's still uncertainty? Because it's the right thing to do, at least for now, until I know for sure.

Right when he's about to kiss me, I unwillingly pull back and turn my face away.

"What's wrong?" he asks, looking confused and a bit rejected.

"I'm sorry. We shouldn't," I say, letting go of him. *Coming here was a mistake.*

"Why not?" he asks as I swim toward the shore.

Because I'm a horrible person. I need to get out of here.

He catches up with me and gently grabs me by an arm. I stretch my legs and feel the bottom of the pool. I turn back to him and look him straight in the eyes. "I may be getting engaged," I say softly. *There. I said it.*

"What?" he asks.

"My parents have arranged something," I say.

"Oh." He looks away, crestfallen. "Why didn't you say something before? It's not like it's a little detail."

"I'm sorry. I had forgotten all about it," I reply, which is partly the truth, and he lets go of my hand.

We get back to the shore and dress in silence.

"When is this supposed to happen?" he asks quietly.

Please stop asking questions. I don't want to talk about it.

"I'm not sure. I don't know if it's even going to happen, but I just want to be respectful," I say.

My father's voice enters my mind again. *Sure, and that's why you're swimming half naked with this other guy.*

"And who's the guy, if I may ask?" Clayton says, pressing with more questions.

"The son of one of my father's coworkers," I reply. "You wouldn't know him."

"What's he like?"

The thought *Spoiled beyond what either of us could ever imagine* creeps into my head, but instead, I say, "I only met him once, so I don't really know." Exasperated with the interrogation, I ask, "Can we please change the topic?"

Clayton nods and then says as he looks at the ground, "You do know this is a big bomb to drop on me, don't you?"

"I'm sorry." That's all I can say. I didn't know he felt that way about me. More importantly, I didn't know I might have similar feelings for him either.

"We should get going," he says, picking up his bag from the ground.

We resume our hike, this time in silence.

🕐 🕑 🕒

As Clayton and I clear the forest, the cornfield comes into view. Rather than entering through our usual walkway, which is wide enough for three to four people to walk side by side, Clayton takes a narrower path wide enough for just one person; clearly, he's still mad at me. I walk behind him, lost in my own head.

Why did I lead him on? What was I thinking? And since when do I like Clayton? Yes, he's cute, sweet, strong, and funny when he's not being a know-it-all, but that's not the point. I might be getting engaged to the mama's boy, and I cannot ruin that for my family. It's the only way to guarantee Mother, Father, and Heidi never have to worry about having food. I'm lucky enough to have been considered, especially when I'm a nobody. And now Clayton's mad. He has every reason to be mad. He's probably embarrassed too. I wonder how long it'll be before he forgives me, if he ever forgives me.

Out of nowhere, he stops and turns around to face me. It's so unexpected I almost run into him.

"Is he rich? I bet he's pretty rich to be able to buy you as a wife," he says with contempt. "I didn't think you were the gold-digger type."

My eyes narrow, and I want nothing but to slap him hard in the face.

He senses my anger and knows he's gone too far. "I'm sorry. I didn't mean that." He tries to apologize, searching my eyes, but the damage is done. I shove him aside and walk past him, hoping I'm heading in the right direction.

How dare he think that of me! It's not as if I'm jumping with joy over this stupid arrangement. This isn't what I wanted. I didn't ask for this.

We finally exit the cornstalks, and I can see Matt's house. As we approach it, I see Rebecca walk out the front door toward us, carrying a small yellow canvas tote.

This is going to be awkward. Just get Daphne and go home. Pretend nothing has happened, I tell myself, hoping Clayton doesn't decide to share with his aunt any of the details from our afternoon. She's been nothing but kind to me and my family, and the last thing I want is for her to think I was trying to take advantage of them. I force my best smile as I approach her.

"Hi, Yvanya." Rebecca greets me, ignoring Clayton and his sour look. "Daphne's back at her house. She wasn't feeling well, so Matt walked her back about an hour ago."

"Okay. I'll get going then," I say, and she hands me the tote. "What's this?" I ask. The bag feels heavy, but I don't want to open it and start rummaging through it here in front of them.

"Some extra stuff we have, plus a few of your parsley leaves, which were ready," she says with her usual smile.

A pang of guilt hits my stomach, and I want to drop the bag and run away. "You don't have to do that. It's too much," I say as I offer the bag back.

"It'll spoil if no one eats it. Take it, and share it with yours," she says.

I nod and say thank you. With that, I start walking back toward the cornfield, this time taking the path I know well. The last thing I want is to get lost in the field.

Less than a minute later, Clayton catches up with me.

"You don't need to come. I know my way back," I say, knowing his aunt must have ordered him to escort me.

"I'm not gonna let you go by yourself," he says.

"Of course you won't. You're a gentleman. I'm the one who's all wrong," I say as I try my best not to cry.

"Yvanya, stop," he says, but I keep walking, pushing a few stalks of corn out of my way. "Stop," he says again, grabbing my hand.

I pull my hand back, trying to set myself free, but he tightens his grip. I stop fighting him, and he releases his hold. His calloused hand lightly scratches mine as he lets go.

"Look, I'm sorry," he says, and the fountains of my eyes open up. Fat tears roll down my face, and I try to wipe them with the back of my hand, but it's no use because the flow is not stopping.

"I didn't mean to hurt you." That's all I'm able to get out.

"I know. I should have known you were too good for me," he replies, making me feel even worse.

I shake my head, but I'm out of words. He pulls me against his chest and holds me tightly. A wave of relief flows through me as I realize I have not lost him entirely. Part of me wants to shout, "Who cares about the arrangement?" and pull his lips against mine, but the rational side of me knows there's much more at stake, and doing so would be selfish and only bring more pain.

"Hey, maybe it won't work out with him," he says with a small smile, releasing me.

"And you're willing to be second choice?" I try to joke, but it comes out as a cry.

He holds my face in his hands and, lowering himself to

my height, says, "For you, I'd be okay with being the last choice if it meant I finally got you."

He releases me, and we hug one last time.

How can he like me this much? I can't help but wonder.

We start walking again, this time side by side, as he carries the canvas bag. We finally exit the cornfield, and the sun is beginning to set. The horizon displays a gorgeous shade of hot pink. We walk quietly near the town, watching carefully for soldiers or tanks, but all is eerily quiet. Not a soul is within sight.

We finally turn onto my street—and abruptly halt in our tracks a couple of houses from mine. In front of my house, partly hidden by the overgrown bushes, an unmarked white van sits in the driveway, which has not seen a vehicle for the past fifteen years.

At once, Clayton pulls me behind a thick maple tree, hiding us from anyone who might be near the van or my house. A door slides open, and I hear a loud thud as it stops abruptly after hitting the end of its track. A chilling scream pierces the air, and without a doubt, I recognize the source. They're taking Heidi.

I prepare to run after them, but Clayton drops the tote and pins me in place against the tree, staring straight into my eyes and shaking his head to remind me that it's not a smart idea. He slowly releases his hold on me, and carefully, we lower ourselves to the ground while peeking around the tree's trunk. A soldier is carrying Heidi, who is barefoot and wearing nothing but her nightgown. She squirms and kicks at him, trying to free herself, but he's much stronger, and her efforts are futile. She lets out another loud scream, and he covers her mouth with his hand. Apparently, she gives him a good bite, and he screams out in pain. For a second, he loses his grip on her, and she drops to the ground. She bounces back and makes a run for it, heading away from Clayton and me. I hold my breath and tighten my fists, praying she gets away.

The man raises his rifle and points it straight at my sister, who is now a couple of houses down the street. I freeze in terror.

"Whitaker! We need them alive!" a second soldier yells. My eyes go to him for a second, immediately noticing his imponent stature. The color of their uniforms also catches my attention: blue. These are our own soldiers, the ones who were supposed to keep us safe. I switch back to the first soldier, who is now lowering his rifle. The second man chases after Heidi.

Heidi is fast for her age, but she's barefoot, and his longer legs have no trouble catching up. She makes it no more than three or four houses before he tackles her, bringing her hard to the ground.

"What the heck is this racket?" a third man yells, coming out of my house.

"The bitch bit me!" the man named Whitaker yells, walking hastily toward the second man and my sister. He swings his rifle over his shoulder and pulls a rag out of one pocket. He reaches my sister and the other man, who are still wrestling on the ground. He covers part of Heidi's face with the rag, and a few seconds later, she stops fighting. The second man stands up and wipes his hands on his pants. He swings my sister's unconscious body over his shoulder, and they walk back to the van. Her long hair flows gently in the breeze.

I can't take it any longer and start to get up. Clayton seems to notice my intention and pulls me down. He lies on top of me and holds down my wrists against my head to immobilize me.

"We need to help her," I whisper with anger.

"They'll catch us too," he replies softly.

"I'll scream if you don't let me go," I say, trying to free myself from his strong hold. His face is inches from mine, and tears blur my eyes as I plead, "Please let me go."

"I can't. I'm sorry," he whispers.

"Do I need to do everything by myself around here?" the man still standing by the door asks, driving our attention back to the soldiers. Clayton eases his hold on me but doesn't let go entirely, still not trusting me to make the right choice.

"Sorry, Rodriguez, but she put up a fight!" Whitaker replies as he shoves her limp body into the van.

"I told you to gag her," Rodriguez replies, and he goes back into my house. A few minutes later, he reappears with another two soldiers carrying my parents' unconscious bodies. They dump them inside the van as if they're nothing but sacks of food. I feel a sharp pain in my stomach, as if someone has punched me, and all the air has come out. I want to cry, but all that comes out is a soft whimper.

"Is that it?" one of the men asks. "I thought they have another daughter."

"If they do, she's not inside," Whitaker replies, wrapping a white rag around his wounded hand.

"Good enough. Let's get out of here before the whole neighborhood wakes up," one of them says, and they all jump into the van. The last guy shuts the door violently as they pull out of our driveway. Screeching its wheels, the van disappears into the twilight. As soon as the van's out of sight, the one streetlight flashes a couple of times before finally turning on.

"You let them take them!" I yell, and I punch Clayton in the chest as hard as I can. Pain shoots through my palm, but I don't care. My face is drenched from tears.

"Yvanya, there were too many of them. And didn't you see their rifles?" he replies, rubbing his chest.

"They took my family—my whole family," I whimper.

"And they would have taken you too if they'd seen you." He tries to reason with me.

"We need to find them," I say, wiping my eyes and nose.

"Let's go. I know the people who can help," Clayton replies. He looks at our surroundings, and after confirming the coast is clear, we start running away from my house, heading the same way we came. We leave no sign of our stop other than the tote of food by the tree.

🕐 🕑 🕒

We run nonstop until we reach Clayton's house. As he fumbles with the doorknob of his front door, I become aware of the cramp creeping through my legs. I've never run this far or this fast without stopping for rest. Although the wind took care of my tears and my face is now dry, my chest still hurts the same as it did half an hour ago. I bend down and rub my calves, trying to dissolve the pain that threatens to slow us down.

Will I ever see them again? I wonder. *Push those thoughts aside, Yvanya. Of course you will. Half the battle's having the right state of mind. Clayton knows people who will help rescue them. Don't give up the fight before it's even started.*

After what feels like an eternity, he finally unlocks the door, and we rush inside.

"Follow me," he says, and I limp behind him. I follow him into the house's only bathroom. I walk in after him, and he locks the door behind me.

"What the heck are you thinking?" I ask, exasperated.

"Trust me," he replies, and before I have a chance to respond, he grabs an edge of the large gray antislip shower mat in the middle of the tub and pulls it up. My eyes widen as it pivots about its opposite edge, revealing an entrance of some sort. The white tub floor now meets gray concrete steps. Not wasting any time, he lifts the lid to the toilet tank and produces two flashlights. He hands them over to me so he can replace the lid. He flicks the bathroom light switch off, and we turn on our lights.

"Watch the steps," he says, and I follow him closely. As soon as I've gone down a few steps, he pulls a lever, lowering the secret door and mat back to their original position, sealing the entrance.

I have many questions, but this is not the time to ask them. We are at the top of some sort of narrow spiral staircase. I'm moving too fast and start to feel as if the walls are spinning around me and the steps are running into one another. I use every ounce of concentration I have to keep myself from falling. I feel a wave of nausea creeping, and my mouth tastes something sour. I remind myself that I need to stay focused on what matters: my family. Getting sick is not going to help them.

After descending for what feels like a lifetime, I hear the noise of a multitude far away. I also see a dim light at the bottom of the seemingly bottomless pit. As we keep moving, the light becomes brighter, and the noise gets louder. We reach the bottom of the stairs, and it takes my eyes a minute to adjust. Slowly, things come back into focus. We're not alone. There are probably more than a hundred people moving around. Women, men, and children of multiple ages and ethnicities are represented. One question after another runs through my mind like a runaway train. *Who are these people, and what are they doing down here? Do they have anything to do with my family's disappearance? Are they running away? What's going on?*

I switch my attention to the room, which seems to be made of poured concrete. A continuous arc forms the ceiling and walls. The ceiling is at least fifty feet high at its apex.

We must be inside a tunnel. The air feels cool and humid, and I wonder how deep we've descended.

"We're a few hundred feet underground," Clayton says, as if reading my mind. "I'll be right back. Stay here."

I can barely hear him over the commotion before he disappears into the multitude. As if I am invisible, people walk in front of and behind me without stopping or giving me a second look. They all head in the same direction, although I don't know where they're going. Most adults are absorbed in conversations. All share one thing in common: no one smiles. Some are clearly in a rush, so I step back, leaning against a wall to get out of their way.

Scanning my surroundings, I tune the strangers out and instead focus on the inanimate objects. As the crowd clears, disappearing through a bend in the tunnel, I notice a huge flag has been hung from a wall: the flag of the former United States of America, the great country we were once part of. It's been years since I've seen an actual flag in person. Back when the protests and demonstrations started to ramp up, the Empire removed them from all public places. Seen as signs of rebellion, they were eventually banned from private property as well. Being found with such contraband could cost you a beating at best and your life at worst.

A draft of wind causes the flag's bottom to wave gently. Its imponent size dwarfs the wall in a majestic and almost mesmerizing way. Seeing this in person is a surreal experience, a feeling that cannot be replicated by even the best picture in a book.

Now that the crowd has entirely cleared, I notice another object: a car. It's not just any car but *the* car. It has to be. It's dark blue and has the same leaping-cat emblem adorning the hood. Right by it, Clayton is speaking to a man who's holding a rolled paper in one of his hands. Looking down, I notice another man sticking out from under the car. He's only visible from the waist down and seems to be lying on a rolling platform. *Enough with waiting here*, I think, and I head over to Clayton.

"What's going on?" I ask, drawing their attention.

"Seems it's not just your dad who's been taken," Clayton says, running his hands through his hair.

"Many of our top people were captured today," the man says, and he extends his hand to me. "Ashton Jones. We haven't met, although I've heard a lot about you."

My eyes widen as I remember the name on the inscription on the picture frame at Clayton's house. "Clayton's dad." I speak the obvious, to which he just nods. At five feet eight or so, with his brown hair and eyes, medium build, cowboy mustache, and recessed hairline, he's not exactly what I was expecting yet not surprisingly different either. If I look hard enough, I can see the resemblance to Clay.

"We're getting ready to go, but we'll need your help," Ashton says, stretching the roll of paper over the car's hood.

As I lean forward to take a peek at the paper, the guy working under the car rolls out.

"I'm done!" he says.

"Preston?" My jaw drops. Never in a million years would I have expected to see him here. *Why is he here? What's going on?*

"Nice seeing you again, Yvanya, although I wish it was under better circumstances," he replies solemnly, rubbing a hand over his forehead and leaving a long streak of grease in its path.

If not in such a tense mood, I probably would have chuckled. His hair is all messed up, and his blue jeans and gray long-sleeved T-shirt have grease stains. He rubs his hands against the side of his jeans, adding a few more black marks. He looks completely out of character from the man I met a few weeks ago. *Is this even the same guy?*

"What are you doing here?" The words finally escape my mouth.

"Changing a belt. It looked like it was about to break, and that's the last thing we need right now," he says, and I give him a confused look. "Sorry—my father is among the abducted. We're working on a plan to rescue them." After clarifying, he picks up a wet rag from a nearby table and rubs his hands on it.

His father was abducted as well? How many people have been abducted?

"You have a little mark," I say, pointing at my forehead.

He rubs the rag across his forehead, but rather than cleaning off the mark, he ends up smearing it even more.

"Better?" he asks.

"Yeah, much better!" Clayton replies, and I can't help but smile.

"Hey, dude, good to see you again," Preston says, giving Clayton a friendly slap on the shoulder.

This is so bizarre. How do they know each other? I hope they don't get the connection between them and me, or it's going to turn awkward very fast. Or is it possible Clayton already knows about Preston and me? No, he wouldn't be acting so friendly toward him if he knew. He must not know. And Preston—is he really a snob who's pretending to be a regular guy now, or was he pretending to be a snob before? And why would anyone in his right mind do that anyway? My head spins as the questions keep piling up. I just want to get out of here and find my family.

"Children!" Ashton calls out impatiently, drawing us back to the paper. We huddle over it. I have no idea what I'm looking at. It seems like the blueprint for a building. "Anderson and McKenzie will most likely be held in here, as it's their highest-security room," he says, pointing at a small rectangular room. "The doors will be guarded. There will be cameras everywhere. We'll need to figure out how to disable them quietly to gain enough time to sneak to the basement floor, where the detention cells are."

"Have you been inside this building before?" Preston asks Ashton, studying the blueprint closer.

"No, but I've seen pictures and videos of the facilities. Your fathers and I have gone through this scenario before, so we have reason to believe it's where they'll be," Ashton replies.

"You knew this could happen?" I ask, still not fully comprehending the big picture.

"We knew it was a risk," Ashton responds solemnly.

I don't want to believe my father has willingly put our family's safety at risk. He's supposed to protect us, not put us in harm's way. *Blaming him is not going to help right now.* I put the negative thoughts away and switch to problem-solving mode. "What about my mother and sister? Where do you think they're being kept?"

"Don't know for sure," Ashton says. "We'll take a look from one of the security rooms once we get there, before we deactivate the cameras. I doubt they'll be with your father. They'll want to keep them separate so they can play dirty mind games with him to get him to cooperate."

My eyes widen with fear at the thought of anyone using my sweet mother and sister as pawns. What do they plan to do with them? Will they hurt them? The thought of someone touching them sickens me. My mind wanders, and I find myself having all sorts of disturbing thoughts and questions. *If faced with the choice, will my father sacrifice my mother and sister to protect the ideals of this group? Where will his loyalty ultimately lie? How far is he willing to go? Did my mother know? Did she approve of this? Is she as responsible as he is?*

"We'll get them out," Clayton reassures me. I want to believe him more than anything, but I'm terrified. What if we don't get to them in time?

"How long do you think we have?" Preston asks.

"No more than twelve hours likely. With your fathers being such high-profile figures, I'm sure they'll want to move them west as soon as daylight comes," Ashton says.

"West?" I ask, although I know the answer.

"The Dungeon," Clayton replies, and I bite my lip. If they take them there, we'll never see them again. They'll be tortured and locked up where no one will be able to free them.

"You said you needed my help," I say to Ashton as a way to distract myself from my worst fears.

"Yes," he replies. "We believe they're being held at the government's EBI headquarters, where your father and Anderson work. To get in without tipping anyone, we need your father's badge. He has a spare in his home office. Can you get it?"

"Where is it? Do you know?" I ask.

"I'm not sure. He said you would know," Ashton replies, and my heart sinks. I don't know. I have no idea where my father keeps anything.

Why would he say such a thing? At least he said his home office, so that's a start.

Do you trust this guy? the voice inside my head asks. *If he were truly your father's accomplice, why wouldn't your father have given him more details about where exactly to find the badge in case of an emergency like this one?*

I don't know what to believe, but the fact is that right now, I don't have anyone else to turn to. This guy is Clayton's father, and whether or not I trust him, I know that at least I trust Clayton. Preston also seems to be on board, so I decide to follow their instructions. I just hope they're not all playing me as a pawn in some sort of delirious insurrection scheme.

"Wait. If they have my father, how do you know they haven't disconnected his badge? What if it doesn't even work at all?" I ask.

"One of the back service doors is on a different server. It has a twenty-four-hour delay, so assuming his access wasn't canceled until today, we should still be able to get in," Ashton responds.

"How do you know this?" I ask. I want to add, "And what's a server?" but I know this is not the time for a crash course in Technology 101.

"Your father and I went through multiple scenarios during our years of working together," Ashton says. He then shifts his attention to Clayton. "Can you go with Yvanya back to her house to retrieve it? Preston and I will get the car ready. Meet us back here within two hours."

Clayton nods, and we start moving. Rather than going back up the same staircase, we run for about ten minutes through a long set of winding tunnels. Different from the first room, they have low ceilings that leave less than a foot of clearance above Clayton's head. The path is narrow, and the lights are now much more sporadic. I can barely see where we're heading. All I know is we're going uphill, sometimes faster than the ceiling can keep up with. I feel more crammed with each step we take. It doesn't take long for claustrophobia to set in.

"Why did we come this way?" I ask, my breathing getting heavier.

"It's safer and will get us closer to your house without exposing us as much," he replies. "We're almost there. Now we just need to get over the hard part."

"Hard part?" I ask, confused. Right as I say it, a whiff of air answers my question. "Sewage?"

"Storm drain. Not as bad," he replies. "Hope you don't have any open wounds."

"Great," I mutter, breathing through my mouth to avoid the pungent smell. In a few more steps, I've got cold water up to my knees. I hope it won't get any deeper than this. I'd hate to find myself swimming in this pool of filth. The light is even fainter in this room.

"There's a ladder on that wall. We just need to climb up,

and we'll be a few blocks from your house," he says, leading the way. A rat's squeal makes the hairs on my back stand up. I can barely see anything, so I follow Clayton closely, holding on to the back of his shirt and hoping none of the creatures come near me. We come to a stop, and he starts climbing.

Once he's cleared me, I stretch my arms forward and feel around until I touch one of the ladder rungs. I grab on to the next one and start climbing behind him. Dirty water drips on me from above, and I close my eyes to protect them. It's a good thing I'm not afraid of heights, because we climb for at least thirty feet. At the top, I hear Clayton groan as he slides the gridded drain cover out of our way. Once we've climbed out, he replaces it carefully, leaving no sign of our entry.

We stand in the middle of an alley a few blocks from my neighborhood. The sun has gone down by now, and for once, the lack of streetlamps in the neighborhood is a relief. The street is completely desolate. We move fast, and my shoes squirt water out with every step. We approach my house carefully. The driveway is empty, but that doesn't mean no one is there. The door's hardware is broken, hanging upside down by a screw. The soldiers must have kicked the door in; a dirty footprint dent has been left as evidence of the violent entry. We gently push the door in and listen for any sounds. The coast seems clear, so we proceed.

"Leave the lights off," Clayton whispers, and I nod.

Having walked these steps in pitch darkness many times,

I know my way perfectly. Clayton goes into the kitchen to fetch us a couple of glasses of water. All the running has turned my throat into a desert. As expected, the door to my father's office has also been kicked open. I turn my flashlight on. The room has been trashed; the chair lies on its side. Files and papers are scattered all over the floor. Half the books from the bookshelves lie on mounds in a corner of the room. Surprisingly, none of the picture frames seem to have been touched, suggesting the soldiers had at least some empathy. I wonder what they could have been looking for and whether or not they found it.

I redirect my attention from the mess back to our quest. *Find the badge; free my family. Where could my father have kept it?* I scout the entire room, opening drawers, running my fingers through the mess on the floor, and pulling the picture frames from the wall and examining their backs. *I can't believe this is happening. Where is this thing? Why would he tell Ashton that I would know instead of just telling him where it was? Father, where is it? Help me!*

"Any idea?" Clayton whispers, touching one of my shoulders.

I jump, startled. I didn't hear him come into the office. "No, I don't know where it is. I don't know where he hid it." I bite my lip hard until I taste something metallic.

"Yvanya, think hard. Is there anything in particular your father would show you? Any hiding spot he shared

167

with you? Any saying he had that could bring a clue?" he says softly.

I see my father's cap on the floor, by the mound of books. I pick it up and hold it against my chest. I put it on, and out of nowhere, I hear his voice in my head: *You girls are the center of my world.* I see him kissing Heidi and me on our heads before tucking us into bed. *Never forget it: you are the center of my world.*

My eyes move to the globe, which, for some strange reason, still sits on the desk. *You girls are the center of my world. Never forget it: you are the center of my world. Center of my world.* The words keep running through my head, louder and faster each time, and my breathing picks up. With a swift motion of my hand, I flip the globe, making it spin about its axis. A soft rattling sound emanates from its center.

At the same time, we hear steps, and the wooden floor creaks above us. We cover our flashlights to make the light dimmer, and I make a gesture to Clayton to close the door behind him. He gently shuts it, and since the lock was compromised when the door was kicked in, all he can do is run the bolt at the top to keep it closed.

Who's upstairs? How many are there? And did they hear us?

There's no time to sit around and wait. I firmly grab the globe, place it between my legs, and squeeze the bottom tightly. I twist the top until it slowly starts to turn. I unscrew it off, revealing a small clear bag. Inside, the badge and a large bronze key are revealed. I look straight up at the family picture, the one in which I'm winking. This time, the wink tells me, *I knew you would find it!*

In all the excitement, I accidentally drop the top of the globe, which, thankfully, falls onto the area rug. The resulting thud is muted. I hope it will be enough not to give us away.

The steps draw near, and now we can also hear muffled voices. Clayton's eyes widen with fear. I spring into action and carefully but firmly move to the family portrait. I swing the picture out of the way, revealing the keyhole. With a decisive hand, I insert the key and twist it until I feel a click. A corner of the bookshelf springs forward by a couple of inches. I remove the key and release the picture, which swings back to its original position. Clayton pulls the bookshelf open enough for both of us to go through it. As we latch it closed behind us, I hear the men kick open the door to my father's study.

A spiral staircase almost identical to the one at Clayton's house comes into view. We run down it, watching our steps as best as we can yet not stopping. It blows my mind to think I've lived my entire life in this house and never known this secret passage was here—a whole new world right under my father's study, so close yet so distant.

Do all houses in my neighborhood have a secret passage, or is it just ours? And if they do, do the owners even know about them? My father had the house built before I was born, so there's no doubt he must have asked for the passage to be added. *For how long has he been sneaking in and out of our house through it? How ironic that I've been sneaking for months to see these people, while he has probably been doing the same, possibly even for years. Does Mother even know? Did she ever join him?* I wonder as her tender, joyful face comes to my mind. *And for how long has Father been conspiring with this underground group? What are their ideals? What exactly are they fighting for?* I have many questions. I hope I get the chance to ask him.

We reach the bottom of the staircase, and between the adrenaline and our speed, I manage to make it all the way down without getting dizzy from the spiral design. "Where now?" I ask. We stand in the middle of a dark, narrow corridor, staring at a fork. There are two corridors to choose from: dark and gloomy to the right and a bit less dark and gloomy to the left. The spiral staircase has left us disoriented, so there's no way to know which way is north or south. We go with our gut and choose left, hoping it'll take us closer to our group's rendezvous location.

An electric wire runs along the ceiling. Every fifty feet or so, a single lightbulb pretends to illuminate the way. Most of the bulbs seem to have a loose connection, casting an eerie show with their flickering. It's still better than total darkness. The ceiling is low enough that Clayton keeps bumping his head into the lightbulbs. Water drips onto my head, and my feet hit puddles here and there. I stick my hand into my jeans pocket and tighten my hold around the bag with my father's badge and secret door key. I need to feel they're safe.

We keep moving, pretending to know where we're heading. We play the guessing game at a couple of other forks, hoping luck is on our side. Suddenly, we spot a sign on one of the walls: an arrow and a bunch of numbers that mean nothing to me but seem to offer good news to Clayton.

"We're almost there!" he says. "I know where we are now."

I'm relieved to see his confidence return. The last thing I want is to get lost in this scary underground world, when my family's lives depend on me. We move faster now, seeing a light at the end of the tunnel.

We end up back where we started, by the navy-blue car. The large, cavernous room made entirely of concrete is now mostly empty, except for the car and a few different groups of people spread throughout the room. I notice tall tables lined against one of the walls, with people clustering over papers and books, seeming to study their contents.

"Did you get it?" Ashton appears out of nowhere.

"Yes. She has it," Clayton replies. "We almost got caught. Some of the soldiers had stayed behind."

"Probably waiting for her," Ashton says, watching me.

"What do we do now?" I ask, not wanting to waste any more time.

"Yvanya, this is going to be a dangerous mission. You should probably stay here," Ashton says.

"I'm coming," I say firmly.

"I don't think your father would want you tagging along. I think it's better if you stay."

"This is my family. It's all I have. I'm coming."

Ashton nods, likely realizing that nothing he says will change my mind. "Here's the plan," he says as Preston spreads the blueprint over the car's hood. We huddle around it. "We'll come in through this back door using Yvanya's badge. There should be no guards, just a card reader. About a few feet down the hall, I'll take the stairs to the electric panel room, where I'll rewire the cameras to show footage from a few hours ago."

"I thought you said we would disconnect them," Clayton says.

"We changed our minds. If we entirely disconnect them, it'll be more obvious to the guards that we're inside. This will buy us more time," Preston says.

"Preston and Yvanya," Ashton says, "you'll keep going down the hall and take the second set of stairs, which will take you down to one of the minor security hubs. There's usually just one guard in there, but he'll be armed, so you'll have to be quick to impair him. Try to subdue him without firing your guns, or you'll alert the entire building."

Guns? I want to ask, but Ashton keeps talking.

"The moment the guard's down, start scanning the monitors. We're looking for any images of your families. Pay attention to the bottom of the screens, which will identify their locations. Write down the locations so you don't forget. The images will change every three seconds. Once you've figured out where everyone is, use this phone to text me. Preston will show you in the car how to do that." Ashton hands me a rectangular apparatus similar to the one I held in Clayton's bedroom. "Upon your cue, I'll switch the images from live to the earlier recordings. That will allow us to avoid the guards at the other stations."

"Like we were saying before," Preston says, "we think

my father and Yvanya's will be in the lowest level of the basement. If that's where they are, there will be many guards around."

"Correct," Ashton says. "I'll head there, as I'm the most experienced shooter." My eyes widen with fear at the mention of shootings.

"You'll need reinforcement. I'll go with you," Clayton says.

"No. I'll be fine; plus, I have a different need for you," Ashton replies. Before Clayton can object, he continues. "Yvanya, you and Preston will go after your mother and sister. The first number on the camera screens will indicate the floor level. The letter next to it will tell you which wing of the building, followed by the room number. Look for signs to help you find your way. Try to blend in; don't call attention to yourselves. Find them, and get out. Send me a text the moment you're out."

"What if we can't see them on the camera monitors? What if we're caught?" I ask.

"We'll just need to improvise. Do whatever you need to do," Ashton replies, and a rock hits my stomach.

Improvise? Do whatever we need to do? They prepared for this type of possible scenario, and this is the best strategy they could come up with? I hate the idea of not having a more robust plan.

"What about me?" Clayton asks, distracting me from my negative thoughts.

"Natasha and you stay outside," Ashton says. "We need you to find a bigger vehicle—a van preferably. We need space for twice as many people. If you can't find a van, just go with whatever you can get, but be ready for us. The moment we come out, we need to jump in and go."

"Who's Natasha?" I ask.

"I am," a female voice says behind me. I turn around to find the Andersons' servant girl, my favorite waitress, the freckled-nosed girl who delighted in my clumsiness. By the way she crosses her arms and looks at me, frowning and pursing her lips, I can tell she still dislikes me. I have nothing but questions, but they'll have to wait.

"Here," Ashton says, passing along some folded clothes. "We're part of the cleaning crew. Remember, try to blend in. In and out, and don't call attention to yourselves."

I unfold my outfit: a pair of beige cargo pants, a cap, and a vest that is clearly too big for me. A name tag is attached to the vest. "Yolanda?" I read out loud.

"It was that or Felipe," Ashton replies. "You look more like a Yolanda than a Felipe."

We change into our new outfits and regroup by the car.

"Let me help you with your weapon," Preston says, and before I have a chance to say anything, he starts messing around with my belt, hooking a holster to the inside of my pants. I notice both Natasha and Clayton giving him looks.

"How much practice did she get?" Ashton asks Clayton, drawing his attention away from what Preston is doing.

"Maybe about a hundred rounds tops," Clayton responds.

"How's her aim?"

"Not terrible for a newbie, but I didn't test her under stress. I thought we'd have more time to practice."

All this talking about shooting is making me sick. I don't feel qualified to handle a gun, but if I complain, then I know they won't let me inside the building and will just leave me behind in the car. I can't stay outside. No one has more to lose than I do. I must make myself useful. I just hope it doesn't require using the gun, because if it comes to that, I don't know if I'll have the guts to pull the trigger.

"How does that feel?" Preston asks, setting the holster in place against my waist. One of his fingers rubs gently against my skin as he pulls his hands away from my waistband. His touch sends a sharp jolt through my abdomen, and I laugh out loud.

"Like you're tickling me," I reply.

"The holster. Is it comfortable?"

"Ah, yes, I guess," I say, realizing what he means. I look around, expecting to get my gun so I can load it into the holster.

"You'll get your gun before we go in," Ashton says, as if reading my mind. "You won't be comfortable sitting with it on."

"What about me? Where's mine?" Natasha asks Preston

in a soft voice, probably hoping he'll help her with her holster as well.

"Sorry, but I don't think you'll be getting one," Preston replies as he attaches his holster to his own belt.

"Why not?" Natasha asks, pouting her lips.

"You have never handled a gun. You don't even know the basics," he replies, dismissing her. For a second, I feel bad for her. She's clearly into him, and he acts as if she doesn't even exist.

Natasha bites her lower lip and gives me an evil look. What little sympathy I felt for her a second ago disappears like a drop of water evaporating on a hot stove. I also can't help but feel relief in knowing she's not armed. Who knows what she'd be capable of doing to me if given the chance?

The rest of the team suit up, and we get in the car, with Ashton in the driver's seat and Clayton on the passenger side. I get sandwiched in the back between Natasha and Preston. The engine roars to life, and we drive down the tunnel. As we leave the large vaulted room, the path gets narrower, the ceiling gets lower, and the lights get dimmer until only the car's headlights illuminate our way. I feel claustrophobic and hope the car won't stall here. I'm not sure we would even be able to open the doors to exit it if we had to. I wonder how many times Ashton has driven this way. Was my father with him during any of those trips?

We drive for maybe a mile or so under these tight conditions until, finally, we exit the tunnel. We come out of what looks like the underground level of an abandoned parking garage. I look back at the entrance as we drive away. Overgrown grass, weeds, and hanging vines camouflage it, making it almost imperceptible against the moldy, stained concrete.

It's darker now. People will be out, some going to work and some heading to school. I wonder if anyone will notice when I don't get on the school bus tonight. Daphne will, of course. What will she think?

Preston shows me how to use the phone, which surprisingly seems pretty intuitive. "I thought the government had removed all cell phone towers used by civilians," I say, running my fingers over the sleek phone.

"They did, but we have taps on the government ones. Our signals are strong and clear, even underground," Preston replies.

"Hey, Clayton, I thought you said you didn't have a way to charge these phones," I say, remembering the first time I saw one in his bedroom.

"These are a different model. I don't have a charger for the one back home," he says.

We drive slowly through town, keeping our profile low, staring straight ahead.

Not having anything else to do, my mind wanders to what it might have been like when the soldiers raided my house. I imagine my mother in the kitchen, dressed in her oversized red robe, the one she bought just because it was red, her favorite color. It didn't matter to her that it was a couple sizes too big; she was infatuated with the color. She was probably preparing breakfast, brewing coffee for herself and my father. They love spending time alone before Heidi and I get up.

I imagine the men kicking the door open and my mother's confused face showing a mix of surprise and fear. She possibly wanted to scream but couldn't; they might have been pointing a gun at her. "Scream and we shoot you," I imagine they threatened.

My father likely walked downstairs to find the men pointing a gun at his beloved wife's head. "Over there," they might have said, directing him to a chair where they could tie him up and then easily subdue him. The soldiers probably then covered their faces with chloroform or some other chemical to make them pass out.

Perhaps the commotion woke Heidi, who walked downstairs to find our parents incapacitated. The men likely didn't see her right away. She might have headed for the door, and as she was struggling to get out, trying to jump barefoot over the pieces of the broken door, they perchance noticed her and chased after her. I picture sweet, innocent Heidi, my dear sister, running down the street, ignoring the pain of the asphalt and pebbles on her bare feet, running for dear life, just to be tackled by men twice her age and two or three times her weight.

I pull myself out of the painful reverie and notice there

are military vehicles everywhere. There are twice, if not three times, as many as we saw earlier today. We pull to a stop sign, and one of the soldiers signals to Ashton to stay put. We hold our breath as the soldier walks our way with his rifle in hand. Out of nowhere, one of his partners summons him from the other side of the street; it looks as if he's found a suspicious individual and needs some reinforcement. We exhale in relief and take advantage of the distraction, slowly driving away. We hear gunshots in the background, and I clasp my hands as my body tenses.

After less than ten minutes of driving, we reach the main gates of the EBI offices. I've never seen where my father works. A large steel sign is illuminated by beams of light coming from the ground: Empire Bureau of Investigation. A modern-looking building framed with glass, steel, and walls that seem to defy gravity sits on the middle of a small hill. Mature trees and bushes surround most of the grounds leading to the hill. A parking lot full of vehicles is on one side of the building; some of them are heavily armored. A ten- or twelve-foot-tall barred fence surrounds the complex; it has barbed wire all around its top. *Is this a working place or a prison?*

We drive past the main gate, circumventing the fence, and enter a back alley lined with garbage containers. The car's headlights illuminate one of the containers as we take a turn, and an opossum or some other large rodent screeches as it runs away. A small, well-lit guard station sits at the end of the alley. We stop in front of the bar as we wait for the heavily armed guard to approach us.

"Identify yourself," he calls out to Ashton.

"We're part of the maintenance night crew," Ashton replies, handing some papers to the guard. The man takes a quick glance and is about to return the papers to Ashton, when he suddenly takes a few steps back and calls another guard. We stare straight ahead.

Out of the corner of my eye, I see Preston's hand slowly reach for his seat-belt-release button, and I tense. *Please don't let us get into a shooting match right here.*

"The maintenance crew came in about half an hour ago," the guard replies suspiciously, holding his rifle with both hands now.

This is not looking good. They're going to catch us.

"Our van broke down; we had to get a different vehicle," Ashton says with a calm demeanor.

"Simon, Yolanda, Michael, Ana, and Juan?" he asks his partner, who is now inspecting a different list.

"Correct. That's us," Ashton replies, and the second guard seems to confirm that the names match his list. After a few minutes, he nods, and the first guard relaxes his hold on his weapon. Preston lowers his hand as well, and I'm finally able to exhale.

"Don't be late again. They don't like it," the guard says to Ashton as he hands him back his papers.

"No, sir, won't happen again," Ashton replies. "Thank you, sir."

The bar goes up, and we drive into the complex. We follow a small service road that leads to the back of the building. The rear facade is nowhere near as glorious as the front. With its mix of concrete and brick, it looks more like a traditional building. We park between two small trucks. Once we're mostly hidden, Preston hands me a gun. I realize then that I've been squeezing my hands so tightly they're almost numb.

"Keep it in your holster," he says. "Hopefully you won't need to use it."

"But if you do pull it out," says Clayton, who has now turned around to face me, "keep your finger off the trigger unless you mean to shoot." I nod as we stare at each other. "Stay safe, Yvanya," he adds, and even in the darkness, I can see the fear in his eyes.

"You can still stay in the car," Ashton tells me.

"I'm coming," I reply before I allow them to change my mind.

"Natasha and Clayton, remember your parts," Ashton says as he, Preston, and I exit the car.

We walk to the back entrance and find it unmanned, at least from our side, just as Ashton said. Ashton swipes my father's badge, and a red light flashes. I hold my breath as I realize it might not be working. He flips it and swipes it again, this time generating a green light. He pulls on the door handle, and we're in.

It takes a few seconds to adjust to the brighter light. We stand in a service hall. The walls are beige, rough, and a bit chipped in some areas. The floor has some stains. There's no one in sight. A pair of brooms and mops lean against a corner. We each grab a broom. Preston lowers my cap a bit. "Try to keep your face low so it's hidden, in case someone might recognize you," he says.

We walk down the hall. In a few feet, Ashton disappears through the first door to the right, as planned, and heads down the stairs. I stick my hand in one of my pockets, feeling the phone Ashton gave me what seems like hours ago. We continue walking down the hall until we reach another door, next to which is a small sign: 1S300. Through it, we enter what looks like a completely different building. Smooth, shiny snow-white walls and floors and glass windows with steel frames surround us. The hall is crowded with well-dressed people who come and go, passing us as if we're invisible. I walk in front of Preston to make our footprint smaller. We get caught up in the mass, trying to keep up the pace while keeping our eyes out for the door we're supposed to take.

Suddenly, I feel Preston pull on my vest, so I slow down until the crowd passes us. To our right is the door we've been looking for, assuming the directions we were given are accurate. We pretend to sweep the floor until a second group of people catch up with us. Once they obscure our presence, Preston opens the door, and we disappear from the hall.

We head downstairs, each with one hand on our broom and one near our holster. We move in silence and stop when we reach a solid white door. On the front is a small black sign with white letters: Security. Preston tries turning the door handle, and to my surprise, it's unlocked. With a soft push, the door swings open without making a sound. Facing away from us, a man stares at some monitors. With narrow shoulders and below-average height, his silhouette does not project much sense of security. A pair of handcuffs hangs from one of his sides. A black metal desk sits a few feet from him with a handgun and walkie-talkie on top. Suddenly, the guard seems to feel our presence and turns around, clearly startled.

"What are you doing here? Cleaning personnel are not allowed here," he says. I feel bad for him. He's clearly no older than I am. I hope he cooperates.

"I'm sorry, sir," Preston mumbles with a different accent. "Me and my partner kind of got lost. We don't know nothin' about this building and don't know how to find our way to the lobby." He moves toward the guard slowly.

"Well, this isn't the way. You need to leave this room," the guard replies, signaling toward the door.

"Come on, sir; just show us the way. We don't wanna be super late, or we'll lose our jobs. We need our jobs," Preston replies, inching closer to the guard with both hands tightly around the broom's handle.

By now, the guard clearly senses that something is wrong and shifts his eyes for a second to the gun that lies several feet away from him. He makes a move for it. Preston quickly swings his broom and hits him straight on the side of his head. The guard drops to the ground as if dead.

I rush to check on him. Around his neck, I feel a strong pulse. *Good. He's not dead*, I think with relief. I reach around him and pull out the handcuffs. I cuff him to his desk. The last thing we need is for him to come back to himself and give us away.

"That's why you should never leave your gun unattended," Preston says, picking up the guard's handgun.

"You're taking his gun?" I ask.

"Two is better than one," he replies with a small grin. "Plus, better for me to have it than him—don't you think?"

"Let's find my family," I say, and we turn our attention to the monitors. There are at least ten small screens, each showing a small black-and-white image. Every three seconds, the images change, just as Ashton predicted. They change too quickly for us to look at all of them.

"You look at the ones on the right, and I'll take the ones on the left," Preston says, and I comply.

I stare as intently as possible, looking at the changing images. I see nothing but empty rooms and random people moving around sterile-looking white corridors and hallways.

The images' resolution is poor, so details are hard to make out. After almost a minute, I see an image of what looks like a young person lying on a bed, covered with a white sheet, with legs tucked in the fetal position. *Heidi! It's got to be her!* My eyes move to the bottom of the screen, and I take a mental picture of the room location: 3W440.

"I think I found Heidi!" I say as I pick up a pen from the guard's desk and scribe the room number on my palm.

"I'm not seeing anything here," Preston replies with frustration in his voice.

Once again, the images change, and out of nowhere, a man is shown running across one of the screens. He disappears as quickly as he came onto the screen. The camera's resolution is so bad I can't tell who it was.

"I think that was one of our fathers!" I say.

"If that's the case, we need Ashton to switch out the images now before a guard at one of the other substations sees them, if they haven't already," Preston replies.

"But we don't know where my mother is," I say.

"We can't wait, Yvanya," he replies, and I know he's right. Our fathers need every split second we can give them.

I pull the phone from my pocket and quickly type, "Go!" I hit the Send button, and a couple of seconds later, I'm notified that the text has been received. We return our eyes to the monitors, and within another couple of seconds, the images change. To most people, it'll look as if the images have shifted as part of their normal rotation. Hopefully they won't notice the images are repeats from earlier in the day.

"Beta station, come in." The radio on top of the guard's desk comes alive.

Preston and I exchange frantic looks. "What do we do?" I ask.

"I think I have to reply, or it'll be more suspicious," he says, reaching for the radio.

"What if they recognize that it's not his voice?" I ask, referring to the guard.

"We don't have a choice. If we don't answer, they'll be here in no time," he says, and he presses the Talk button. "Beta station here. Copy," Preston says, changing his voice a bit. I keep an eye on the unconscious guard. If he's pretending to be down and plans to make noise while Preston's talking, I will have to silence him.

"Is everything okay, Beta station? Copy," the voice on the radio says.

"Yes, everything's normal. Copy," Preston replies.

"Roger that. Seems we had a false alarm. Over and out," the radio voice says, and the line goes silent.

"I can't believe you fooled them," I say with relief. Preston and I return our gaze to the monitors. Although the scenes are from earlier in the day, assuming she hasn't been moved, we might still be able to learn where they're keeping my mother. Before a minute has passed, we hear running steps approaching. Someone's coming. I guess Preston wasn't as convincing as I thought he was.

I run to the door and lock it. It's a solid door, so it should buy us some time. For a second, I let panic take over, but then I see Preston scanning the room for an exit and spring back into troubleshooting mode. The guard lies unmoving in the same place where he first dropped. There are no windows and no other doors. Up on the ceiling, I notice an air supply vent. It's about eighteen by eighteen inches maybe. Can we fit? I might, but what about Preston? It'll be a tight one. I hate being in confined spaces, but it's better that than getting shot. There's no other choice.

The steps outside the door have now switched to pounding fists. "Lewis, are you there? Open up!" someone yells, frantically rattling the door handle.

With no time to waste, Preston drags the desk—and, with it, the guard—so it's located under the vent and climbs onto it. He stretches his arms and, with a strong push, loosens the grill. He calls me over with a hand signal, and I obey.

Suddenly, as I try to climb onto the desk, I feel a hand wrap around one of my ankles.

"Let me go," I whisper, shaking my leg, but the guard's hold only tightens.

"Don't make me shoot you," I hear Preston say, and as I look up, I see him pointing the guard's own gun at him. With fearful eyes, the guard immediately releases his hold on me, and I'm able to climb onto the desk. At this point, I'm relieved I took the time to cuff him.

Preston wraps his arms around my lower thighs and lifts me up to the vent. I squeeze through the tight entrance and then crawl on my stomach to one side to make room for him. He follows soon after, although with much more difficulty. His broad shoulders get stuck, and I hear him grunt as his shirt's fabric tears. Once up, he replaces the vent, and we're on the move.

We move out of the room right as the other guards burst through the door. Their shouting becomes fainter the farther away we move. Luckily, they don't seem to have any intention of chasing us through the vents. I hope that doesn't mean there's a fan or some other dangerous mechanical component along our path. It's pitch black here, so we have no idea what lies ahead.

As expected, my well-prepared partner produces a small flashlight, which helps illuminate the way. We make some turns until, a few feet away, we see light shooting up through a vent. We turn off our light and get closer. Looking down, we see that we're over a restroom facility—over a toilet stall, to be exact. A couple of men are talking by the sinks, and we hear a toilet flush. We wait until they exit the restroom to quickly make our way down into the room. Preston lowers himself first and then guides me down. I replace the vent on my way down.

We sneak out of the restroom as fast as we can. *Good*

that no one walked in while I was in there! I think, and then I refocus on our mission. *Where are we now?* I wonder. We continue to walk down a hallway with our heads lowered, trying to figure out where to go next. People come and go, but no one seems to notice us. Finally, near a conference room, I spot a room numbered 3E520. I look at my palm to confirm where we need to go. The writing has become blurry, but it's still legible: 3W440. At least we're on the right floor. A plate by another room confirms we're moving in the right direction.

"Yolanda?" A woman stops me. She's dressed in a black suit with a tucked-in white blouse. The wrinkles on her face make her look tired, and her eyes show confusion.

"Yes, ma'am. How can I help you?" I ask softly, remembering my name tag. I keep my eyes low to avoid showing my face too much. Preston has distanced himself from me, likely to avoid drawing more attention.

"I need you to take this to 3W660." She relaxes her gaze and hands me a medium-sized box. I'm surprised how light it is.

"Yes, ma'am, on my way," I say, and I continue moving before she has a chance to say anything else.

Good. At least now I have a reason to head over in that direction, I think, moving faster. Preston catches up with me shortly after. We make it to the west wing, and I drop off the box by the 600 area. The numbers are going down. We continue moving, looking for the 400 area. *Where is 440?*

I anxiously scan every room number. Finally, at the end of the hallway, I spot room 440. There are no windows on the door, so we don't know what awaits us inside.

With no time to waste, I turn the door handle, which, thankfully, is unlocked, and slowly push the door open. The light is on. The room is empty except for a figure curled up on a bed.

Heidi! I found Heidi!

Relief rushes through me. I run to her—and then realize it's not Heidi.

11

"Daphne? What is Daphne doing here?" I ask Preston, who seems just as perplexed.

He shakes his head with confusion. "Who's Daphne?"

"My friend," I reply, and then I turn my attention to her. "Daphne, wake up." I shake her softly at first and then more vigorously when she doesn't respond.

"Did you know she was also missing?" Preston asks.

"Of course not!" I exclaim louder than I intend to. I check her pulse, which seems normal. *What have these people done to her?* I wonder angrily. "And where are my sister and mother?" I ask, knowing it's a rhetorical question at this point.

Suddenly, we hear what sound like gunshots, and within seconds, an alarm goes off. A voice on the PA system announces that the building is on lockdown. *We're gonna get caught!* I fear the worst.

"Yvanya, we need to go now," Preston responds, picking Daphne up. I help him shift her body until her weight is balanced across his arms and then pull the sheet from the bed and throw it over her, tucking it in a few places so there's no risk of it coming off while we walk. I cover her entirely and hope no one notices us carrying a limp body down the hall.

Back in the hallway, people are running in all directions. We pick up our pace to match theirs, hiding in plain sight for a while. Another round of gunshots makes the hairs on my back stand up. I keep an eye out for the room numbers, making sure we don't miss our exit. We enter the south corridor, and by now, there's almost no one in the hall. People have retreated to wherever their lockdown protocol directs them, probably their offices. We see them slamming doors and sticking something under them, most likely barricading themselves. We find the stairs and leave the main corridor.

Once on the first floor, we check around before entering the main hall. The coast seems clear, so we keep moving. I walk in front of Preston so it's not obvious he's carrying a person. We stand a few feet from the door to the service corridor, the one we came from initially, when three guards show up out of nowhere. They're heading in our direction. I lower my face, hoping that if I don't make eye contact, they'll just ignore us, but our luck seems to have run out.

"You two," one of them says, blocking our way. The other two continue moving.

"Yes, sir?" I reply, keeping my face low.

"We're in lockdown; you need to follow protocol. Go to your safe room right now," he says.

"Yes, sir, that's where we're heading," Preston replies.

The guard stares at Preston's load and seemingly is about to inquire what's under the blanket, when his fellow guards call for him to hurry up. He gives us a second look and then heads toward them, leaving us behind.

Yes, thank you!

We take a deep breath and resume our escape. Once out of sight, we run through the service corridor and out of the building. Clayton awaits us behind the wheel of his father's car. We lay Daphne on the backseat with her head on my lap. Preston climbs into the front. Clayton is as dumbfounded as we were about finding Daphne, and we share with him the bad news of not having found my mother or sister. We wait anxiously for news from Ashton and our fathers.

A few seconds later, a third-floor window near our vehicle bursts into pieces. Fragments of glass rain all around us. We see two figures jump out from the building into a nearby dumpster. Immediately after, they climb out and run to a small dark-colored van, whose side door is wide open. A hand sticks out, signaling for us to follow them.

As if on cue, Clayton presses the accelerator, and we're moving.

"Only two came out! Where's the other one?" I cry. *Please let one of those be my father!* I selfishly plead.

"Don't know, but they said we need to go. Keep your

heads low," Clayton says as he maneuvers the car through the tight alley. A bullet makes a hole in our rear glass, and I get as low as I can, shutting my eyes tightly.

"Hold on!" Clayton yells, and I hear wood breaking as we hit something, most likely the bar at the security checkpoint. I can hear sirens right behind our tail the entire time, but I don't dare look up.

We continue driving as fast as we can through the town until the road widens, and Clayton's driving becomes less erratic. I raise my head to see the small van beside our car. Their inside light is on. My father sits in the front passenger seat. *He's alive! My father's alive!* I rejoice in my head. I watch as he communicates with Clayton through signals. Soon after, he turns off their inside light, and I no longer see him. Looking around, I notice that the vehicles following us are no longer there.

"Why aren't we being followed anymore?" I ask.

"They're probably planning to intercept us ahead. Too bad for them—we're not going where they think," Clayton responds.

With a stronger sense of security, I dare to sit upright now. I cradle Daphne's head on my lap, running my fingers through her dark hair. "Wake up, girl. Wake up. Daphne, it's me—Anya. Wake up," I whisper into her ear. She doesn't bat an eyelash, but her rhythmic breathing gives me hope that she'll eventually be okay. She has to.

Questions about my mother's and sister's whereabouts

run through my head, and I feel sick to my stomach as I imagine the worst. *We will find them, and they will be just fine.* I try to stay positive.

I look ahead and see that Preston and Clayton both have some funky-looking sunglasses on top of their heads. I don't think much about it and instead stare out my window, trying to see my father. All I can make out is his silhouette in the passenger seat.

Out of nowhere, all goes dark. Both cars have turned off their headlights. I can't see a thing. *We're going to crash!* I fear the inevitable.

But instead of crashing, Clayton slows down the car to a crawl and makes a sharp right turn.

"How can you see where we're going?" I ask him.

"We've got night-vision lenses on," he responds. "Plus, I've done this route many times. I know it like the back of my hand."

"Where are we going?" I ask.

"The Joneses' farm. We're picking up more supplies and don't want anyone to see us approaching," Preston responds.

We drive for another ten minutes or so in pitch darkness. I feel more relaxed by now, given we haven't hit anything yet. Gradually, a faint orange glow appears in the distance. The longer we drive, the larger and more defined it gets. Both of our vehicles stop at the entrance to Clayton's family farm. No one within our car speaks a word. *I hope everyone made it out alive.*

I want more than anything to jump out of the car, run to hug my father, and ask him if he knows where my mother and Heidi are, but I refrain from doing so, out of respect for Clayton. This is not the time.

"I can't believe this." Clayton finally breaks the silence, his voice choking as he tries to contain a cry.

"Man, I'm sorry," Preston says, placing a hand on his shoulder.

I'm speechless. *Who could have done something like this?* Of course, I know the answer.

Clayton takes a deep breath and shifts the car back into drive. As we drive away, I look out the back window to see the flames completely engulf what's left of his community.

12

"What do we do now?" I ask with anxiety creeping in.

"We go to our rendezvous location," Preston replies.

As we turn away from the farm, we pick up speed. We drive silently for about ten minutes. The car's headlights are still off, so I can't see anything. The way we suddenly start turning around corners makes me think we're back in town.

We enter an old concrete structure and soon find ourselves driving underground once again. Clayton turns on the headlights. He's driving a bit too fast for my comfort. The sight of the walls speeding past our car gives me motion sickness, so I lower myself in my seat and focus my eyes on my unconscious friend. I continue running my fingers through her hair.

Eventually, we make it to the large chamber where we started. We exit the car to find ourselves surrounded by an even larger crowd than the one I saw before—maybe two hundred or three hundred people. I can't tell for sure, but the place is packed. Once again, adults and children are moving nonstop. Most of them carry large bags of what I assume must be food and ammo supplies. Some of them stack the bags against the walls, where others pick them up and take them somewhere else. The crowd moves in a disorganized fashion. I have no clue where they're heading or where they're taking all these things. A mother runs after her rowdy little boys, trying to stop their horsing around. She grabs each by a wrist, pulls them toward a wall, and sits them away from the main traffic. Nobody rests. The tension in the air is even higher than it was a few hours ago. I keep wondering, *Who are these people, and what exactly is going on?*

"Dad!" Clayton yells, catching a glimpse of his father. They rush to each other, and Clayton's father pulls him into a tight hug. As the embrace gets tighter, I see Ashton pull back as if in pain. That's when I notice the bloody rag tied around his upper arm. He must have gotten hit or cut during the rescue mission. Other than that, he seems unharmed. I look around for my own father.

"Yvanya!" I hear his sweet voice.

I turn around, and tears cloud my eyes. He's dirty and sweaty, with dried blood stamped across his forehead and a few bruises by his mouth and nose.

"Father," I mouth, but no sound exits my lips. He pulls me against his broad chest, and I start whimpering. For a minute or two, I'm lost in his arms. Part of me was convinced I would never see him again. I breathe in his scent, the scent that fathers have after a long, laborious day. Memories of my childhood, of cuddling against his chest as he read stories to Heidi and me, flash in front of my eyes.

"Where are Mother and Heidi?" I finally ask when I'm able to speak.

"They have them, but we'll find them," he says, holding my chin up so our eyes meet. "I promise you." Just as he always promised me I would be fine after a scraped knee, I have no choice but to believe him.

"McKenzie, we need to go," Ashton says, interrupting us.

"What's happening?" I ask Clayton as he starts stuffing bags into our car's trunk.

"We need to leave. This location has been compromised," he says, throwing a few more bags in before slamming the trunk shut.

I look up and notice a long row of vehicles behind our car. *Where did all these cars come from?* Slowly, a band of smoke starts creeping into the chamber, and people start screaming and running toward the vehicles. Doors slam as the vehicles fill up. I see Preston standing a few feet from us, seeming to search through the crowd, and I immediately realize his father is the one who didn't make it out of the EBI building. I hope that means only that, as with my mother and sister, they're keeping him elsewhere. Preston is probably wondering where he is and if he's okay. But there'll be time to think about that later. Right now, we need to go.

I wave Preston over. He seems to hesitate for a second and then rejoins us. We climb back into the car; Preston,

Clayton, and I are in the back, with Ashton riding shotgun and my father driving.

"Where's Daphne?" I ask, realizing she's gone.

"We reunited her with her parents. They're in one of the vans behind us," Preston replies. "Natasha, Matt, and his mother are with them. They'll follow us to our next base camp."

I have more questions than answers, but given how stressed out everyone in the car is, I decide to hold them. Clayton, on the other hand, opens up with no intention of stopping. "Okay. So what exactly is going on? Where is everyone going? What happened to the original plan? What happened to the farm?"

Ashton interrupts him, turning his head to face him. "Son, we believe there was an informant within the group who gave us away. Our own government soldiers ransacked our homes, dragging many of our opposition leaders and their families out. Some were taken, others were beat up badly, and the least fortunate were killed."

"Where's my father?" Preston finally asks as my father zigzags through the tight tunnel.

"Let's talk when we get to our next stop. We need to focus on driving," my father replies, and he and Ashton put night-vision glasses on as our headlights go out. I hate being left in the dark, literally and figuratively.

As we exit the tunnels, I notice some of the cars behind us turning in different directions. We're splitting up.

We drive for a while, maybe for an hour. It's hard to keep track of time when you're on edge. After a while, I notice taller buildings around us. We must be heading toward the downtown area. I've never been here but have heard of it: tall abandoned buildings, pretty much a wasteland. It's dark outside, but the full moon casts enough light to make out some shapes and silhouettes.

"We're heading to the Delta compound," my father says. "We're splitting up into teams throughout the city. That way, we can keep casualties low if we're discovered." I swallow hard, not liking the sound of this. "We weren't supposed to get activated until next month, so we weren't entirely ready. We'll have to improvise and make choices as we go."

How's improvising working out for us? I think.

My father drives the car into an underground garage and turns the headlights on once we're a couple of stories under street level. We pass some old cars covered in mounds of dust. Their tires are deflated; they've been abandoned for who knows how many decades. I turn my eyes straight ahead and see glowing eyes ahead of us, and I panic for a second. A pack of raccoons freeze in place, startled by the unexpected visitors. A few seconds later, they run away. The garage is empty except for about a dozen cars and pickup trucks, most covered with scratches and dents from years of wear and tear. We park our car near the staircase and carry the contents of our trunk up a couple of flights before heading toward the building's lobby. The staircase is dark and has a musty smell. We illuminate our steps with the help of a few flashlights.

The door to the lobby makes a loud creak as we open it, and once inside, we're greeted by friendly faces. Women and men of different ethnicities rush to help us with our supplies, freeing our hands the moment we're inside. They set some of the items in a corner and carry others away. The room is packed with people, bags, and boxes.

"Mr. McKenzie, it's a pleasure to finally meet you." An older Asian man shakes my father's hand vigorously.

"And whom do I have the pleasure of meeting?" my father asks him.

"Jordan," the man replies. "Whatever you need, sir."

"Jordan, can you help find us a first aid kit?" my father asks, and after nodding, Jordan disappears into the multitude.

A middle-aged woman offers me a glass of water. I drink it gladly, realizing it's been hours since I've wet my throat. Slowly, the crowd starts to dissipate; most of them take the bags and boxes that clutter the room with them, and I can finally take a look at my surroundings. We're in a completely enclosed lobby. There are no windows around, just marble floors and walls all over. The emergency lights are on, casting enough light to illuminate our area.

We're in an old hotel. I read the old decaying sign by what used to be the front desk: The Millennium Hotel.

Large black plastic bags cover the windows, keeping us hidden from anyone outside. A large wooden desk with a stone counter sits in the center of the room. The floors are partially covered by an old stained carpet with a floral pattern. An empty vase has been moved to the edge of the counter; dried-up stems stick out from a garbage can. Large mirrors with golden frames line one of the walls, reflecting what little light we have.

A few minutes later, Jordan reappears with a short fifty-something-year-old woman who carries a small rectangular case.

"Yvanya, do you mind helping Josephine with Ashton's arm?" my father asks me.

I nod and walk with them to a corner right under one of the emergency lights. Jordan pulls a chair for Ashton. Josephine puts on a pair of gloves and hands me another pair. She removes the bloody rag around his arm. I want to vomit. I've never seen so much blood in my life.

"It's really bad, isn't it?" I ask, forgetting that Ashton can hear me.

"I've seen worse," she replies with a chuckle, pulling a pair of tweezers from a hermetically sealed bag. "Hold this for me, dear." She hands me a roll of gauze and then continues to clean his wound. "Okay, here's where it's going to hurt," she tells Ashton. "I need to remove the bullet. You must not scream." Before giving him a chance to reply, she digs into his upper arm, twisting a pair of pliers. Ashton

205

jerks his head back, holding in what otherwise would have been an agonizing scream. As quickly as she went in, she pulls out the pliers with a brass fragment between them. She drops it onto a white rag, staining the rag with blood. Blood starts squirting from his arm, and I feel like I'm going to pass out.

"Dear, apply pressure to the wound," she tells me as she pulls a small bottle from the kit. She applies some of the liquid to a clean rag, and by the smell of it, I can tell it's rubbing alcohol.

Ashton is not going to like this one bit, I think. He quickly confirms my assumption by twisting his whole upper body as he holds in another painful scream.

Josephine works as fast as she can, rubbing the alcohol on his wound. "I'm so sorry, Mr. Jones," she says, putting pressure on his arm, "but I really don't want you to get an infection."

Josephine finishes dressing his wound. As I'm throwing away the bloody rags and gauzes, I see my father pull Preston aside. They walk to the opposite side of the lobby, away from all ears. My father sets his hand on Preston's shoulder, and I can imagine what he tells him, because as soon as he talks, Preston crumples to the floor. He covers his face with his hands and shakes gently as my father tries to comfort him. I turn around and walk away to give him some privacy. I can't help but think it could have been my own father.

Soon after, Daphne's parents arrive. I see some men greet

her father at the door to the staircase, taking her from him. They disappear behind a wall. I'm not sure where they're taking her, likely somewhere more private. Daphne's mother follows closely behind. Matt and his mom join Clayton in a corner. The last of the group to enter the lobby is my best friend, Natasha. She scans the lobby as she enters, locking her eyes on mine for a second. A woman offers to help her with her bags, but she refuses the help, pulling the items close to her chest.

A bit later, I find my father in a room by himself with his face buried in a map. He's sitting on a red velvet couch. One arm of the couch has been torn, and stuffing protrudes from it. A floor lamp illuminates the room. "Who's in charge of this whole thing?" I ask him.

He lifts his head, staring at me for a few seconds. "You're looking at him," he replies with a blank face, and I stare back at him with unbelief.

"You? By yourself?"

"Together with Jones and Anderson, yes. Anderson and I provided the inside intel. Jones coordinated with the farmers and the rest of the opposition. We're the leaders of the Daylight Militia."

My eyes widen. I've heard that name many times before but always associated it with terrorists—hateful people seeking to destroy what's left of our country. Any connection that involved my father was beyond my imagination. Anger seeps in as I realize he has been living a double life. I think of all the lives lost so far and wonder if the status quo would have been better.

"Why? Why not just leave things as they were?" I ask, trying not to show any emotion, although my face is likely telling a different story. "Yeah, things were bad, but at least people were alive. Now people are dying."

"Yvanya, you don't understand. You don't know what we know, what our own government, let alone the Empire, were planning—what they're still planning—to do. Abductions. Unethical, cruel scientific experiments. Mind-controlling. Poisoning of our citizens. For goodness sake, these are the people we elected, and they've turned against us, the ones they were supposed to represent. This is not a war we wanted to start. We had no choice," he replies, but his words don't fully sink in.

"Preston's father is dead and most likely his mother too," I say.

"I understand that. Many people are dead, but many more will be dead if we don't continue with our cause. It's not going to get better. I'm not pretending it's going to be easy. I'm no fool. Everyone who is part of this revolution understands the risks and the consequences, but we need to try. We can't assume a defeated attitude," he says, seeking my understanding.

"Heidi and Mother. They're helpless," I say.

"Heidi, yes. She's completely helpless, and we need to

find her as soon as we can," he says with a concerned look. "But your mother?" He chuckles.

"What about Mother? How is that funny? How can you laugh right now?"

"Yvanya, your mother is not helpless. In fact, I would be afraid if I were the soldiers who took her," he replies as he scratches his head, and my eyes open wide.

"What are you saying? I don't understand."

"Yvanya, your mother can take care of herself. Said simply, she's a deadly woman," he says, and then, clearly seeing the confusion in my eyes, he continues. "She's well trained. She could kill a man with her bare hands. Technically, she's a weapon."

"Why are you telling me these lies?" I ask. Certainly he must be making this up to make me feel better. I know that Mother is in good shape and has good muscle definition, but a weapon capable of killing? Impossible! "Where is this coming from?" I ask, more confused than ever.

"Your mother is well versed in multiple martial arts. She was also my Krav Maga instructor. That's how I first met her."

Martial arts? Krav Maga? Since when do you guys know how to fight? "You told me you met in high school," I reply.

"Well, yes, that's technically true, although I didn't know we went to the same high school until after the fighting class," he says. "Your mother was partnered with me to teach me how to fight. She was as adorable as she was quick. She beat the crap out of me that weekend. I was sore for over a week. I actually enjoyed it, though." The memory brings a smile to his face.

"What?" I can't help but say. I run through memories of my mother, searching for anything that might support my father's story. I recall a time when we were all seated at the table. I was playing with a glass salt shaker she cherished dearly. She had inherited it from her grandmother.

"Don't play with it," she told me.

Ignoring her, I kept passing it from one hand to the other, until I accidentally dropped it, and it rolled down the table's edge. As it was about to hit the ground, her hand moved at what seemed to me supernatural speed and caught it right before it shattered into a thousand pieces.

"Mother reflexes," she joked as we stared at her in astonishment.

"The point is," my father says, interrupting my trip down memory lane, "she's strong and quick and can take care of herself. We need to rescue her, but she'll be okay. As long as Heidi is with her, she'll be fine as well."

"Hold on. If Mother's such a good fighter, how come she let the soldiers take you all?" I ask.

"They got to Heidi first. Your mother and I were in bed, and we heard the door open. We thought it was you sneaking back inside, so we didn't move. Soon after, we heard Heidi scream, but it was too late. They had a knife to her neck by the time we came into your room. They threatened to kill her if we as much as moved a finger. We had no choice. They subdued your mother and me with chloroform. I don't recall what happened after that. All I know is that I woke up in one of the cells in the basement of the EBI building with Anderson by my side. I heard some of the soldiers say they might be keeping your mother and Heidi at one of the downtown buildings, so that's why we're here. We're not entirely sure, but it's the best lead we have so far."

"You knew I was sneaking out?"

"Of course." He laughs.

"But I was so quiet." *I thought I was being so clever and getting away with it this entire time!*

"Trust me, we knew exactly what you were up to."

"Then why did you make such a big fuss about the suntan mark?" I ask, remembering how angry he was when he noticed my tanned wrist.

"I was hoping you'd stop sneaking out and risking getting caught for an adrenaline rush."

"I didn't do it for the adrenaline rush. I really enjoyed visiting the farm. I enjoyed my friends' company. I've felt more alive these past months than I've felt in years," I say, realizing for the first time what those escapes really meant to me.

"I know. In part, I was hoping I would scare you enough to stop you from heading the direction you were going. I saw too much of your mother and me in you. We shouldn't be surprised, though; it's part of your DNA, I guess. Anyway, I became afraid. Being part of the opposition is not an easy life. It's not free from risks or heartache. We were hoping you and Heidi would learn to conform, to find happiness in what you had and what you were, so we'd be able to keep you sheltered. That's why we tried to set you up with Preston, thinking that maybe if you got married, he would take you far away from all this mess and the destruction that is to come. We would have sent Heidi with you to keep you all safe. I guess that's out of the question now."

"What about that day when I followed you into town?" I ask, still wondering how much he really knew. "Did you know I was there?"

"Of course. I would be the worst spy in the world if I didn't notice such an obvious tail."

"Why did you keep going then? Why not stop or call me out?"

"I had Jones waiting for me. He needed the blueprints to the EBI building; plus, I thought it would be good practice for you—part of your training."

"Training?" I say, confused.

"I asked Clayton to take advantage of the time you were spending with him to train you on a few basics. Tell me—did he ever get to teach you the basics of shooting?"

"Since when do you know Clayton?" I ask. The more answers I try to get out of him, the more questions I get.

"I've known those boys for years," he replies, as though not giving it a second thought.

Does he know how Clayton feels about me? I bet he doesn't.

I can't believe my father not only approved but also was behind all of this. "Yes, he taught me the basics," I reply.

"Hopefully you won't need those skills," he says, and he starts to walk away from me.

"How did Anderson die?" I ask, stopping him in his tracks.

"They shot him soon after I woke up. They don't take treason lightly. They wanted to make an example of him. They kept me alive, hoping I would give up our intel."

I close my eyes and think of Preston, of how sad and alone he must be feeling right now. "What about his mother? Where is she?" I ask, trying to take the mental picture away. "Is she alive?"

"I'm not sure. I haven't seen Elizabeth since the dinner party at their house," he replies. He then lowers himself to my level, holds my face on his hands, and adds, "Listen, I'm sorry to have to share all of this with you. I wish there was an easier way or, even better, that this wasn't even happening, but I need you to trust me. We will do everything we can to rescue Heidi and your mother. I need you to believe that."

I give a slow nod as I do my best to hold tears in. He then gets up and leaves the room.

They shot and killed Paul Anderson, Preston's father. It could have just as easily been my father. How would my life be different right now if it had been the other way around? I sit on the velvet sofa, rest my face on my hands, and let a new stream of tears flow down my face.

13

A few hours go by, during which my father and Ashton are in meetings. Preston and Clayton are invited, along with Matt, Daphne's father, and a few other men. They use one of the conference rooms as their meeting place. A sign on the door reads, "Private. Do not come in." I feel a bit hurt that I'm not included, but as all of this is new to me, I conclude it's probably best to leave the planning to them. With nothing else to do, I decide to give myself a tour of the place.

I walk aimlessly around some of the common areas and then stop to check on Daphne. There's been no change in her condition. Outside her room, Rebecca, Matt's mother, stops to tell me I've been assigned a room. They've cleaned a few rooms on the first couple of floors. Mine is room 206. I'm surprised to hear about this, as I had no idea they were so organized or even that someone was taking care of these seemingly mundane details.

"We've been planning this for months. It's taken a lot of coordination, and although it's not perfect, we're in pretty good shape, considering everything that's going on," she says. "I think you'll find that we have most of the basics covered."

"How many people are involved in this?" I ask.

"Locally, a few thousand, but throughout the entire country, it's hard to say—maybe a hundred thousand. We don't keep formal records, for everyone's safety."

She gives me a small LED lantern and walks me to my room. We climb up the dark stairwell, our steps echoing through the dark concrete shaft. The hall is empty, with peeling beige wallpaper. We stop by the old elevator. The door to my room is ajar, and the security bar has been pulled backward to prevent the door from closing.

"Leave it like this when you're out, or you won't be able to get back in," she says.

I push on the heavy door and enter the room, illuminating my way with the small lantern. I see two double beds and a small night table in between them. A lamp hangs from the wall over the table. Opposite the beds is a long dresser with an old television set on top. There's a musty smell in the air. I wish we could open the windows to get some fresh air, but of course, that's not an option, as it could give away our whereabouts.

"Remove the bed covering, and set it by the corner. It's dusty, but the sheets underneath should be fine," she says. "There should be water in the bathroom. Don't use it for drinking or brushing your teeth, though."

"Thank you, Rebecca," I say, and I give her a small hug. It's been a long day, and we're clearly both tired.

As I pull away from her, she places a hand on my upper arm and says, "Yvanya, I'm so sorry your mom and sister are missing. I'm sure your father and the other men will have a plan to rescue them in no time."

I nod sadly, hoping she's right. She turns to leave, when I ask, "Did you hear about the farm?"

She turns, and her facial expression shows a mix of tiredness and sorrow. "It's a shame they would do that. The barns and silos were filled with grain. It could have fed so many. Such a waste. I still can't believe we won't be going back, but then again, we kind of knew that once things were put in motion, nothing would ever be the same. Get some rest, dear." She leaves my room.

After pulling the covers off one of the beds, I lie down to rest. The mattress is old, but it's more than I expected. I can finally get some sleep.

As I start to doze off, I hear the door open loudly, and I sit up quickly.

"Who's there?" I call out, reaching for my lantern.

"Great. I have a roommate," a voice responds.

I turn on the light to see Natasha.

14

"Cricket, wake up."

I hear Clayton's voice in the distance. Slowly, it gets closer, until I feel him shaking my shoulder.

"Yvanya, come with me," he whispers.

Where am I? I think, disoriented, and slightly open my eyes. Clayton holds a small lantern, and the soft light emanating from it illumines my surroundings. *Ah, right. A hotel.* I slowly roll out of bed. I'm exhausted. My watch reads 5:30 p.m. GTZ; it's early morning. I glance at Natasha, who seems sound asleep. *What could possibly be so important that it can't wait a few hours?*

"How did you get into my room?" I whisper as we leave my room.

"Your door was ajar. The security bar was holding it open," he responds. Natasha must have left it like that. Clayton produces a second lantern and hands it to me.

"Where are we going?" I ask as he leads me back to the dark staircase. Instead of heading downstairs as I expect, he starts climbing.

"You've got to see this," he says, tugging on my hand.

It had better be worth it, I think, following him.

We climb five or six floors, and by now, I'm feeling pretty awake. My leg muscles, on the other hand, don't appreciate the strenuous exercise without prior stretching or warming up. "How much farther?" I whine.

The stairs are dark, and we can only see the few feet our lanterns illuminate ahead of us. I hope these people have enough spare batteries because I'd hate to be stuck in this old hotel with no light. Something about this building makes me feel uneasy. I keep getting the feeling I'm being followed and watched. Our footsteps resonate across the entire shaft. I bet no one has been up here in many years or maybe even decades.

"Only a few more floors," he says, but I'm sure he's just saying that to keep me from turning back.

We climb maybe another ten floors or so. By now, I've lost count. My legs have finally had enough, and they cramp up, so we stop for a quick rest.

"Do I need to carry you?" he jokes, out of breath himself.

"Now you offer?" I laugh, restarting our climb.

After a few more floors, we reach the top level. He opens the door, and a golden aura surrounds him.

"The sun is out!" I move past him so I can see better.

"Sunrise," he says.

We're on the rooftop. A veranda surrounds the entire perimeter. An old bar sits behind the door to the stairs. The counter is made of stone, and pieces of it are chipped away here and there. The whole place is empty except for some dried leaves and twigs scattered all around. The wind must have blown them here, I assume, given there are no trees or plants around. I walk to the edge of the building and set my hands on the veranda railing. I look down, but it's still too dark to see anything with any level of detail.

"Here." Clayton produces a cup and hands it to me. In his other hand, he has a thermos. He pours a cup of coffee for each of us. I take a sip; it's still warm. The rich smell brings a sense of comfort, and I smile.

"Where did you get this?" I ask.

"The kitchen," he says in a serious voice, and we both laugh. "I brought it up a little while ago but thought you would enjoy the view, so I went back downstairs to get you."

"So you went up all those stairs twice already? That's quite a workout," I reply, and he laughs.

We watch the sunrise in silence, standing next to each other. As it gets brighter, buildings of different heights appear around us. Their deteriorated facades and broken windows offer a clear visual symbol of our society, broken and damaged by years of neglect and abandonment. The old Ohio River runs in the distance, its bank twisting, bending, and stretching beyond where the eye can see. The famous yellow bridge spans the river, extending to the other side, where another ghost town sits. A second bridge existed, but half of it collapsed into the river on a cold winter night more than a decade ago. Thankfully, there were no fatalities, or so the public was told. Right after that, they inspected the other bridge and found similar deficiencies, so traffic was limited to lightweight and pedestrian traffic. Some of the remnants of the bridge still stand, and their sight stirs a feeling of sadness and longing for a life in this once vibrant city I never got to enjoy.

I switch my attention to the more pleasant view. Across the horizon, the sky gradually changes from dark purple to red to pink, with splashes of orange, yellow, green, and, finally, light blue. The steady change of colors is fascinating. I haven't seen a spectacle like this in a long time. A flock of geese fly over us, honking as if saying hello. I lower my right arm, letting it hang by my side, while I hold the warm cup with my other hand. Clayton does the same, and his arm slightly touches mine. The hairs on our skin intertwine, and I smile as I feel electricity cross between us. I'm certain he feels it too, because his breathing pattern changes for a few seconds.

"You shouldn't be so close to the edge." A voice startles us, and I look back to find Preston standing by the door. His hair looks messed up; he likely just woke up as well. "You might be seen."

"It's still dark enough," Clayton says.

"The sun is coming up. It'll get bright enough pretty soon," Preston responds, and we step back away from any potential prying eyes. "Can I speak with Yvanya?" he asks

Clayton, who, although he looks disappointed, assents and turns toward the door.

"See you around, Cricket," Clayton says, and he leaves.

"Cricket?" Preston lifts an eyebrow.

"It's what he calls me. Inside joke, I guess."

"Beautiful sunrise, no?" he asks, staring at the horizon. I notice his eyes look red and a bit swollen. He must have spent the past few hours crying.

"How are you doing?" I say, ignoring his question.

"Hanging in there. I think it still hasn't fully sunk in. I need some distraction, though. Please, let's not talk about it. I can't think of that right now," he says, avoiding my eyes.

He's trying to look strong, I think, and I agree to change the topic. "Why did you disappear on me?" I surprise myself with my choice of question.

He turns to me, apparently not expecting this question, especially not at this time. "Disappear? When?" he asks innocently, or maybe he's just confused. I can't tell.

"After our initial meeting. It took over a month for my father to hear back that you were still interested in me," I reply with my eyes glued to the horizon.

"It's complicated," he says, but then he seems to sense my annoyance and shifts gears. "It wasn't my choice. I had already made up my mind that same night. I wanted to move forward. There were other things keeping me from taking the next steps, though."

"Your mother," I say. "And by the way, where is she?"

223

"We got separated. She was out when I got notice from my father that they were coming for us, so I couldn't wait for her. I took Natasha, and we went straight to the Alpha compound, where we ran into you. My father had recently shared an escape plan with her, so I'm guessing she's at one of the other compounds."

"Is she trustworthy?" I ask, wondering if there's any chance she could have been involved in what led to my family's kidnapping.

"Absolutely," he replies without hesitation. "She loved my father and loves me more than anything in the world. She would never do anything to put us at risk."

"So she hates me." I stir the conversation back to where I was heading before.

"*Hate* is a strong word. She doesn't hate you, but I have to admit she's not your number-one fan." He starts to say more, but I interrupt him.

"Because I'm not rich. Because I'm not well manicured." I state the facts, pretending not to care about having been so strongly rejected. A strong gust of wind blows my hair into my face. As I straighten it, out of the corner of my eye, I think I see movement by the door. *Clayton. I bet he's hanging around eavesdropping on us.* I decide to ignore it.

"It has nothing to do with your social status, although I'm sure she doesn't love that part. I think it's mostly because you speak your mind and don't conform to what our society expects from a lady," Preston says.

"And of course, that's a sin," I reply, still staring ahead. "No one warned me that having a brain and a bit of social conscience was so undesirable."

"It's not the intelligence or empathy that turns some people off; it's displaying it in a way that contradicts or challenges the approved norm. We live in a society where the upper class has the power, and they're not interested in giving it up. My mother thought that long term, your nonconforming spirit could jeopardize her way of life—our family's way of life. She's not a bad person. It's just that her priorities are not the same as yours."

"Or anyone else's, as a matter of fact," I say.

"She had a rough beginning in life and wants to make sure her family doesn't end up going back to that. Nevertheless, sharing your controversial thoughts is a bad thing if you're looking for my mother's favor. If instead you're looking for mine, then it's quite the opposite," he says, rubbing his index finger down my arm. I smile for a second, as his touch sends shivers through my body.

Don't look at him, I think, but even without seeing his face, I know he saw my smile.

"The engagement is off, you know. Not that it was ever on to begin with," I say. With that, I walk away, leaving him by himself. *Is that the type of distraction you were seeking?*

"What did he want?" Clayton asks as soon as I walk into the lobby. I haven't seen this jealous side of him before.

You should know; you were eavesdropping. "He wanted to check how I was doing with my mother and sister missing," I lie, although I tell myself it's not a lie. I'm guessing that had I not derailed the conversation the way I did, eventually, he might have asked me about that.

"How is he doing?" Clayton asks.

"Acting tough, as if nothing has happened. Why don't you ask him yourself? He might talk to you about it."

"Yeah, I will. By the way, Daphne's awake."

My eyes widen, and I sprint to her room. An older man gives me an annoyed look as I nearly knock him over. I don't have time to apologize. My friend is up, and I want to see her. I need to confirm she's okay.

I climb the stairs two at a time. By the time I reach her room, I'm completely out of breath. The thick, old burgundy curtains are open, allowing light into the room. The sheer curtains remain closed, guarding our whereabouts from the outside world. Daphne's mother sits on the edge of the bed, right by her side.

"I heard she's awake," I say, approaching them.

"Anya," Daphne softly moans, raising her head a bit, acknowledging my presence.

"She is, but she's feeling very nauseated," her mother says.

"Hey, I'm here." I grab one of her hands. It's cold and

limp, not what I expected. Within a few seconds, she gives me a small reassuring squeeze.

"What happened to her? Has she said anything?" I ask, letting go of her hand and sitting on the edge of the bed across from them. The mattress sinks heavily under my weight.

"She spoke a bit a few minutes ago." A voice startles me. It's Matt, coming out of the bathroom with a damp towel on his hands. He approaches Daphne and places it over her forehead. He continues talking as he helps her sit up. "She said that when she walked in after I dropped her off, two men were waiting for her inside the house. They gagged her and drove her to a building, which we're assuming was the EBI building. There, she was forced by several women to take some medication—a couple of bright pink pills. They told her the pills would calm her down and threatened to hurt her when she refused to take them. Eventually, they lost their patience and forced them down her throat. She said that within half an hour, she started seeing weird colors and objects moving, hallucinating, and soon after, she lost consciousness. She doesn't know anything that happened between then and a few hours ago, when she woke up."

"She's lucky to be alive." Josephine enters the room. It seems she's been standing by the door this whole time, listening to Matt's story. "I didn't want to interrupt, but I believe they gave her Nitrotussin. It's a very potent drug."

Josephine explains that drug addicts used to take it

about twenty or thirty years ago to induce hallucinations, and in small amounts, it can cause a feeling of euphoria. In large amounts, though, it can cause unconsciousness and stop a person's heart entirely, or worse, the person might stay in a permanent trip and never come out of it. The thought of living the rest of my life in such a state seems far worse than just dying from an initial overdose.

"Will she be addicted to it?" I ask, worried about potential dependency or long-term side effects.

"Not long term. For the first few days, she might crave it just to feel normal again. And she will most likely experience withdrawal symptoms, such as sweating, vomiting, and shaking. These should fade within a week, and as long as she doesn't take it again, she should be able to recover fully," Josephine says.

"How do you know these things?" I ask her.

"I used to be a nurse," Josephine replies. "I worked at the town hospital. We saw many overdose cases decades ago. The use went down as the population became aware of the negative effects. We heard stories here and there about research going on with inmates at the Dungeon. The rumors were never confirmed, so I'm not sure if there was truth to them. I don't understand why the Empire would be using it on anyone, let alone on innocent youth. Not sure what threat they could possibly believe she would pose for them to do something like this to her." Josephine's words bring a deep frown to my face. She places a hand on my shoulder as she reassures me. "But don't worry, honey; your friend will get better. I've seen many worse-looking people fully recover. She just needs to rest."

I walk toward Daphne and give her a kiss on the top of her head. "Get better soon. We have so much to catch up on," I whisper, pulling her against me in a gentle embrace. "Please keep me in the loop on her progress," I say to Matt, who replies with a nod.

Daphne's mom hugs me on the way out. I walk away from Daphne's room feeling somewhat relieved now that it seems she's going to recover. Out of nowhere, a terrifying thought creeps into my mind. *What if they've done the same thing to Heidi and my mother? What if they don't recover? What if they're forever lost?*

What little relief I felt for Daphne's improving condition is immediately smothered by the renewed fear for my mother's and sister's well-being. I can't envision any ethical explanation these sinister people could use to justify forcing dangerous drugs down the throats of innocent citizens. For how long have they been doing this? I feel an unbearable repugnance and become engulfed with deep contempt toward our government and the Empire. I've never fully trusted our world leaders, but I never imagined they could be so depraved. I walk down the hall, tightening my fists as hard as I can, with my nails sinking deep into my skin.

15

What's going on? I wonder as I enter the lobby. A crowd stands in the center of the room. Others stand near a wall, whispering and pointing at the crowd. A couple of men move out of the way, and I can now see my father's back. The crowd parts, and I'm able to see what the fuss is about: Elizabeth Anderson, Preston's mother. She has made it to our compound somehow.

Am I seeing clearly? Is this really Elizabeth? I eye her up and down. She wears a tight blue dress and sky-high heels, one of which is broken. She limps as she walks on her broken shoe. Yes, I'm seeing correctly. There's no doubt. Holding her by one of her upper arms, my father guides her through the lobby and past me. Neither of them seems to notice me. Her looks are uncharacteristic: her hair is in disarray, and her face is dirty. I bet she's unaware of her appearance. Everyone stares at them, shaking his or her head, and people lean toward one another, clearly gossiping. She keeps her head high, still acting as if she's above everyone. My father ignores the onlookers and continues to walk her across the lobby. As they turn down the hall, they disappear from our view. A few men rush past me, following my father.

"What are people saying?" I ask a group of women huddling in a corner.

"It's that woman. We can't believe she dared to show her face here, of all places," a brunette who looks to be in her fifties replies. Her leathery skin and the deep bags under her eyes make her look tired. They've probably been up all night.

"I know—the nerve of her. They'd better tie her up," a blonde woman says. She sports a choppy, uneven, short haircut, most likely done by herself. Cutting one's own hair is not an uncommon practice, considering few people have spare money for professional haircuts.

"What do you mean? What has she done?" I ask.

"Honey, word in the street says she's likely the reason we're all here ahead of schedule. The coup wasn't supposed to happen for another few months. The names of our key officials were leaked, and everyone believes she was responsible," the brunette responds.

My eyes widen upon hearing this. *This is nothing like what Preston told me. Could it be possible?* I wonder. "What are they going to do with her?" I ask.

"If it were up to me, they'd tie her up in a dark, empty room and throw away the key," the brunette responds.

"No one would miss her—that's for sure," the blonde says.

I step away from the group and chase after my father.

The hall is dark and empty, and the flowery wallpaper is missing in many spots, revealing patches of the cream-colored drywall underneath. Most of the conference rooms on this wing are empty except for long, rectangular wooden tables and cushioned chairs that likely have not seen a human in decades. I turn the corner and notice a dim glow escaping from underneath one of the doors. It's the same room where they were meeting before. The pale light appears and disappears as people move inside the room. The "Private. Do not come in" sign is still taped to the door. I carefully lean against the door, trying to listen in. I hear only muffled voices, one of which belongs to a woman. I can't make out any words. I decide to head back to the lobby, as there's no sense in getting caught eavesdropping when I can't even discern the information.

Back at the lobby, I see Clayton sitting on the floor near a corner. He's eating a bagel. I realize I haven't eaten anything, and my stomach grumbles in response.

"Hey, Cricket, want some?" He offers me one of the bagel halves.

"I sure do," I reply, taking it without hesitation. "Thanks." The soft cheese coats my teeth with its delicious creaminess.

"See? I know what you want and what you need," he replies.

"Really? And what's that?" I ask with laughter in my voice.

"Bagel, of course," he replies, and I shake my head in amusement.

"Did you know about the rumors concerning Elizabeth?"

"I had heard, but for Preston's sake, I have been giving her the benefit of the doubt."

"Do you think he knew?"

"Hard to tell. He didn't say anything, but there's a possibility," Clayton replies, taking another bite of his bagel. I smile as cheese gets all over his cheeks. He immediately wipes it off with his wrist.

"How long have you known him?" I ask, leaning against his side. He lifts his arm and places it around my shoulders. I enjoy his company, as he makes it easy for me to be myself. He doesn't judge me or try to shut me up when I go off while standing on my soap box.

"For many years now—way before he left for college. His father used to bring him down to the farm when he was a teenager. He used to hang out with us. Helped my father and me fix up one of the tractors one time. He's pretty good with mechanical things," he says. "When did you meet him?"

"Some months ago, my family got invited to his house for dinner," I reply, keeping all the other details to myself.

"He's the one you were getting engaged to, isn't he?" Clayton asks, and I can sense the unhappiness in his voice. I nod, confirming what he already knows.

"That was the original plan, but it never materialized," I reply.

"He passed on you? What a dumbass. I think I've lost all respect for him," he says, gently squeezing my upper arm as I smile.

An hour or so goes by, and I walk back to the conference rooms, hoping to get an update from my father. I get to the interrogation room to find the lights still on. I ignore the unwelcoming sign on the door and walk into the empty room, wondering what's so important that they want to keep secret. Some chairs have been rearranged to form a small semicircle in the middle of the room. Across from them, a single chair faces the others. I walk quietly, imagining what probably took place. I picture Elizabeth sitting in the singled-out chair, facing questions and accusations from the men. I wonder how she took it—if she broke down and took responsibility or if she denied their claims.

As I stare at the walls of the room, I see a piece of wallpaper sticking out. It draws me as light draws a moth, and I grab it firmly between my fingers and slowly start peeling it off. The sound of the paper tearing is soothing to my ears.

"You're not supposed to be here." Natasha startles me. I didn't hear her come in. I wonder how long she's been following me. The thought that she can so stealthily sneak up on me raises goose bumps on my skin.

"Neither are you," I reply, eyeing her outfit: tight blue jeans and a striped light-blue-and-gray long-sleeved shirt.

"Well, no one tells me anything, so I guess I have no choice but to find out what's going on by myself."

"Then that makes two of us," I say.

"No, no. We're nothing alike. You've no idea what it's like to be me. Don't you even pretend. You've probably never worked one day in your life."

Where is she going with this? I wonder.

"Your parents didn't sell you into a life of servitude." She starts to say more, but I interrupt her with a loud gasp.

"You were sold? I'm so sorry. I didn't know that people were still being sold," I say.

"Yes, I was. It's still happening all over the place, so don't look so shocked. And I'm not seeking your sympathy. The Andersons rescued me from my abusive owners. If you weren't living in your self-centered world, you would know that not everyone has enjoyed the privileged life you've had."

"Natasha, my life hasn't been perfect either." I start to say more, but she cuts me short.

"Yes, I'm sure you've had a horrible life. You, with your perfect family and your precious, perfect skin and beautiful hair. You think you can just sweep in and take whatever you want. Don't you? You don't know one thing about him."

Of course. She's still hung up on the whole Preston thing. Doesn't she realize it's all over?

"I've known him for over ten years. During every single

one of his milestones, during each of his accomplishments, I've been there, dreaming and fantasizing about the day when he finally realizes he's always been in love with me. I've suffered in silence when I've seen him pursuing other girls. Well, I'm not gonna let you get in the way. Now it's my turn, and you can't have him," she says.

There's no reasoning with her. "Be my guest," I reply, lifting my arms. "I don't want him. I'm perfectly happy alone."

"Sure, and that's why you continue to flirt with him, making sure he's watching your every move, trying to make him jealous with your loser boyfriend."

"When have you seen me do that?" I say, challenging her.

"Earlier this morning on the roof, for one," she replies.

Oh, so that was her eavesdropping on us, not Clayton, I realize.

"I'm so tired and fed up. I can't take it anymore. You're nothing but a skank."

I feel an adrenaline rush. I'm done with this vicious girl. "How dare you call me names? You're psychotic! Listen, it's all in your head. I have no interest in Preston. Even if I did before, it's all over. Look around you. Look where we are and what's become of our lives. The only thing I'm concerned about right now is finding the rest of my family. Getting a boyfriend is the least of my worries." I should stop there, but for some shameful reason, I choose the low road and add, "Plus, it's not as if his dearest mother would approve of you either." I feel regret right away and wish I could take my words back. I know it's a low blow. Natasha can't help her condition, but I wish she could see how ridiculous she's being.

"Elizabeth loves me," she says, and I raise my eyebrows. "Why do you look so surprised? I've been her number-one maid forever. Trust me, she would rather see him with me, who has been loyal to her all these years, than with a gold digger like you."

"Funny—that's what I think of you. Now, leave me alone," I reply, and I start walking away from her, but she grabs my wrist tightly.

"You're going to regret this," she says, sinking her fingernails into my skin.

"Should I be afraid?" I ask as our faces come within inches of each other.

"You'd better sleep with an eye open," she says with vile spitting from her eyes.

"You're threatening me?" I yank my wrist from her grip. "You'd better never —"

We're interrupted by voices approaching the room. We quickly separate and hide behind two columns by the back of the room.

"Why are you really here?" a male voice asks. He's speaking softly, but the empty room amplifies his voice.

"Sweetheart, I came for you," a female responds, and I'm almost certain I know who the speakers are.

Oh, we shouldn't be here. What if they notice us?

"Mother, I'm not going anywhere with you," the guy responds.

"Preston, we need to leave now, while we still can," Elizabeth says.

"What do you mean?"

"They're coming. They're going to be here tonight, and there will be nothing left. This whole place will be obliterated."

"Who's coming?"

"The Empire. They know the rebels are downtown, just not in which exact building. They're coming late tonight with heat-seeking equipment so they can screen the buildings from the outside. They'll be using the same technology they used to find that Mitchell guy in the west. They'll be able to pinpoint this location in no time. They plan to storm this place by surprise—to ransack it and bomb it maybe. Who knows? That's why I'm here. I came to warn you and get you out of here while we still have time."

"Mother, how do you know this?"

"I have my sources."

"Sources? I need you to answer one question for me, and I need you to tell me the truth." He pauses for a few seconds. "Did you give Father up?"

"Please don't ask me that."

"Tell me. Is it true what they're saying? Did you?" he pleads.

"They were on to him already. I just confirmed what they knew in exchange for immunity. Immunity for all of us, even your father, if he chose to repent. How was I to know he would betray us?"

"Mother, he didn't betray us. You betrayed him! He confided in you because he wanted you by his side as his wife. He wanted our family together, and instead, you outed him. They killed him! You killed him!" Preston yells.

"Lower your voice! I did not kill him. I did not," she says, sobbing loudly.

"I don't know what to say to you," Preston replies, his voice breaking. I hear him sob for a few seconds, and then they both stay quiet for close to a minute. Finally, Preston breaks the silence. "The only thing we can do now is warn everyone. We need to get them all out of here."

"No. There's no time. If the Empire sees them moving, they'll move in quickly. They'll attack right away, and most likely, you and I won't make it out. We need to go now, before it all unfolds."

"We can't do that. We can't leave these people here. They're innocent. There are children, elderly, and Yvanya. I won't leave her."

I smile at the sound of my name.

"Forget the little brat. You'll meet other girls—more reputable ones. You'll get your pick," Elizabeth says.

"No, you don't understand. This is madness. And what about Natasha?" he asks, and I turn my face to her. She's leaning against her column, clearly listening as intently as I am.

"Leave her. We don't need that burned one," Elizabeth responds, and my mouth drops open.

"Wow, you're unreal," Preston says, and I hear him start to walk away.

"Darling, wait. What are you doing?" Elizabeth asks.

"I'm doing the right thing. I'm talking to Jones and McKenzie," he responds, and he walks out of the room.

"Preston!" she calls, limping after him.

I stare at Natasha. Her head is down. Tears roll from her face onto the floor. Leaning against the wall, she slowly rolls down and pulls her legs against her chest. I feel bad for her.

I shake my head in sadness, leaning it against the column. Once I feel the coast is clear, I walk over to Natasha, who is wiping her tears away.

She stands up and, with the same hatred, says, "Don't you dare pity me." With this, she leaves the room with her head held high.

16

It's been a few hours since all the commotion, and I'm exhausted. Knowing that Preston will be sharing with my father the news of the Empire's plans, I head to my bedroom to take a quick shower. The pipes have been dry for so long that it takes a minute to get all the air out and get a consistent flow of water. There's so much excitement pertaining to Elizabeth's arrival that I just need to get away for a bit to recharge.

I take the steps two at a time and walk into my room, hoping not to run into Natasha. To my benefit, the room is empty. It's too empty, though. I notice that her stuff is gone. We didn't come with much, but I remember her last night dropping a bag of toiletries and a small brown notebook onto the night table. "Touch my things, and I'll cut your fingers off," she warned me. I was in shock from the unnecessary threat, but given how tired I was, I decided to ignore it at the time.

Maybe she switched rooms. After our fight, there's no way she'd want to stay in the same room with me. I take a shower and change into a new set of clothes Josephine or one of the other ladies has laid out for me. I'm guessing they have been planning this event for a while now, because they've taken care of many little details. Clean towels and sheets, water, food, spare clothes—there seems to be an abundant supply for such an old hotel that hasn't seen an actual guest in decades. The dark gray tank top feels a bit tight, but the camo jeans fit just right. I put my sneakers back on and brush my wet hair.

I head back downstairs in time for lunch. We're gathered in the hotel's restaurant. Paper plates are passed around with servings of rice, chicken, and green beans. I see Elizabeth sitting at a table by herself with her face low. She moves her food around with her plastic fork, not eating much. She's changed from the blue dress and broken heels to an oversized brown sweater, loose blue jeans, and flat shoes: a commoner's outfit. I bet she's dying inside, and I bet they gave her that outfit on purpose just to spite her. I look around and notice that some of the men are keeping a close eye on her. I bet they recognize she's a flight risk. I wonder what she told them and if Preston mentioned to others what she said to him. Should I say something? I make a mental note to connect with my father after lunch to see what he knows.

Josephine and some of the other ladies join me at my table. I recognize the blonde one from earlier today.

"Did you move Natasha to a different room?" I ask them.

"Who's Natasha?" Josephine asks.

"My roommate. The Andersons' maid," I reply.

"No. There are no other clean rooms available," one of the other ladies says, a redhead with long, wavy hair. I assume Natasha has taken residence in one of the dirty rooms and continue with my lunch.

"I guess she's too good for chicken," one of the women says, referring to Elizabeth, who continues to push her food around on her plate.

"I heard she had a fight with her son," the blonde woman says. "Where is he, by the way? Such a nice view to look at."

What? Did I hear her right?

"Jeanette!" Josephine exclaims as she and the others laugh. "That's not an appropriate thing to say."

"Hey, I'm just saying he's lucky I'm not in my twenties—or thirties, as a matter of fact," she replies. "I'd be all over him."

Wow, cougar alert!

"Stop it. You're making Yvanya uncomfortable," Josephine says. I realize then that my mouth is wide open from the shock. I quickly close it and feel my face flush.

"What about you, Yvanya? You should go for him. I haven't seen him with anyone. I bet he's single," Jeanette says, and I can feel my face blush even brighter.

"Leave her alone. She's with the other boy. He's cute too," the redhead replies, and she winks at me.

"Oh yeah, the one with the strong arms," Jeanette says, and I can feel my ears burning red by now.

"I'm with no one, actually. Perfectly happy by myself," I say. *What is wrong with these women? Why don't they mind their own business?*

"Exactly. She's a strong, independent woman. Who needs a man by her side?" Josephine says.

"I do!" Jeanette replies, and they all burst out laughing again.

I smile at them and politely excuse myself from the table. Despite feeling a bit annoyed by their nosiness, I'm glad to see them in good spirits. It provides a bit of a distraction from the constant tension and gloomy mood.

I run into Clayton as I'm leaving the restaurant. I casually look at his arms and laugh on the inside as I think of Jeanette and her pack ogling him.

"So what's the plan?" I ask him as we walk into the lobby. "When are we rescuing my mother and sister?"

"They're deliberating on the best plan of action. They think they know where they're being kept, but there's no certainty," he replies.

I need to talk to my father to confirm that Preston told them everything he heard. "Do you know where my father is? I need to talk to him," I say, but before he has a chance to reply, Preston joins us.

"Hey, have either of you seen Natasha?" he asks.

"No. She moved out of our room, but I'm not sure where she went," I reply.

"What do you mean she moved out of your room?" Preston asks.

"We were roommates. We had an argument, and when I went back upstairs later, her stuff was gone."

"What stuff?"

"Some toiletries and an old notebook. Nothing much, really."

"That's my notebook. I need it back."

"What did you fight about?" Clayton asks.

"Nothing important," I reply, trying to dismiss the questions. *Why did I say we had a fight?*

"Yvanya, I really need to speak with her. What happened between the two of you?" Preston says.

"She was upset, crying, and since then, I haven't seen her again," I reply, avoiding his eyes. *Please stop asking me questions.*

"You look like you're hiding something. Please look at me. Why was she upset?" he asks, but I stay quiet, not sure how to explain what we witnessed without making the situation more awkward than it already is. "Yvanya, this is important. You need to tell me," he says, and I look at him. My heart accelerates, and I can feel my eyes wide open, giving him a fearful look. "Please tell me."

Fine. I'll tell you, but you're not going to like it. "We were in one of the conference rooms, arguing. She was accusing me of something unimportant, and then we got interrupted by you and your mother. We got startled because we knew we weren't supposed to be there in the first place, so rather than letting you know we were there, we just hid—and ended up accidentally overhearing your conversation. I'm sorry. I didn't mean to intrude on your privacy."

Preston's eyes widen. "And Natasha—are you certain she heard us as well?"

I nod, looking straight at the floor. I feel so embarrassed that I just want to get out of here.

"How much did you guys hear of that conversation?" he asks softly, sounding more embarrassed than angry.

"The whole thing," I mumble.

"How upset would you say she looked?" he asks.

"What's going on? What was the conversation about?" Clayton asks.

"Pretty upset. Devastated," I say.

"Yvanya, I'm sorry you overheard that conversation. I'm going to ask you to please keep what was said confidential," Preston says.

"Did you talk to my father about it?" I ask.

"Yes. He knows. But right now, we need to focus on getting that notebook back. We need to find Natasha immediately. Is there a chance she moved to a different room?"

"She didn't get reassigned to a new room, but it's possible she's hiding somewhere else in the hotel," I say.

"Then let's split up and ask folks around. Someone might have seen her," Preston says.

I check with some people, but most of them don't even know who I'm talking about. Those who do know who she is don't remember having seen her today.

I approach a little older lady sitting by one of the lobby doors. Her gray hair is tied up in a bun; freckles and sun marks cover her skin. She must be in her seventies at least, and her back is bent with a hunch. I'd be surprised if she weighs more than a hundred pounds. She seems to be observing everyone around her and smiles as I take the seat next to hers.

"Excuse me, ma'am. I'm trying to find a friend. She's about my age and has freckles and light-colored hair," I say.

"Oh yes, I remember your friend. A nice young lady. She left the hotel about an hour ago. She looked a bit unsettled. I assumed she was going out for fresh air, but she hasn't returned," she says.

"Clayton! Preston!" I yell across the lobby, waving at them. They immediately join us.

"Did you happen to see if she was carrying anything?" I ask the lady.

"I think she was carrying a small bag and a little book. I remember because she dropped it and then quickly picked it up. She seemed to be in a hurry. I'm guessing it was probably her diary. You know, girls can't go anywhere without their diaries. I used to have one back when I was younger. I don't know what happened to it, though."

"Preston, what's in that notebook?" Clayton asks the moment the woman pauses for air.

"Clay, we need to talk to both of your fathers right away," he replies, and he turns and runs away from us. Clayton chases after him.

"Are you completely sure about this?" I ask the woman.

"Absolutely. I may be old, but my memory hasn't failed me yet. It must be because I played with puzzles my whole life. Do you know they can help prevent dementia as you age?" she asks.

"I didn't know that, but thanks for the tip," I reply. "Did you notice if my friend left alone or if someone else was with her?"

"She was by herself. That's why I thought she was just going out for fresh air. You know, it can be hard being inside this hotel all day. There's little ventilation, so it can get stuffy."

"Okay, I need to go now. But thank you, ma'am," I say, and I run after Preston and Clayton.

"Lucy—that's my name!" I hear her yell.

"Thanks, Lucy!" I yell without looking back or slowing down.

I enter the hall with the conference rooms, looking for signs of the men. I find my father, Ashton, Matt, Preston,

Clay, and a few others in the room where Elizabeth was interrogated a few hours before—the same room where Preston and his mother had their argument and where I last saw Natasha. The chairs have been moved, returned to their places by the long table. I quietly stand by the door, unnoticed.

"I can't believe you let her hold on to that!" My father raises his voice at Preston.

"With the rush, she was helping me carry some things last night, and I completely forgot about it," Preston says, rubbing his forehead. "I'm sorry."

My father takes a deep breath, probably trying to control his anger. "Preston, Clayton, find that girl, and get that notebook back," he says in a voice that's calmer yet just as urgent. Preston and Clayton nod. "You need to get to her before she's captured. We don't know her state of mind, and she could easily give us away."

"We understand," Preston says.

"What about me? How can I help?" I ask, drawing their attention as I cross the doorway.

A deep frown takes over my father's initial surprised look as he seems to consider the options. "Go with them. I want you out of here in case she's compromised our location. We are under martial law, so stay hidden, and do not get caught. And, Yvanya, follow their commands." He points at Preston and Clayton. I have not seen his eyes this fearful. My confidence drains.

"Father, what's in that notebook?" I ask.

"Yvanya, there's no time to talk now. Go with them." He pulls me into a tight hug and kisses my forehead as we separate.

"Do you still have your phones?" Ashton asks Clayton and Preston, who nod in response. "If you find reason for us to immediately evacuate, send notification at once. If you can give us five to ten minutes, it'll be appreciated. If we need to go, we'll head for the Tango compound. Remember where it is?"

"I do," Preston replies.

"You have until 8:00 a.m. GTZ to get back here. We need to leave right after sunset. We can't risk having them find us," my father says.

"A couple of the other guys and I will head to the roof to see if we spot her or anyone else near you guys or the hotel. Keep an eye on your phones for any updates," Matt says. "Make sure they're set to vibrate." At once, Clayton and Preston switch their phones to vibrate mode.

"I'm hoping you won't need these, but just in case," my father says, passing out spare magazines.

Clayton and Preston attach them to their belts, and I notice each is wearing a concealed gun with a holster. I had no idea they were armed. *Are all these folks armed?* I wonder.

"Take this as a last resort only. Don't try to be a hero," my father says, handing me a gun and a couple of magazines. He helps me suit up and hands me a light jacket to wear over them. Clayton and Preston pack additional ammo, water bottles, ropes, and a few other essential items in dark backpacks.

Everyone says a quick goodbye, and we take off. *Will they still be here when we get back? Will I ever see my father again?* I push the dreaded questions out of my mind, as I need to focus on the task at hand.

It's 1:00 a.m. GTZ when we leave the hotel. We use the same door Natasha used, a heavy glass door lined with black garbage bags. The brass handle feels cold against my hand. Immediately after we go through, we hear the bolts locking it from the inside.

My father has ordered everyone to take all essential items to the cars. If Matt spots anyone suspicious approaching the hotel, they will need to leave at once. This way, at least they'll be able to take their critical things with them. I hope it doesn't get to that. I hate the thought of getting separated from my father again. I want my family reunited safe and sound under the same roof, not spread throughout the city, wondering if the others are even alive. After what they did to Preston's father, I have no reason to believe they would spare any of us if they managed to get their hands on us. I count on them believing that my mother is harmless. With her thin, petite figure, I still can't reconcile my father's description of her. "She's a weapon," he said. They clearly have no respect for the young either, based on what they did to Daphne.

We wait for half a minute while our eyes adjust to the harsh light. The sun is shining brightly, although it's not as hot as it was the day before. Preston and Clayton look at their phones, confirming they have strong signals.

"Which way do we go?" I ask.

"That way." Preston points to the right.

I assume his guess is as good as mine, but thinking he might know where we're heading makes me feel more optimistic. We walk close to the buildings, staying under awnings and sills as much as possible to conceal ourselves in case someone happens to be keeping watch from the top of a nearby building. The sidewalks are full of cracks and overgrown grass and weeds, and tree branches and fallen leaves are everywhere. The wind blows, and a small tumbleweed rolls in front of us. Signs of restaurants and shops are now dim. The store windows are so dirty we can barely see through them. The place is a total ghost town. At a corner, a sculpture of a colorful pig with wings looks out of place.

We keep moving for a few more blocks and come across a plaza. A three-tiered bronze fountain sits in the middle. A statue of a woman with her arms stretched out stands proudly at the top. As I admire the prominent fountain, I see Preston bend down and pick up a piece of paper from the ground.

"What's that?" Clayton asks, noticing it too.

"It's a paper I had stuck in the notebook. It must have fallen from it. But most importantly, it means Natasha came this way," Preston says as his face brightens with hope.

"Where to now?" Clayton asks as we look in all directions.

Buildings surround us on all sides. Although we're mostly hidden under a large tree, I'm starting to feel vulnerable and exposed, afraid someone out there might be watching us.

Clayton's phone vibrates. He takes a quick peek at its screen and follows with an immediate order: "Hide! We need to hide!"

At once, we run and take cover behind some overgrown bushes by one of the buildings. We kneel close to the ground, trying to stay as low as possible.

"What's going on?" I ask softly.

"Over there," Clayton says, pointing toward the corner opposite where we stand.

I stick my hands in the bush, separating some of the branches enough to take a peek. Across from us, a couple of Empire soldiers are walking toward the fountain. One, likely of Asian descent, has almond-shaped eyes and short, straight dark hair. The second one is Caucasian and sports a buzzed haircut. With their broad shoulders and muscular figures, they seem to carry their large rifles with little effort. They pause for a second and look around. Seemingly not finding anything out of the ordinary, they resume their walk and head straight toward us.

"What are we gonna do?" I whisper, grabbing one of Clayton's arms. There's nowhere else we can hide now. We're stuck behind the bushes.

The men walk closer to us, and I can now hear them loudly. Unfortunately, they're speaking in a foreign language, so I have no idea what they're saying.

I slowly turn my head to look at Preston and notice him with his hand by his waist, ready to go into combat mode if needed. A pigeon lands a few feet from us and starts cooing, as if trying to give us away. The soldiers stop talking and turn their gaze in its direction. I try shooing it away without making a sound or moving too abruptly but am unsuccessful. It continues to look straight at me. I've never been a fan of pigeons, and this one is not helping their case.

One of the soldiers' walkie-talkies goes off loudly, scaring the bird away. The soldiers must have gotten startled as well, as I hear the radio drop to the ground. They quickly retrieve it and answer the call. They then retreat at once, running away in the direction from which they came.

I let out a loud sigh of relief once they're out of sight. "Do you think that call was about her?" I ask.

"All I could make out was the word *pergola*," Preston says, pulling out a small map of the downtown area.

"You understand their language?" Clayton asks the same thing I'm thinking.

"A bit. I took a couple of semesters in college, but their accent was very strong—difficult to follow," Preston responds, studying the map. "I've seen some old pergolas here." He points to a spot on the paper. "We're here. There are a few different ways we could get there. This street has no covering, so we would be exposed from above, not to mention it's the same one those guys took." He draws an invisible line on the map. "This other one has buildings with awnings. They're mostly torn, but it's better than nothing."

We study our potential routes for a few minutes and align on the one that, according to Preston, offers the most concealment.

We stay as close as possible to the buildings, moving in single file, with Preston in the front and me in the middle. Clayton covers us from behind. Preston wasn't kidding when he said this route had better concealment. Large trees line the street, and with large trees come large roots. The sidewalks are broken, with parts of them cracked or elevated, after years of neglect and the pressure from the expanding roots.

"Watch your step," Preston says.

Not long after, I trip on a root and bend an ankle. A sharp bolt of pain shoots through my leg, and it takes a big effort to hold in the scream.

"Are you okay?" Clayton whispers, rushing to my aid.

I rotate the ankle a few times to see if it helps, but it has the opposite effect. I take deep breaths to avoid crying.

Clayton pulls one of my arms over his shoulders to help stabilize me. Preston signals to Clayton, asking him if we're good to proceed, and Clayton assents.

We continue for a few more blocks, with me limping and leaning on my human crutch, while Preston scouts our surroundings. By the time we get to our destination, I'm able to put more weight on the ankle and can let go of Clayton.

We lie low as we take our first look at the landscape. We're by the edge of an incredible courtyard. Wooden pergolas line the square. Thick vines, ivy, and wildflowers twist around them, creating a magnificent and fragrant curtain. Pavers of different colors, some of them stained with moss, mark the path under the pergolas. Overgrown grass and weeds stretch across the courtyard. Wild daisies form a carpet of yellow and white, giving birth to a small meadow in the middle of this concrete and asphalt wasteland.

"This place is gorgeous," I say, running my hands over thick vines that twist and bend around a pergola post. A ladybug lands on one of my hands, and I carefully guide it to an ivy leaf. While I'm taking in the beauty of this small oasis, Preston and Clayton leave me momentarily to scout the area for signs of life. I try to stay low, hidden from any potential onlooker. With all the tall buildings around me, it would be a lot easier for someone high up to spot me than for me to spot him.

I stay put for another five minutes or so, when Preston and Clayton return with good news. They've spotted

Natasha entering one of the buildings. It's time to go get the notebook. A glimmer of hope creeps through me, and I finally feel as if there's a chance all this craziness will work out in our favor.

We move toward the building, staying under other building sills to keep a low profile. As we cross a block, I'm able to take a good look at our destination: a building featuring twin towers maybe twelve to fifteen stories high, each with a pyramid-looking structure at the top. The building's facade is made of concrete, limestone, and white rock, likely marble. The towers are joined by a two- to three-story-high entry pavilion that faces a smaller garden. The left tower is attached to a rectangular building via a walkway that extends across the street. The complex of buildings forms a large letter *L*. The architecture is impressive, but lots of the windows are broken.

As we draw closer to the building, we notice two Empire soldiers approaching from a different direction. They seem to be in a hurry and have their rifles in hand. They must have seen Natasha or heard she was there. What little hope I had immediately sinks. We duck behind bushes and wait a few minutes.

Once we feel the coast is clear, we sneak closer to the building and enter through the same door the soldiers took. The door is large and heavy. We hold on to it as it closes to make sure it doesn't close with a loud sound. We scan the pavilion entrance for any signs of life. Other than tree branches and leaves, the area is clear. A large empty fountain sits in the middle of the room. There's an old circular desk to its left, which is probably where visitors and others checked in before entering the main building.

"Where are you? Come out!" one of the soldiers yells. His accent is strong, likely Eastern European. A loud echo resonates throughout the empty building, making it hard to tell exactly where the voice is coming from.

Not wanting to take any chances, we retreat a few steps and take cover in a large walk-in closet. Clayton goes one way; Preston and I go the other. We hide behind a pile of old boxes, some of which have cords and other electronic parts sticking out from them.

"Miss, we just want to talk to you," the second soldier says in what seems to me a forced softer tone.

The men continue walking and calling out to her. I wonder why she would go through the trouble of running away with the notebook, knowing it is so important to Preston, only to enter the enemy's territory and hide.

Suddenly, one of the soldiers starts to close in on us. His voice gets louder and louder, until he's standing in front of the closet. I take a peek and see his back. The man is huge. His imponent figure is easily more than six feet tall. I estimate he's probably more than 250 pounds of solid muscle. One of his arms rests by his side; the veins on it bulge, as if the muscles underneath are pushing them out. I pull my head back, fearing he'll turn and catch me, and hold on to Preston's hand, squeezing it tightly. Based on what I've seen from Preston so far, my guess is that his other hand is right by his holster. If push comes to shove, I know he'll have no problem using force. My concern is that any shots fired might do more harm than good, as they'll draw the attention of other soldiers to us.

The second soldier approaches the first one, and we hear their voices clearly. They speak in short, quick bursts in a foreign language, so I can't understand a word they're saying, but it seems Preston might be able to. He stares without blinking at a blank spot on one of the boxes, clearly focusing all his attention on what he's hearing. The men speak for less than a minute and then split up, each taking the stairs to one of the towers.

Clayton sneaks into our area, and Preston brings us up to speed. "I didn't get everything, but from what I was able to piece together, it seems they think Natasha must have gone up to one of the towers. Their orders are to capture her, get every piece of information they can out of her, and then kill her. I think they also said the rest of their squad is heading this way and should be getting here in a few hours. It's led by some guy named Max, and by the way they talked about him, he seems to be a pretty vicious guy, not someone we'd want to cross paths with. We need to find Natasha and get the heck out of here before they show up."

"We should abort," I whisper.

"Yvanya, did you not hear what I said? If they find her,

they're going to coax everything she knows out of her and then kill her. We can't let that happen," Preston replies.

"And if they catch us, they'll kill us as well," I say.

"I know you're scared, but we're armed, and Natasha is not. It's not right to leave her like this," Preston replies. I know he's right, and I admire his loyalty to those he cares about, but I really want to avoid being in the middle of a shooting. "Stay behind me," he says, drawing his weapon.

Clayton leaves the closet and hides behind a column about fifteen or twenty feet away from us. Preston signals to Clayton, who signals back to him. After a few exchanges, they both nod. I have no idea what they said, so I'll have to trust that they know what they're doing. I also need to ask them later to teach me sign language. I hate not understanding people.

Clayton draws his gun, and we separate. I keep my right hand near my waist in case I need to draw my weapon too.

Preston and I take the stairs to the left tower. I slowly close the door behind us, making sure it doesn't make any noise. *This building is huge. How are we ever going to find her, especially before the rest of the soldiers show up?* I think with dismay.

We stop at the first floor, scanning the rooms for any obvious hiding places. Other than desks, chairs, and old electronics, the floor is pretty much empty.

"Natasha," Preston whispers.

Nothing. If she's here, she's not coming out.

To my right, I notice a rustling sound. I follow it, hoping it'll lead me to her. Instead, I find a thick open book, its pages turning as the wind blows. My heart sinks at the discovery, and I go back by Preston's side. We go up to the next floor and then the next one. Each floor takes us a good ten to fifteen minutes to clear. Other than books, useless electronics, and dirty sheets of paper, there's nothing of interest. There's no sign of Natasha.

We're back at the stairs, halfway to the next floor, when we hear the voice of one of the soldiers. "Bitch, come out now! I'm done with this game!" he yells in English. He's clearly lost his patience. His voice gets closer as he heads down the stairs.

We backtrack as fast as we can, keeping our steps inaudible. Once we're back on the previous floor, we find a hiding spot within earshot of the stairs. We listen as the second soldier comes up to meet the first one near our floor. They exchange some abrupt words and then head back downstairs. It seems they might have given up on their search.

Soon after, I hear a light buzz, and I see Preston pull his phone from his pocket. He texts back and forth with someone before turning to me. "The Daylight Militia has located your mother and sister. Seems they're being held at the old abandoned zoo."

"At the zoo? How did they find out? And do they know how much longer the soldiers will be keeping them there?" I ask, keeping my voice low.

"Not sure for how long. They tapped into the government's cell phone towers and were able to infiltrate their systems. They have people at one of the other compounds listening in on private conversations," Preston says.

We stay put for a little bit, waiting until we're certain the men are gone. Preston corresponds with Clayton by text, sharing our location. Soon after, Clayton pops onto our floor. He confirms he found nothing in his tower, and we catch him up on what we recently found out.

"Let's go, guys. We need to get back to the hotel before they leave," I say, hoping this time they'll agree with me.

"Yvanya, Natasha's likely still here. We need to find her and get the notebook before she changes her mind and turns it in," Preston says.

"The notebook. The notebook! What's in the stupid notebook? Why is it so special? Why is it so important that we get it back?" I ask with frustration in my voice.

Preston sighs. "The notebook contains the exact locations of every single compound for the Daylight Militia."

My jaw drops. "You mean to tell us you wrote in a single notebook where all the rebel hiding places are and then gave it to Natasha?" I ask in disbelief.

"I didn't write it. I have a map in it with the information. And like I told your father, I didn't give it to her on purpose. It accidentally ended up in her hands with all the chaos from our unplanned departure."

"Yes. Thanks to your mother." I immediately wish I

could take it back, as I see the hurt in his eyes. "I'm sorry. I didn't mean to say that."

"That's beside the point," Preston says. "Many lives are in danger now, so we need to find the notebook and the map and keep them out of the Empire's hands."

I'm starting to doubt Natasha is still in the building, when we hear a loud crashing noise from above. "That's gotta be her," Clayton says, and we chase after the sound, splitting up to facilitate our search.

"Natasha, it's me—Preston. Please come out so we can talk," he whispers.

We scan a few more floors, calling out to her, but our search leads nowhere. We stop to rest on the sixth floor. I carefully take in our surroundings. The room we're in is probably fifty feet by thirty, give or take ten feet. A bunch of white office desks and black rolling chairs are evenly spread out throughout the entire room, all covered with a thick layer of dust. Some of the desks have old computer monitors attached to them. A couple even have personal items left behind: a picture frame of a large family and a forty-year work anniversary award plaque. A sheet of paper hangs by a tack on a cushioned board. Upon examining it, I see that it's an old drawing with "I love you, Daddy" scribbled in poor calligraphy over a stick-figure family. I turn my attention away from the drawing and notice a sharp nail sticking out from one of the desks. I push the desk back, getting it out of the way. I'd hate to scratch myself on the nail.

By now, it's dark outside. The broken windows are letting the wind in, and the temperature has started dropping. We sit on the floor by a corner, pull out some protein bars and fruits from our bags, and make that our dinner. Above us, we hear soft steps and a thud, accompanied by a loud, high-pitched scream of "Ouch!" as someone seems to bump hard into a desk; then everything goes quiet again. Preston grabs a flashlight and heads back upstairs to see if he can locate Natasha.

Ten minutes later, he returns with nothing but a bar wrapper in his hands. It's the same type as the ones we have at the compound. It's 8:00 a.m. GTZ. Clayton texts our fathers, who indicate they're leaving. They can't wait for us any longer. The soldiers will show up anytime with their heat-seeking instrumentation, and then everyone's life will be at risk. We'll need to reconnect with them ahead.

"Ask him if we should meet them at the Tango compound, as previously planned, or at the zoo," Preston tells Clayton.

After a few minutes, we get a response. "He wants us to head to the zoo, but he's insisting that we don't leave without the notebook," Clayton says. "We'll have to stay put. And by the way, my phone battery's dying."

"Mine's low too," Preston says after inspecting his own phone. "Let him know we're turning our phones off to conserve power."

We sit in silence for a few minutes. It's very dark by now,

and it's hard to see anything. We have our flashlights by us, but we don't turn them on unless absolutely necessary. We haven't heard a noise from upstairs for at least an hour, and I'm starting to worry Natasha might have left, leaving us behind to waste our time in this pitch-black mausoleum. The rational side of me finds it hard to believe, though. She probably doesn't have a flashlight, and without it, it'll be impossible for her to find her way out. Most likely, she's just fallen asleep somewhere. We'll need to get up early to resume our search—hopefully before she's up, so she doesn't get the chance to continue moving around on us.

I lie down, using my backpack as a pillow. It's uncomfortable, but it's better than putting my head straight on the dusty, hard floor. Eventually, I doze off into a dreamless sleep.

🕐 🕑 🕒

I wake up a few hours later, shivering from the cold. The temperature must have fallen another ten degrees or so. I stretch my arms out, feeling for my friends, but am greeted with nothing but the empty, cold floor. *Where's everyone?* I turn on my flashlight and scan the area around me. It's empty.

I slowly walk around the floor until, around a corner, I catch a glimpse of a faint beam of light. I switch off my light and proceed carefully, not sure whose light it might be.

I carefully peek around the corner and am relieved to find it's Preston. He's sitting on the floor, leaning against a wall.

"Hey, where's Clayton?" I ask softly, trying not to startle him. He looks up at me and smiles, so I walk over to him and sit by his side.

"Doing a round, hoping that Natasha has fallen asleep and we can catch her," he says.

"What about you? Not tired?" I ask.

"Nah, I've got too much on my mind," he replies.

"I'm so sorry for what you're going through. And honestly, I don't understand how you're keeping yourself together. I know I wouldn't be coping as well if it were me," I say.

"I'm taking it one day at a time and trying to stay focused on our next steps. I guess I'm also kind of in denial. I'm secretly hoping it's not true—that my father isn't dead and that my mother didn't give him away. No one other than the soldiers claims to have seen him die, so there's a chance he's still alive," he says while staring straight ahead.

I'm a bit surprised by how open he's being with me and wish I could offer him some comfort, but I don't know what to say that will make him feel better. I've never been in this type of situation before, so we sit in silence for a minute.

He turns to me and breaks the silence by saying, "I know you probably think I'm being crazy for believing this, but I'll believe it for as long as I can if it helps me get through this ordeal. And I promise I'll do whatever it takes to reunite you with your family. That's my number-one mission right now. I might have lost all I held dear, but if I can keep you from going through the same, I'll do it in a heartbeat."

"Why are you so kind to me, when you barely know me?" I ask, looking him in the eyes.

"I feel like I know more about you than you think. You're smart, brave, caring, and beautiful, all in one package," he says, and I smile. I'm glad we have poor lighting, so he can't tell I'm blushing. "I know Clayton also likes you. I can't blame him. And I wish I could just step down and give you up, but I can't. I've been looking for someone like you for a very long time. I have one favor to ask you, though."

"What's that?"

"Please just give me a chance. Get to know me—the real me—before you make a choice."

"If we ever make it out alive," I say, looking down at my hands.

"*When* we make it out alive. We will," he says, and I smile.

"I hope you're right," I say, getting up from the floor. "I'm gonna try to get some sleep."

I find my way back to our impromptu beds and lie there with my eyes closed, thinking of the things he said and hoping to eventually fall asleep. A few minutes later, Preston lies down next to me. He senses me shivering from the cold and wraps his arm around me. I smile and cuddle against him, letting his heat warm me up as I finally doze off again.

18

"Guys, wake up." Clayton's voice rouses me from my sleep. "I hear rustling sounds, like someone moving around. I think it may be Natasha."

"Or what if it's not her? What if the soldiers are back?" I whisper with fear in my voice. I feel Preston's arm still around me, and I move it, conscious of how it might make Clayton feel.

"That's possible," Preston responds, stirring as he becomes more alert as well. "Let's keep it down until we know for certain."

We slide our night-vision glasses on. Although everything looks a shade of green, I can see pretty well. We move with ease around the room, navigating our way to the stairs so we can listen better. *Be Natasha. Be Natasha.* The plea runs through my head. We lean against a wall, staying out of view in case someone flashes a light in our direction. Not only would it expose us, but because we have the night-vision glasses on, it would blind us for a minute or two, leaving us out in the open, incapacitated.

The noise is coming from below, and as the tones become more evident, it's apparent to us that the sounds are not from Natasha. *The soldiers are back, and we still haven't found Natasha or the notebook*, I think with dread. *But we still have the night-vision glasses, and they likely don't have any, so at least that gives us an advantage.* I try to see the positive side, but that thought lasts only a second, because immediately, I hear something that makes my skin crawl: high-pitched howling. Whatever is downstairs is howling, and by the sound of it, it's not alone. There's a pack. We take a peek down the stair shaft and see them coming up the stairs.

Where do we go? I start to freak out as I hear them drawing closer. My legs freeze, and I can't move. Thankfully, Preston and Clayton are in better control of their bodies, and seeing them sprint into action knocks me out of my stupor. We run through the floor, seeking a place where we can hide. I don't recall having seen any suitable places while we were searching for Natasha earlier. *Where can we hide? Where can we go?* The howling gets closer, and I start hyperventilating. I run too close to the desk with the nail sticking out, and I feel it cut through my pants. A burning sensation creeps through my leg.

We find a small break room area with a glass door. We go in and, with no time to lose, shut the door.

"Were those coyotes?" I ask, trying to catch my breath.

"I don't think those are coyotes," Clayton responds, panting as well.

"Then what are they? They sure sound like a pack of coyotes, and there should be no wolves in this area."

"I think those are coywolves."

"What the heck is a coywolf?" Preston asks, pacing from one side of the room to the other.

Clayton explains that they're hybrids that emerged when coyotes mated with eastern and gray wolves who ventured into our region more than half a century ago. They're not as big as full-size wolves, but they're much larger than typical coyotes. Contrary to actual wolves, coywolves are not shy around humans, so it's not uncommon to see them in urban areas. To top it off, they're known for having the same vicious predatory behavior as their wolf ancestors.

"Ah, that's great. Combine the best of the two beasts to give us a smaller but more vicious and courageous predator. That's just perfect!" I exclaim, sitting on the floor to examine my thigh. The burning sensation builds as my adrenaline starts to wear off. I run my hands through the area, feeling something damp on my jeans. "Can I please get some light here?" I ask, taking my night-vision glasses off.

Clayton draws his flashlight from his pants pocket and shines the light on my leg. A large bloodstain covers half my right thigh. My jeans have torn, exposing a deep scratch. I hope I don't need stitches. Clayton moves the light to illuminate the floor, following the path we took into the break room. A trail of small blood droplets crosses the glass door and disappears around the corner.

"Just what we need," I say.

Preston kneels by my side, producing a small first aid kit. Clayton holds the light, illuminating the area, while I keep my eyes glued to the door, expecting to see the animals any second. With a quick and forceful motion of his hands, Preston tears my jeans further. He puts on a pair of sterile gloves and proceeds to clean and disinfect the cut. I realize I still don't know what he studied in college. The way he handles himself around blood makes me think he might have studied medicine, although he's likely too young to be a doctor.

"By the looks of it, I don't think you'll be needing stitches." His words bring some good news to me. "Please tell me you're up to date on your tetanus shot, though," he says, and I nod, grateful those shots are still mandatory. With people living in the dark, accidents are fairly common, so the Empire demands we all get our routine shots as a preemptive measure. For once, it's a mandate that actually makes sense.

Once the cut is clean and the area is dry, Preston has me apply pressure as he wraps a bandage around it. This requires an awkward motion, as he has both his hands inside my pant leg. Clayton gets distracted, and the light wanders off, no longer illuminating my leg.

"I need some light here, or I won't know where I'm going," Preston says.

"Well, we certainly don't want you getting lost in there," Clayton replies dryly, bringing the light back. I can tell he's burning with jealousy, not that I'm enjoying this one bit. Maybe if my leg wasn't throbbing and wild animals weren't trying to eat us alive, it would be a different story.

"Good as new," Preston says, giving me a pat on my good leg once he's done.

"I think they might not have noticed us," Clayton says, turning his attention to the door and shining the light outside our safe room.

I get on my knees and press my face against the glass to get a better look outside, and out of nowhere, a ferocious creature pounds on the door, making me jump a few feet back. My heart races at a billion beats per second, and a deep, terrified scream freezes inside my throat, unable to escape. The paws move frantically across the glass, leaving behind a smeared red mess. Claws scratch the glass, producing a high-pitched racket. Growling adds to their hair-raising orchestra. The animal is joined by at least another two, further increasing the blood smear on the glass.

"Kill the light!" Preston yells some sense into Clayton, who also seems to be frozen in place. At once, Clayton complies, and we're left in pitch darkness. We continue to hear the animals growl and howl outside our door.

"What are we gonna do?" I cry, clinging on to Preston's arm.

He turns his light on, draws his gun, and then checks to

confirm it's loaded. As if aware of the risk they're suddenly facing, the coywolves stop their howling and growling, and all but one retreat quietly away from the door. As Preston gets ready to open the door and turn the hunt around, we hear loud voices inside our room. I follow the sound to an air duct vent on one of the walls. I can't tell for sure if the voices are coming from the same floor or how many there are, but they clearly are male voices. "The soldiers are back," I say, stating the obvious. They're likely oblivious to the killing beasts hovering a few floors above them. We can no longer shoot the animals, as doing so would give away our whereabouts. We're trapped in here until the coywolves decide to move on.

We look around the room, searching for a way out. There's a small window in the back, but we're about six or seven stories up, too high to jump. I shine my light back at the glass door, and it hits the animal's eyes, making them shine in the dark. *What an eerie sight, you hideous animal.* As if it's heard my insulting thoughts, it pounds menacingly on the door, pushing down on the door handle. The door begins to open, and two of the coywolves stick their heads into the room. The three of us lurch toward the door at once, trying to push it closed; however, the animals' snouts are in the way, so it won't close. They yelp and snap at us. I try to kick the one on the bottom, but I miss, and it catches my shoe, biting the sole.

"It's got my shoe!" I yell as I shake my foot, but it only

holds on harder. Clayton kicks it on the snout, and it finally releases its hold on me. Finally, both coywolves give up their fight and pull back, allowing us to shut the door.

"Are you okay?" Preston asks.

"Yes. Thankfully, it just got my shoe," I reply.

There's no lock on the door, so I stand guard, holding it closed, as Clayton and Preston rummage through the room, looking for something to secure it. They find a small filing cabinet, wiggle it across the room, and park it by the door. The two of them go back to looking through the room for a way out while I continue to stand guard.

Two of the coywolves are now out of sight, leaving one standing in front of the door. *There's no way I'm taking my eyes off you.* I stare at the animal through the dirty glass. Its strong jaw hangs slightly open, exposing long, sharp yellowed teeth. Stringy drool hangs from one side of its mouth, threatening to fall at the smallest jerk of its head. A second coywolf returns, and the first one turns to it. They start fighting over something the second one is holding in its mouth. Eventually, the first one rips it from the second one and drops it in front of the door. I look down and gasp. It's a large piece of blue-and-gray fabric—the same pattern as that of Natasha's shirt. Half of it is covered in a dark red substance, most likely blood. I feel my stomach revolt. The second coywolf pounds on the door again, leaving a new smear of fresh blood on the glass. A better look at its face shows blood dripping from its snout. Its front legs are drenched in blood. I turn away and start hyperventilating.

"What's going on?" Clayton comes to my side, and I point to the door. "Where? Oh my goodness, is that part of Natasha's shirt?"

Preston joins him, takes a quick look, and then runs past us and loses what little dinner he has left in his stomach in a trash can.

"I think so," I mumble.

Natasha. Her name comes to my mind, and I turn toward Clayton's chest, where, cradled by his arms, I cry silently. Even though friendship was not something she and I shared, there's no way I would have wished an end like this upon her. She didn't deserve this. No one does. *Was she attacked in her sleep? Did she feel anything? Did she try screaming? How much blood did she lose before she finally lost consciousness?* The gory questions run through my mind, and I can't help but put myself in her place, picturing what her last moments might have been like.

"We need to find her, to help her," Preston says with his head still over the trash can.

I let go of Clayton and sit in a corner, pulling my legs against my chest. "There's a lot of blood. If it's hers, she's gone," I say as I wipe my tears, trying to pull us back to reality. *Even if we knew she was still alive, there's no way to get past the animals without letting the soldiers know we're here.*

Clayton stares out the door and then suddenly points

across the hall. "Guys, over there by the wall. Was that there before?"

I get up from the floor and join him at the door. I look past the bloody mess in front of the door and follow the direction in which he's pointing. He shines his light, and we can clearly see a small brown book with blotches of the red substance on some areas.

"I don't recall having seen that there before," I say, making space for Preston, who's trying to get a look.

"That's it! That's the notebook! It has to be," he says.

Terrifying screams break the silence, followed by gunshots and more screaming. It seems the soldiers have finally met the other building tenants. *Should we shoot the remaining coywolves? Should we make a run for it now? Are all the soldiers dead? Even if they're not all dead, will they notice our gunshots if we fire at the animals right now?*

We ponder our options, when suddenly, the shooting stops, and we hear voices coming through the air duct vent again. *The soldiers are not all dead, and to make matters worse, they're calling for reinforcements.* I don't know whether to feel upset or relieved by the news. Regardless, the moment has passed, and we can no longer shoot the animals. If we do, the soldiers will likely take notice and come after us. With the additional support, they will have us rounded up in no time.

Preston sits in a corner with his head between his legs. I sit next to him. I don't know what to say, so I say nothing.

I rest my head against his shoulder and rub my hand over his back, hoping to bring him some comfort. "I might not have felt the same way she did, but I still cared about her. She was like family," he says softly.

In the meantime, Clayton is still looking around the room, trying to find an alternate way out. He calls us eagerly to show us another door he's found. It is hidden behind a large cabinet and connects to the same hall as the first door, although around a different corner. He quickly shares his newfound idea. The guys will hold the second door open long enough to attract the animals' attention. Once the coywolves abandon their guard on the first door, I'll open it enough to retrieve the notebook. We'll need to be quick enough to shut our doors in time to avoid allowing one of the animals inside. It could work. No, it will work, because it needs to work. It's our only chance.

"Let's finish this," Preston says, seeming to be resolved on succeeding and moving forward. My admiration for him continues to grow as I take in his perseverance amid all the adversity he's faced so far.

Would I have the stamina and courage to keep going if I were in his place? I know deep inside I wouldn't. Being certain of the death or betrayal of everyone I love would have made me give up by now. I'm not a fighter. I've never been one. I'm only standing because I still have the hope of being able to rescue my family. If I knew for a fact they were all gone, I would run away from it all or turn myself into the hands of the Empire. Either way, I would call it quits.

We wiggle the small cabinet out of the way, allowing enough slack for me to open the door and stretch my torso across the hall to reach the notebook. I kneel on the floor, facing the glass door, ready to go. Preston stands behind me with gun in hand, ready to shoot if I don't make it back inside in time. Preston and I turn our lights off and put our night-vision glasses on, hoping the darkness will give me a few more seconds before they realize I've opened the door. Clayton stands by the back door, ready to shine his light into the hall. We take deep breaths and kick off our plan at Clayton's command.

Clayton opens the door and calls out to the animals as he throws a ball of crumpled paper across the hall. He's made sure to throw something that is light enough to distract the coywolves but that won't draw the attention of the soldiers downstairs. We hope the ripped pages of the book he found will be enough.

For a few seconds, we fear the plan is not going to work, as the coywolves seem to ignore him. Then they decide to go for it.

Rather than running after the ball, as we hope, they run toward the door. Clayton shuts it in the nick of time, almost catching one of their snouts. I take advantage of the break and swiftly but surely crack open my door, stretch across the hall, and wrap my hand firmly around the notebook before pulling myself back inside. I shut the door right as the coywolves turn around and head back toward me. They go wild, more rabid than before, pounding and scratching the glass with a renewed hunger for blood.

I hand over the notebook to Preston as I wiggle the cabinet back against the door, ensuring it stays shut. Clayton moves his cabinet back over the second door, ensuring no intruders are able to come in that way. I wipe the blood from my hand on my jeans.

"The map's here," Preston confirms with relief. He stuffs it into his backpack, and we resume our search for a way out of the room. The air vents are too narrow for us to fit through, so those are not an option. Whether we like it or not, the only way out is through the back window. We fear that breaking the glass might attract unwanted attention, but we have no choice.

Preston uses a paper weight he finds on a shelf to break the window. He clears it as best as he can and then climbs onto a cabinet by the window to get a good look outside. He confirms we're six or maybe seven stories high, but to our benefit, there's a fire-escape ladder outside the building nearby. The only challenge is that the ladder starts two stories down and is offset a few feet to our right. If we're able to get to it, we should be able to get close enough to the ground to jump to the street without severely hurting ourselves. The thought of a hard landing with my injured thigh makes me cringe, not to forget my injured ankle I twisted earlier. It's going to hurt—there's no doubt about that.

We go through our backpacks and come up with two ropes. Clayton and Preston estimate that combined, the ropes should get us close enough to the escape ladder. The hardest part will be swinging the couple of feet to the right to land on the ladder.

"Who wants to go first?" Preston asks, probably expecting Clayton to volunteer. To everyone's surprise, including my own, I volunteer. They both oppose my decision, but I firmly insist, arguing it'll be safer because there will be two people to help lower me instead of just one. Eventually, they agree.

Clayton clears all the glass remnants from the window, pulls a piece of carpet from the floor, and folds it over the window to reduce the friction between the rope and the window. A grim image of the rope breaking and me falling to my death creeps into my mind. I imagine myself hitting the ground, my legs breaking upon impact, and blood flowing away from my cracked skull. I pull myself from the gruesome reverie and try to focus on what I'm doing.

Preston loops the rope around my waist and thighs and under my butt, creating a rudimentary and uncomfortable seat. He ties the two ropes together in a convoluted knot and then ties the remaining free end to a large desk anchored to the floor. He assures me it'll hold; plus, he and Clayton will be there to lower me slowly.

"Cricket, ready to rappel down the building?" Clayton

asks me, trying to ease my fear yet looking as worried as I feel.

"Not really, no," I say. I regret having offered to go first, but that ship has sailed. We need to get moving. If the soldiers heard the glass break, they might be on their way up.

Clayton helps me climb up to the window, and I stick my head out to get an idea of where I'm supposed to be heading. The full moon illuminates the night, so I can see all the way down. I'm typically not afraid of heights, but usually there's a guard or other safety barrier keeping me safe on firm ground. Dangling close to a hundred feet above a cement sidewalk while depending on nothing other than a rope to keep me alive is a different story.

You can do this. Be brave. I take a deep breath and step out the window. A cold blast of air fully awakens all my senses. I breathe in and out slowly for a few seconds, not daring to look down.

"Try walking down the building," Clayton says.

I rest my feet against the wall and slowly lean back, staying in a semiseated position. My hands let go of the window, and I hold on to the rope instead. The rope tightens around my body, casting a sharp pain on my injured thigh. I hope it doesn't cause the bleeding to resume. I switch my focus to my descent. Slowly, they begin to lower me.

This is not so bad! I think with relief as the distance between myself and the ladder shrinks. I'm soon a few feet above it, but the real issue is getting to it. Even if I stretch out my arms wide, I am not able to reach it. I'll have to swing.

I slowly start moving from side to side, each time a little harder. I stretch my hands and push against the building as hard as I can, further increasing the distance I'm able to cover. I swing a bit farther, until I'm finally flying over the ladder. Right on cue, Clayton and Preston suddenly drop me the remaining few feet, and I land softly on the ladder.

I did it! I made it!

But it's not over yet, as the other two need to join me.

With quick hands, I untie the rope, something I'm happy to do since it is cutting into my skin. I check on my leg, feeling around for signs of wetness as an indicator of more bleeding. The bandage feels dry, so I assume the gauze and fabric are containing any potential new blood flow.

Clayton and Preston have already retrieved the rope. A few minutes later, Clayton's head appears on the window. He slowly climbs out, and my anxiety resumes. *Please don't fall*, I pray silently.

Preston lowers Clayton a bit faster than he lowered me, seeming to have caught the hang of it or maybe wanting to get this ordeal over with. Just as I did, Clayton swings from side to side until he's over the ladder, and Preston drops him the remaining feet, a bit faster and harder than they dropped me. I help Clayton untie the rope, and Preston recalls it.

"Hold on. How is he going to get down? Who's going

to lower him?" I say as the complexity of the third descent suddenly hits me.

"He'll have to lower himself." Clayton's obvious response raises even more questions, but I hold them as I see Preston exit the window. I hold my breath and squeeze Clayton's hand harder than I intend to.

To my relief, Preston seems to have no problem lowering himself. He's wrapped something around his hands, which appears to help with his grip. Soon he's dangling a few feet from us. It's time for him to start swinging. He starts rocking back and forth, each time getting closer. *A few more feet. Come on. Hurry up*, I repeat in my head, hoping it'll help him get to us faster.

Unexpectedly, the piece of carpet bent over the window to protect the rope from chafing comes loose and falls down. It misses Preston by a few inches, startling him. He continues swinging back and forth, trying to get closer to the ladder, but it seems that without the carpet's dampening effect, the friction between the rope and the window is too high, and the rope finally reaches its breaking point. Preston starts falling, not yet having cleared the ladder.

All the air leaves my body as I see him fall past us. Within a nanosecond, we feel a hard jerk, and the ladder shakes vigorously. He's managed to catch the side of the ladder's base and is no longer falling. We hurry to pull him up. He's a lot heavier than I expect, but Clayton and I manage to get him to safety.

"I almost had a heart attack," I say, wrapping my arms tightly around myself, now that I know he's safe.

"Yeah, almost made Clayton's life easier, though," Preston replies, laughing. I pretend not to understand what he's talking about.

"Dude, don't joke like that," Clayton responds, punching him gently on the shoulder.

Preston unties what's left of the rope and stuffs it into his backpack. We then proceed to climb down the rest of the ladder and jump the last few feet to ground level. Preston catches me so I don't have to land hard on my injured leg. Once he sets me down on firm ground, I turn to him and give him a tight, long hug. "Thanks for not dying," I whisper softly into his ear.

"You're very welcome," he responds, grinning from ear to ear.

We stand by the building, hiding among the shadows, as we wait for Clayton to send a message to his father and mine to let them know we've successfully regained the infamous notebook and map. It's 4:00 p.m. GTZ. We still have a few hours before sunrise.

"Great. Now we need to head to the zoo," Clayton says, turning the phone off and stuffing it back into his backpack.

"And how do we get there?" I ask.

"The tunnels, of course," Preston responds.

We reach into our backpacks, retrieve our night-vision glasses, and start running, with Preston leading the way.

19

"How's your leg doing?" Preston asks as we stop for a rest break.

"Throbbing a bit, but I can keep going," I reply as he pulls out a water bottle. He lets me drink from it first and then takes a couple of large gulps himself.

In the meantime, Clayton takes advantage of the stop to consult his map. He takes off his night-vision glasses and illuminates the map with his flashlight. Preston and I remove our glasses to avoid straining our eyes with the bright light.

"The zoo's a bit over three miles from where we started, so we should be about halfway by now," Clayton says, putting the map away. "We need to stick to the right at the next fork."

"Where did all these tunnels come from?" I ask.

"Some were built by breweries back in the days before refrigeration to keep the beer cool. Others were built during the prohibition era to move alcohol and other forbidden items around the city. The Daylight Militia built the ones by the suburbs over the past fifty years, anticipating the need for a time like what we're going through," Clayton responds.

"What made them think they would need something like this?" I ask.

"If you know anything about history, you know that it tends to repeat itself. Every empire goes through the same cycle: the empire expands with wonderful promises; the people realize reality doesn't meet their expectations; they suck it up for some time with the hope that things will turn around; and finally, the people reach a breaking point, which leads to rebellion and, if they're successful, liberation."

"Let's hope we're able to reach the final phase," Preston says.

After satiating our thirsts and giving my leg a short break, we're ready to resume. We speed-walk through the tunnel, following the route Clayton has set. The sound of water dripping has become such a normal background noise by now that I no longer notice it. The area of the tunnel we've been walking through for the past hour is pretty wide, maybe ten feet or so, with the ceiling reaching heights of up to fifteen feet. However, when we reach the exit by the zoo, the tunnel shrinks to the point that we need to move in single file. Preston and Clayton have to slouch to avoid bumping their heads on the ceiling. The air feels heavier, and thoughts of being trapped here during an earthquake send shivers down my spine. At last, we reach the exit and come back up to the surface. The crisp air feels refreshing and energizing—exactly what I need right now.

Sunrise won't happen for another hour and a half or maybe two hours max. We need to be quick to stay hidden as long as possible. We climb the small hill and take a good look at the entrance gates. A green triangular roof sits over ten white square columns. Half the letters in the name are either missing or hanging by a thread. The iron gates are tilted, likely weakened by corrosion. The trees and foliage are overgrown. Many of the stone pavers are raised, having lost their war against the strong tree roots that refused to stay underground. The zoo is one of the oldest in the pre-Empire days and one of the few that boasted a botanical garden; everyone in the city used to love it. Now it's just a dump the Empire seems to have turned into a secret base. I wonder what else is happening here and how many other prisoners they're keeping. My mother and sister can't be the only ones.

We cross the main gates, keeping our eyes wide open for any sign of soldiers. The calm and quiet make the air feel spooky. My gut tells me we're walking into an ambush. I hope I'm wrong.

We walk into the central plaza; old buildings surround us. I read the signs on a couple of the buildings: Welcome Center and Zoo Shop. As before, we keep our steps away from the open areas and as close as possible to the building structures.

A short walk from the central plaza, we reach a small lagoon. Around it are the remnants of train tracks that have endured years of weathering and neglect. The tracks themselves are slightly thinner and closer together than the tracks I've seen in the past; I wonder what sort of smaller-scale train used to commute here and for what purpose. We stand at an old bridge next to a portion of the train tracks. Out of nowhere, a couple of Empire soldiers start moving toward us. We look back and forth, trying to find a place to hide. Without seeming to think twice, Preston and Clayton jump down to the tracks from the bridge and immediately disappear under the bridge. *Thanks for the warning!* I want to yell. A second later, I follow after them.

The bridge is not too high, but my leg and ankle are still sore, so it takes a good amount of effort to keep silent as a current of pain erupts upon impact. About half a minute later, the soldiers walk over the bridge. The boards are spaced out enough that we can see them.

Preston remains laser-focused on what they're saying and is able to pick up some valuable words from their conversation as they approach. "Girl at the gorilla cages," he whispers.

It's not a lot, but it's enough for my heart to accelerate. *It has to be Heidi. It has to be her.*

All of a sudden, one of the soldiers stops abruptly over us. He says something I don't understand and then bends down to the ground, and the three of us freeze. *Can he see us?* I wonder, holding my breath as my eyes open wide.

"A penny!" he exclaims in English, and then he adds something else in the foreign language. He laughs as he stands up and places the penny in his pocket, and they resume their walk. The three of us exhale loudly.

"We need to get to the gorilla area. I also heard them say they're keeping *them* separated, and I assume they were referring to Heidi and your mother. Do either of you know where the gorilla area is?" Preston asks, and Clayton and I shake our heads. "Okay, then we'll have to divide and conquer. We need to find them and get the heck out of here before it gets bright."

"Yvanya and I can follow the road to the left, and you can go to the right," Clayton tells Preston. "I'll text my father to let them know where we're heading. If they get here before we're done, they can back us up."

"Sounds like a plan," Preston says. He then turns to me and asks, "You okay with all of this?" I nod, so he turns to Clayton once more. "Take care of her. I mean it."

"Like I wouldn't," Clayton replies.

We climb up to the bridge. Right before we split up, Preston grabs my hand and gives it a strong squeeze. "Be safe," I whisper, and he takes off. Clayton and I head in the opposite direction.

I'm grateful for all the overgrown vegetation, as it provides ample cover along the way. We pass what a sign discloses to be the old reptile house: a circular stone building with a three-level white dome lined with windows. A red metal roof sits on its top. Assuming snakes and gators lived in there, it would have been my least favorite part of the zoo. Something about the way snakes move—how they seem so unpredictable—makes my skin crawl.

A short walk ahead reveals another sign to my right. Ivy has grown all around it, but I can still make out the words: Cat Canyon. A picture of a tiger's face makes it obvious that domestic house cats were not the cats on display. Clayton taps me on the shoulder to get my attention. A little ahead to our left is a different sign: Gorilla World. A picture of a grumpy-looking, muscular gorilla sits on top of the words. To the left of the sign is a narrow concrete path half covered with branches, moss, and leaves. We check our surroundings, and after confirming no one's within sight, we move quickly down the path. It takes us to a covered structure made of rock and bamboo trunks.

A thick floor-to-ceiling viewing glass separates the visitors' area from where the animals would have been kept. On the other side of the glass is a large indoor habitat and play area. Ropes, rocks, and tree trunks and limbs, probably made of concrete or some other artificial material, create a large jungle gym for the primates who once called this their home. All the way to the left, I see a set of cages. I can easily see into three of them, and to my disappointment, they're empty. One of them is tucked in a corner, which I can't see well from my vantage point. I move to the right, trying to get a better angle. At least from what I can see, it's also empty.

I start to feel crestfallen, when I notice another cage to the far right. Lying down on the floor near the gate, I see a mess of clothes, blankets, and blonde hair. *Heidi!*

I tap violently on the glass, trying to call her attention without having to yell. After a few seconds, she finally stirs and looks in my direction. Her surprised face is priceless. *I'm here, Heidi! I'm here. We're getting you out. You're going to be safe!* I start crying out of relief.

But out of nowhere, her beautiful grin turns into muted screams. *What's wrong?* I yell in my head.

"Yvanya, we have a situation," Clayton says as I turn around. His gun is out, and his shoulders are squared—he's ready to engage.

Coming around the corner with rifles drawn, five soldiers quickly surround us. Four of them wear the black Empire uniform, while one of them wears our country's bright cobalt-blue uniform.

"Stop, or I'll shoot," Clayton warns.

"Drop your gun, or we shoot her," one of the Empire soldiers replies, and three of them point their rifles at me. The other two continue pointing their guns at Clayton.

"Don't, Clayton. Don't drop it," I say softly, thinking I might be able to pull my gun out of its holster and shoot them before they have a chance to shoot us. But who am I kidding? The thought that I could pull off something like that with my lack of experience is preposterous.

"No, Yvanya," he replies, as if reading my mind.

"Drop it now!" one of the soldiers, a kid most likely no older than we are, yells.

We stare at the soldiers, who in turn stare at us. The group is a mix of nationalities and ethnicities, with none of them older than Preston. Their thick arms hold on tightly to their weapons. The tension's so sharp we could cut it with a knife. One of the soldiers, the one with *Region 12* embossed on his uniform, starts to shake. This is probably the first time he's been engaged in this type of situation. Realizing that nothing good will come from firing—and likely afraid I might try something stupid—Clayton drops his gun, and we lift our arms in surrender. Big, fat tears roll down my face.

So close! We were so close.

"I'm sorry I failed you," Clayton says as the soldiers surround us.

Once they've secured Clayton's gun, they pat us down to check for additional weapons. They find mine and strip me of it. They also take our backpacks away. Once they feel confident we're no longer armed or dangerous, they walk us through a small door into the indoor habitat, where the jungle gym and the cages are.

"If you try anything funny, I'll blow her spine," one of

them warns us, pushing the barrel of his rifle against my back.

One of the other soldiers opens one of the small cages across from Heidi and pushes us into it. He closes the door and pulls on the latch a couple of times to confirm it's locked. They throw our backpacks into a corner of the main enclosure, hang the key to our cage on a nail by the glass, and finally walk away.

Clayton sits in a corner, and I move to the bars and stick my arms out, waving at Heidi, who, with a sad face, waves back.

"Are you okay? Did anyone hurt you?" I yell at her.

"No. I'm hungry but otherwise okay," she responds.

"How long have you been here?"

"I don't know. Ever since I woke up, I guess."

"Where's Mother? Have you seen her?"

"I don't know. I'm not sure where they're keeping Mother or Father."

"Father's safe," I say, trying to bring a bit of relief to her. "We shouldn't talk too much, in case they're listening."

She nods, and I move away from the bars. I sit next to Clayton and pull my legs against my chest. He places his arm around my shoulders, and I start to cry quietly.

"I'm sorry," he says again.

"We should have known they would be waiting for us. It seemed too easy," I reply softly.

A middle-aged Asian Empire soldier walks in, and I pull

my legs tighter against my chest. He has short black hair, and a prominent scar runs across his left cheek, ending less than an inch from his eye. He stands in front of our cage for a few seconds without saying a word and then gloats at our misfortune. "You other McKenzie girl? We been waiting for you. Now you mother has two reasons to start talk," he says in broken English, and then he leaves.

I hide my face against Clayton's arm, and he responds by pulling his other arm tightly around me.

"It's not over. You know that," he says softly.

Preston is here, hopefully not caught. He'll rescue us. The encouraging thought runs through my mind. I don't want to say it out loud, for fear our cage might be bugged. The last thing we need right now is to alert them to his presence, if they don't already know. *Our fathers should be arriving in a few hours as well. If Preston doesn't free us, they will.* I try to keep my thoughts focused on an optimistic outcome.

Suddenly, I feel very tired. It feels like an eternity since I last slept on my soft, warm bed. I can't go anywhere right now, so I might as well take a nap. Hopefully it'll recharge my battery. Once Preston or our fathers get us out of here, we're going to need all the energy we can get to leave this place behind. I shut my eyes and immediately doze off.

20

I stand by a gray block wall with my eyes fixed on Preston, who's in front of me, as still as a statue. His eyes are glued to mine, daring me to a staring contest. Whoever moves his or her eyes away first loses. His stare makes me blush, and I want more than anything to look away, but I won't give him the satisfaction. I won't let him intimidate me, or at least I won't let him know he intimidates me. He moves closer to me. When his eyes are less than a foot away, I suck my lips in, doing a terrible job of withholding a smile. For a second, his eyes move down to my neck.

"I win!" I exclaim victoriously, but my outburst lasts only a second because immediately, he closes the small gap between us, pinning me against the wall. He lowers his lips to my neck and kisses me slowly. I freeze, not knowing what to do. His touch sends shivers through my body—the good kind of shivers. My legs feel wobbly. He slowly moves up to my lips; my eyes are tightly shut. I kiss him back. He gently pulls his head back, and I open my eyes. I'm surprised to see it's no longer Preston. He has turned into Clayton. I close my eyes and let him kiss me.

"Yvanya, wake up," Clayton says.

"Huh?" I ask dreamily before becoming alert.

"You were talking and moaning."

"What was I saying?" I ask innocently, hoping it wasn't anything embarrassing.

"I couldn't tell. You were just mumbling," he replies to my relief. "What were you dreaming about?"

"I can't remember anymore," I lie. *Oh, Clayton, if only you knew.*

A few hours pass without any sign of Preston. He wouldn't leave without us—that's for sure. *Could he have been captured as well?* I begin to fear. *Positive. Stay positive. No sense in worrying about what you can't control,* I remind myself. *Maybe start thinking of plan B.*

I look around our cage, trying to find anything that might prove helpful. The key is too far from us, and there's nothing inside or near the cage we could use to reach that far. The only realistic option would be to overpower one of the soldiers when he opens the gate and then quickly make a run for it. Unfortunately, that would leave little time to rescue Heidi, and I'm not leaving without her. It's unlikely a soldier opening our cage will be alone, so the prospects of that plan don't look good anyway.

I consider sharing my thoughts with Clayton, hoping he might have a better plan, but by now, he's the one who has fallen asleep. He's barely gotten any rest, so I decide to let him be. I watch his face as he sleeps, studying the freckles on the top of his nose and the long lashes that softly flutter as his eyes move underneath his lids. Now he's the one dreaming. *Hopefully nothing too wild*, I think coyly. Across the room, Heidi sits quietly in her cage. *The poor kid must have been so scared.* I wish I could wrap my arms around her.

It's around 12:00 a.m. by now. The sun has turned the habitat into a greenhouse. My stomach starts to grumble. I hope that starving us to death is not part of the soldiers' strategy to get us to talk. I wonder when they will start our interrogations. If they haven't gotten anything out of my mother, I'm sure they'll try to get as much as they can from us. Will I be able to stay quiet? I hope so, but I'm not entirely sure. If they resort to torture, how much pain will I be able to endure before I give in? Or worse, how much will I allow them to do to Heidi before I fall apart and talk? Will they use me as bait to get Clayton to talk? How much are we willing to sacrifice to protect the greater good?

I'm lost in my head, when out of the corner of my eye, I catch movement by the small entry door to the habitat. My first thought is that soldiers are finally coming with food, but then, to my delight, I realize it's not soldiers. Preston and my mother are here. My beautiful mother! She's alive, and judging by how quickly she's moving, she's doing well. Whatever they might have done to her has not stopped or broken her.

"Over there!" I whisper, pointing at the key that hangs by the glass. I try not to yell, as I'm not sure how far away the soldiers might be. I shake Clayton, who immediately wakes up. Preston rushes to get the key. My mother goes to the monitoring camera and, with a firm grip, rips it from the wall. She then heads toward Heidi.

Within thirty seconds of their entry, deafening alarms go off. *They know. They probably saw them on the video monitors. How soon before they get here?* I wonder.

My question is immediately answered, as two soldiers run into the habitat with rifles in hand. To their surprise, my mother is waiting for them by the door. She tackles them the moment they set foot in the room, knocking their weapons from them. She kicks the rifles out of their reach, and they chase after her, unarmed. I gasp in fear as one of them grabs her by her shoulders and, swinging his arm around her, puts her in a choke hold.

The motions seem to be well engraved in her mind, because immediately, she drops to the ground and kicks the man off in what looks like an effortless choreographed dance. The second man is waiting for her, though, and surprising her with a blow to the head, he knocks her down to the ground. She quickly covers her head with her forearms, avoiding the punches from her assailant, who is now sitting on top of her abdomen, trying to pin her down. When the man least expects it, she thrusts her hips up and sideways, making him lose his balance and throwing him face-first to the ground behind her.

She jumps up from the ground and, like a ninja in the middle of the night, proceeds to climb onto one of the fake trees and run through the branches with the speed and balance of a mountain lion. They follow after her, but they are much slower as they struggle to keep their balance. Once the men are standing on the middle of one of the limbs, she turns and surprises them with a set of kicks and punches to the face before jumping into the air as a gymnast would on a beam, kicking them off the tree branch. They land hard on the ground.

I'm so amused by the show, never having seen this side of her, that I forget what I'm supposed to be doing.

"Get Heidi," Preston tells me, handing me the key. Preston and Clayton then run to retrieve the soldiers' rifles.

By now, my mother has incapacitated the men, but as expected, the trouble doesn't stop there. A new group of four soldiers show up. Preston, Clayton, and my mother fight them off until they are also disarmed and incapacitated.

In the meantime, I fumble with the key, trying to unlock Heidi's cage.

"Come on. Come on," she says.

Finally, I get the door open, and she comes out and gives me a quick, tight hug. In addition to her nightgown, she's wearing a pair of sneakers that seem too big for her. I run to grab our backpacks, and I toss one to Clayton and then wrap the other around my back. Preston hands me his handgun, and with that, we run out through the door.

The path is clear for now, and my ankle no longer hurts, so we move as fast as we can. In the distance, we see a group of soldiers heading our way. We hide behind some rocks and wait until they've passed. With all the overgrown plants, we're able to stay hidden until we reach the zoo entrance. From there, we rush back to the tunnels.

We're safe! I can't believe we made it out, I think. My mother leads the pack, followed by Preston and then Heidi and me. She holds my hand tightly, likely afraid we'll get separated if she lets go. Clayton watches our backs.

A few yards into the tunnel, we hear approaching steps. We freeze and lean against the wall, waiting to see who's coming. *Friend or foe? Please be friend. Please.* The steps on the other side suddenly come to a stop as well. Preston pulls out his phone and sends a text. Within a few seconds, we hear a bell sound. "Ashton! McKenzie! That you guys?" Preston yells.

"Yes, it's us!" I hear my father's voice. We run to each other with joy.

"Where's Paul?" my mother asks.

"My father's dead," Preston replies softly.

"When did he die?" she asks, confused.

"Almost two days ago at the EBI building," Preston says. "He was shot."

"He was shot all right, but he's not dead. I saw him earlier today. They were keeping him at a different interrogation area. I thought you knew and had released him," my mother says.

"We just got here. Beatrice, are you certain he's alive?" my father asks.

"He was when I saw him today—a few hours ago maybe," she says, clearly starting to lose her patience in repeating herself.

"You told me he was dead." Preston turns to my father.

"That's what the soldiers told me at the EBI building. I didn't see him, but I had no reason to believe otherwise," my father responds.

"We need to go back for him," Preston says, probably still not fully believing it.

"We will. All of you go straight to the Tango compound, and Ashton and I will get him," my father responds.

"I want to go with you," Preston says.

"No. You're the only one who knows how to get to Tango. We need you to lead them there," Ashton replies.

"We won't leave without him," my father says, and Preston finally agrees to the plan.

I hate the idea of separating once again, but it's the right thing to do. We can't leave Preston's father there. My mother gives my father a tight hug and a kiss and then draws a quick map for him of where she believes Paul is being held. Rather than entering the zoo the way we did, they decide to take the underground tunnels that run under the zoo, hoping to stay hidden longer. My mother shows them where she saw exits near the area where Paul was being kept. My father looks at my mother, Heidi, and me and says, "You girls are the center of my world. Never forget that."

I smile at him and reply, "Yes, that came in handy already."

With a wink, he tells me, "I knew you would figure it out." He gives Heidi and me a hug and a kiss, and with that, he and Ashton hurry past us, heading back toward the zoo.

We speed-walk through the tunnels for a couple of hours until we make it to a large vault where a couple of vehicles await us. We cram into one, with Preston behind the wheel. Safe in the backseat, I continue to hold on tightly to my sister's hand as my mother runs her fingers through my hair.

"I didn't know you knew how to fight," I whisper to her with a smile.

"There's a lot about me you don't know," she says before kissing my cheek. "And there's a lot I'll be teaching you in the next few weeks."

Her words make me smile. I rest my head on her shoulder with the images from her earlier performance still running through my head.

21

It takes us a few hours to get to the Tango compound. The mountains around it keep it hidden from outsiders. A thick canopy of trees spreads through it, adding extra coverage from the skies. A small field has been tended, and vegetables and fruits are ready for picking. In another area is a barn with chickens and other small farm animals. A pumping well provides fresh drinking water. The taste is different from the water at home—more metallic. I'm sure I'll get used to it eventually.

Many log cabins have been built throughout the compound. They're small but meet the intent. Upon our arrival, Rebecca, Daphne's parents, and some of the people we met at the downtown hotel receive us. They show us to our cabins and help us set up. In my family's cabin, there's a bunk bed for Heidi and me on one side, and a small bedroom with a double bed for my parents is on the other. A bathroom and a small kitchenette fill the rest of the space. It's much more than I anticipated.

As we didn't bring much with us, we are fully unpacked

in less than five minutes. The women take us to see Josephine, who concludes that other than being food deprived and a bit dehydrated, my mother and sister are just fine. She orders them to rest, eat, and drink plenty of fluids. She also inspects my leg for any signs of infection. There's nothing so far, but she disinfects my wound and puts on a fresh bandage just to be sure.

Daphne and Matt come to see us soon afterward. By now, Daphne's nausea has started to subside, and she's able to keep food down. She's expected to be back to normal within a week. I can't wait for that. There's so much I want to tell her and so much I want to ask her.

The three hours that go by as we wait for our fathers feel like an eternity. I want to stay positive. I need to. I can't imagine going again through the same ordeal and experiencing the fear and anguish of not knowing whether I will ever see my family again.

Out of nowhere, we hear clapping and cheering. Heidi, my mother, and I run from our cabin to the center of the valley, where the clamor seems to be coming from. A large group of people block our view. We move through the multitude, with people stepping aside to let us through, until we make it to the front. Standing in the center of it all are Ashton Jones, Paul Anderson, and my father. We rush to hug my father. *He made it!* I can barely believe it. Tears of relief run down my face. Clayton is already by his father, and Preston is by his. In the middle of the crowd, I notice Elizabeth with tears in her eyes.

🕐 🕐 🕐

Walking by myself among the cabins, I see a group of children kicking a ball in the central plaza. Their laughter can be heard throughout the entire compound. I pass them and notice Anderson and Elizabeth walking hand in hand on one of the paths. One of his arms is cradled by a sling. *Does he know what she did? How it almost cost him his life? How can he just hold her hand like that?* I shake my head with reproach.

A short distance ahead, I run into Preston. "Are your parents back together?" I ask him.

"Yes, they are," he responds with a smile, as if nothing out of the ordinary has happened between them.

"Even after what she did? He's able to just look past it and go back to her?"

"No one's perfect. She truly realized the mistake she made and asked for forgiveness, so he put his pride aside and forgave her. That's what true love is: the ability to see past the imperfections of your loved one and accept them for who they are."

Will I ever be able to love like that? I wonder. *Will I be able to forgive someone who has wronged me so deeply?*

We keep walking in silence. Butterflies and bees fly over the wildflowers that line the path around us. The fresh breeze mixes the scents of the woods with those of the valley below as it plays with my hair. We hike up a small hill that ends at an overlook. To our surprise, Clayton is there, staring down at the valley.

"What are you watching?" I ask him, and then I fall quiet and stand by his side as I notice it. Preston stands by my other side. Down in the valley, in the central plaza, people are gathered by the flagstaff. Slowly, as an act of defiance and proof that the people's spirit will not be crushed, they're raising the forbidden flag. In unison, their voices come together, singing "God Bless America," an iconic song we all have learned at some point in our lives but never have been allowed to intone.

The sun is beginning to set, casting a spectacle of colors in the sky. As we stare in awe at the waving flag, Clayton and Preston simultaneously reach for my hands. Once again, I'm firmly reminded that someday I'll have to choose between them. Lucky for me, that's not today.

EPILOGUE

The first thing I notice when I open my eyes is how white everything is—not fancy white like the Andersons' house but sterile, cold white like a laboratory facility. I sit up and study my bed. It's narrower than a twin-size mattress. It's squeaky and bouncy—not the most comfortable surface, but I've slept on the floor before, so it's not the worst either.

The air is freezing, which immediately makes me realize I'm wearing nothing but a cream-colored gown. I look underneath it to realize I'm not wearing underwear. *Crap. Someone changed me. Someone has seen me naked* is the first thing that pops into my mind. *Great, Yvanya. You don't even know where you are or what they're gonna do to you, and your biggest worry is your coyness.*

The door opens, and a middle-aged Asian woman walks in. Her long black hair is tied up in a tight bun. She's wearing her glasses so low that they threaten to fall off. As if reading my mind, she pushes them up with one of her fingers. She wears a doctor's gown, or maybe it's a laboratory gown.

"Hi, Yvanya. I glad to see you awake. Welcome to

Dungeon. We very happy you here," she says in broken English, speaking in a scripted tone.

Who is this woman, and what does she want with me? How does she know my name?

"Now, be a dear, and open mouth wide," she says, approaching me as she reveals a small paper cup in one of her hands.

"What's that? I'm not taking anything," I snap.

"Now, now, don't be difficult. Here is medicine to help you calm down," she says.

As she draws closer, I can see the contents of the cup: pink tablets—probably Nitrotussin, the same hallucinogenic drug they gave to Daphne.

I get up and move as far away from her as I can, into a corner. Now I'm trapped with nowhere to go. *I can still fight her. After all, I'm my mother's daughter. I should have inherited some of her abilities—I hope.*

"Get away from me! Let me go!" I yell, knowing that my protests are in vain because I'm all by myself, barefoot, and seminaked. *How far could I make it like this?*

"Now, if you no take by yourself, I ask for some help. Whether you like or not, you will take. It make you feel better. I promise."

"No, that's Nitrotussin. It'll make me sick, and I will become a slave to the drug," I say, hoping my words will stop her from approaching me.

"Oh, so you hear about this medicine a bit. That's good,

but don't worry. At these amounts, it will only give you good sleep." She inches closer to me as she explains they've been working on a new version of the drug that will make people like me much more agreeable to doing what we're told. It'll make us more complacent and overall more grateful for all the gifts the Empire has showered us with.

I square my legs and shift my balance a bit forward, prepared for hand-to-hand combat with her. She realizes I don't plan to play nicely and, pressing a button on the wall, calls for additional support.

Within half a minute, three female nurses enter, all dressed in light blue gowns. The first two, whom I've never met, are probably in their thirties or early forties. My mouth drops when I take a glance at the third one: Natasha.

"Natasha, you're alive! You're alive!" I scream. "Please help me! Help me!"

"I'm alive no thanks to you. You left me there for the wolves to eat. I was injured, and you left me," she replies, lifting her gown's sleeve to show me the scar on her arm, which stretches from her wrist to her elbow. Whoever stitched her up did a bad job, as the wound left a nasty scar.

"No! We thought you were dead! There was so much blood. If we'd known you were still alive, we wouldn't have left. Please," I plead.

"It was the soldiers who rescued me and kept me alive. I bow my allegiance to the Empire now. And you, Yvanya, are a traitor," she says with hatred in her eyes.

"No, please help me. Please," I beg as the first two nurses take a firm hold of my arms. I try to free my arms and kick the nurses off, but they easily overpower me, pulling me back to the bed, where my kicking and thrashing are of no use.

"Open wide," Natasha says, but the anger in her voice is gone, replaced by a heartless, stoic tone. She forces my mouth open. The doctor approaches me and drops a couple of pills into my mouth. I try to spit them out, but she pours water right after, too fast for me to spit. I start to choke. She pushes my head backward, opening my throat and forcing me to swallow.

"You soon find this medicine works very fast," the doctor says. "Let me know how you like."

Within less than a minute, the room appears to start moving, and my tears start rolling. I focus my eyes on Natasha's face, which slowly becomes distorted as I lose myself to unconsciousness.